THE TRUTH
ABOUT
PARALLEL LINES

Jill D. Block

D1444622

This is for MoMD,
the man of my dreams,
my best friend, my partner, my love.
Thank you for showing me the way to happily ever after.

In this unbelievable universe in which we live,
there are no absolutes.
Even parallel lines,
reaching into infinity,
meet somewhere yonder.

—Pearl S. Buck

Jenna

CHAPTER 1

June 9, 1981

"Holy shit. You're having sex with Mr. Peanut?" Beth asked, just a little too loud, leaning forward in her chair. "Get out of here."

"Wait, who?" asked Kristen, looking first at Beth and then at me. "You mean the dad? How *old* is he?"

"Shhh, you guys. God." I looked around the dimly lit room. There were two ladies a few tables away. They looked like they could be mother and daughter. Or actually, with their pearls and sensible shoes, more like grandmother and mother. There was a guy sitting alone at the bar, sort of hunched over, with a folded up newspaper in front of him. I imagined that he was secretly out of work, drinking up their savings while he was trying to figure out how to tell his wife. There were two other guys, businessman types, at a table by the stairs, probably planning to take over the world or something.

It had been Beth's idea to come to Peacock Alley, figuring it was an appropriately grown up place for our first legal drinks. Our birthdays had always been a pretty big deal, and we always tried to do something special, something momentous. It was this freaky thing, that we were three best friends, and we had the same birthday. We'd skipped out of school early, cutting our last two classes. But who really cared? We were seniors, and graduation was two weeks away.

Over our first round of drinks we'd talked mostly about the prom, which was less than a week away. Beth and Kristen both had pretty serious boyfriends, and there was some big after-party at somebody's father's summer house in the Hamptons. I was going to the prom with my friend Kevin, but we were going to skip the party. We weren't a couple, and it would have been awkward. I was pretty sure he liked boys, but for now he was keeping that to himself.

Even though I had a little buzz from my drink, I started feeling bored, antsy, irritated maybe, listening to them go on and on about this stupid party that I was pretty sure was going to suck anyway. Was I jealous? I guess. No, not really. I don't know. Maybe a little. I really didn't care about the party, but I was starting to feel like their little sister. Like Beth and Kristen had outgrown me.

When the waiter came over with another round of drinks, I stopped listening to them, and started thinking about next year. Beth was headed to Emory, where she would for sure end up being class president and dating the son of the richest guy in Georgia, and Kristen was going to Michigan, but if I had to guess, she'd probably transfer to be with her boyfriend by the end of freshman year. And me? I was staying right here.

Then I reminded myself, for the four thousandth time, that Columbia is an Ivy League school, that the Creative Writing program is one of the best in the country, and that they are giving me a big scholarship because of my book. My book! Okay, so it was a kids' book, and not really much more than a comic book. But, still. I wrote it, and now it is totally being published.

It was this really big deal for a while. It seemed like everyone who knew me was talking about it, and people were totally impressed, and proud of me. It made me feel really proud of myself. But everything was taking so long. The publication date was still so many months away. It was like no one even remembered anymore. Like I was becoming invisible. Maybe that's why I told them.

"But wait a minute. Isn't he like married?" Kristen asked.

"Stop. Let her talk. Go ahead," Beth said to me. "Start at the beginning."

September 24, 1977

I was lying on my bed, drawing a picture of Shaggy from Scooby Doo instead of doing my homework. I could hear my mother on the phone in the kitchen. The usual—my dad and Deirdre. The bastard and the whore. I stopped listening. I swear, she'd been having the same conversation for the past six months. I wondered who she could be talking to, who she knew who hadn't already heard it all before.

"Hold on. I'll ask her. Jenna?"

She spoke so loudly, it was like she was calling to me from across some vast country estate.

"Yeah?" I spoke softly, proving a point, knowing she could hear me through the door.

"I'm on the phone with Laura. Can you babysit tonight? For some friends of hers? Their sitter just canceled."

"Boy or girl?"

"Honestly, Jenna. Does it matter?"

"How much will they—? Okay, fine. Whatever."

That was how it began.

Chloe seemed nervous when I arrived that night. Like she wasn't confident her parents had done an appropriate level of diligence on this teenager in whose care she was being left. Her wide eyes darted back and forth, following the conversation.

The mom and dad were beautiful. Both of them. They were all dressed up, him in a tuxedo, her in a sparkly dark blue gown, looking like they had just stepped out of a luxury car ad in a magazine. But there was definitely a weird vibe. Like they had argued before I arrived, or maybe they were dreading the event they were attending.

I apologized for being underdressed, but the mom either didn't hear me, or didn't get my joke.

"Chloe has a nut allergy. You didn't bring any food with you, did you? Candy? Or sunflower seeds?"

I patted the pockets of my jeans. "Nope. No food. I am certified nut-free."

"All of the food here is safe, so you don't have to worry. But please don't order in. Or take her out."

Take her out? What, like to a disco? Oh sure. It's Saturday night. Maybe Chloe and I could hit up Studio 54. I wondered if maybe the mom was a little crazy.

"Chloe already had dinner, and she can have a snack if she wants. She can show you."

Chloe nodded, without making eye contact. The mom kept talking.

"There are adrenaline shots in the desk drawer. By the window. Do you know how to give an injection?"

Did I know how to give an injection? Was she kidding? The look on her face made me feel like I'd been caught in a lie. Like, *How dare you call yourself a babysitter when you are not certified in adrenaline injection?* I wondered if I should lie or if it was better to say no. I guess I just stood there and stared at her.

"You don't. Okay, I can show you. But first call 911. Then give her the shot. And then call me. I left the number of the hotel where the dinner is. Tell them that we are attending the—".

"Mara, enough." He was standing by the door, holding her coat. "There are no nuts here. She isn't going to need it. And if she does, she will read your step by step instructions. Jenna, you do know how to read, don't you?" He rolled his eyes, and followed it with a wink.

The wink totally saved it. It softened the eye roll, made it less mean. It said, in a fraction of a second, *yeah, I know she's crazy, but she's my wife, and I love her.* I smiled at him.

Chloe warmed right up after they left, like she was relieved we'd all survived the encounter. She introduced me to Oscar, the cat, and explained, without my asking, that no, he isn't a grouch, that there used to be a Felix, too, but he had fallen out the window, and they didn't know if he landed on his feet, but even if he did it didn't matter because fifteen floors was too high for a cat to fall, and cats don't really have nine lives, so now it's just

Oscar, and they keep the windows closed and use the air conditioner. I swear she said all of that without taking a breath.

I asked her about school, and she gave me a tour of her bedroom. We put on outfits from the dress-up box and talked in funny accents and called each other Darling. They had this unbelievable record collection, so we put on some music, and choreographed a dance routine in the living room. We dipped carrot sticks in maple syrup and drank apple juice out of wine glasses.

At bedtime, I told Chloe the story of Peanut Girl, about a little girl named Zoey, who everyone believed was allergic to peanuts. But that was just the story she and her family told in order to protect her powerful secret. The truth was that peanuts gave Zoey magical powers, whatever magical powers she needed at the time. She could become invisible; she could have superhuman strength; she could fly. But she could only use her powers for good. If she abused them, they would be lost.

There wasn't much to the story, but Chloe liked it. I promised to tell her more the next time.

Once Chloe was asleep, I took my time checking things out. It was a big apartment in a pre-war doorman building, not far from mine but on a much nicer block. I figured out that the dad ("Call me John") was a lawyer. Some of his business cards were on the dresser, and there was a cardboard box next to the adrenaline desk that was filled with copies of the November, 1977 issue of the Journal of Intellectual Property Law. November, 1977 hadn't even happened yet, but then I saw from the cover that he had written one of the chapters.

There were golf clubs and tennis racquets in the front closet. And I could pretty much tell from the kitchen that the mom didn't have a job. There were lots of cookbooks and pots and pans and complicated food processors and blenders. She had some really nice clothes and bags. With labels from designers I only knew about from riding the bus up Madison Avenue. And three pairs of cowboy boots, which just happened to fit me perfectly. There was a packet of rolling paper in the drawer of the dad's bedside table, but I didn't find his stash.

I was careful to put everything back exactly where it had been long before they were due to get home. I washed and dried the dishes we'd used, and wiped the counter. I pushed back the dining room chairs and turned off the lights other than the lamps in the living room where I settled onto the couch with my homework. I could tell they were pleased with what they came home to, and I knew that Chloe would give them a good report in the morning.

November 5, 1980

I'd learned a lot about them, by poking around in the drawers and closets when Chloe was asleep, but also just by being around. Like, I learned from chatting with Mara that John had been married before and had kids from his first marriage. They sometimes came over for dinner, and they were all going on a trip together over New Years, John and Mara, Chloe and his two boys. I wondered how the first wife reacted when he got together with Mara. And I tried to imagine how bad my mother would freak out if my dad and Deirdre got married, if they had a kid.

By the time I'd been babysitting for Chloe for more than three years, we had a regular thing where I picked Chloe up once a week after ballet, plus I would babysit sometimes on a weekend night. On ballet days, Chloe would do her homework while I made us dinner, usually just heating up something that Mara had left. After dinner, we would hang out a little and play, maybe watch some TV. After her bath we would pick up where we left off with The Adventures of Peanut Girl. Sometimes, if one of us had thought of something really good, we would start the story while we ate, and keep at it, going back and forth, telling and retelling, until she had to go to bed.

Even though she was just a kid, Chloe had become a big part of my life. I really looked forward to seeing her. She was sweet and smart and curious. And funny—she could crack me up. And if she would reach up and take my hand, or when she gave me a hug at bedtime, I felt a weird flutter inside, like my heart was melting a little. It felt like I was the big sister she should have had, or maybe the big sister I wished I'd had. Sometimes I imagined I was her stepmom.

When I did the first Peanut Girl drawing, I tried to make her look like Chloe. It was for my Drawing and Painting class—the assignment was to depict something in an exaggerated style, so I drew her as a cartoon super-hero. I'd shown it to Chloe and she loved it. Then the next week John asked me to bring it by so he could take a look.

Until then, I hadn't even known that Chloe told them about Peanut Girl, and I was pretty self-conscious about it. I'd never written any of it down and the story sounded so lame if I tried to say what it was about. But without even knowing the story, my art teacher said the drawing was really good. And he was a hardass, so maybe it was.

John absolutely flipped over it. Mara didn't seem that interested but it didn't matter because of John's reaction. It turned out that Chloe had told him the Peanut Girl story, that she updated him over breakfast the mornings after I babysat. He said that even before he saw the drawing, he was thinking that I should write it down. Now that he saw my drawing, his idea was for me to do a "graphic novel", which I guessed was sort of a cross between a book and a comic book. He described it as a picture book for readers. He said that if I would give him a few pages, story and pictures, he would "send it around and see what kind of interest it generates". What? That was nuts. It was just my goofy bedtime story. But it felt so good to talk to him about it, to be taken seriously. I think right then I fell in love with him a little.

He told me that his ex-wife's husband was an entertainment lawyer. John told him about me, and set up a meeting for the three of us, me, him and Roger. I couldn't say what freaked me out more—that these men, these lawyers, wanted to have a meeting with me to talk about my story, or that John and Roger seemed almost like friends. John explained that they are all adults, and this is business. I swear, when he said that, it made me think I should ask him to talk to my mom.

The craziest thing of all was when Roger called me to say that Little, Brown wanted to publish the book. My book. The Adventures of Peanut Girl. First, though, I had to write it. And get my college applications done. And finish high school.

June 9, 1981

I told Beth and Kristen everything. And they were absolutely captivated. It was a really good story. I'm actually kind of surprised the two business guys and the mom and grandma didn't pull over their chairs so they could hear better, because that's how good it was. It was like a modern-day Romeo and Juliet. There was sex and romance, and secrets and lies, and love and betrayal, and the potential, in equal parts, for heartbreak and happily ever after. It was funny and it was sad. I told them about the time John and Mara's neighbor came into a restaurant where we were, and how we had to just throw a bunch of money on the table and sneak out before our food even came. And how he said that he and Mara had been unhappy for a long time, how they didn't make each other laugh anymore. And that he believed it was more important for Chloe that her parents be happy, even if they aren't together. I told them that he is smart and funny and really into music and movies, and how, compared to him, the boys at school look like idiots. And I told them that we were trying to figure out how we might be able to get away for a weekend together sometime.

The thing is, none of it was true.

I didn't mean to lie to them. It really just came out. And then, once I got going, it didn't even feel like I was lying. It was an easy story to tell. I guess I had been imagining it for a long time. After almost four years, I felt like I was a part of their family. I wished I was. And really, who could blame me?

I was the product of a broken home. And by broken, I don't mean snapped in two pieces, like a breadstick. I mean shattered. Smashed. Like a glass that got stomped on at a wedding, but without all the cheering and mazel tovs. It was broken beyond recognition, beyond repair.

I could still remember back when we were a family—a mom, a dad and a happy little girl. From the outside, I guess back then we looked a lot like John and Mara and Chloe. Even when we were happy, though, my dad worked all the time, which really bugged my mom. But he's a doctor, and doctors work a lot. And it was his work that paid for the apartment, the vacations and the private school. Even when I was just nine or ten, I knew the script by heart.

He moved out right after my bat mitzvah. And it was fine for a while, better actually than when he was home and they were fighting. I stayed in my same school, and I saw my dad a couple of times a week. Eventually, my mom and I moved into a smaller apartment, which really wasn't so bad, but she hated it. You would think that having to take the elevator to the laundry room in the basement was the worst thing in the world. I would hear her on the phone—"I am 39 years old and feeding quarters into a dryer. Can you imagine?"

But the Deirdre thing changed everything. I remembered her from before. She was an intern at my dad's hospital. I'd only met her a couple times, but I remember hearing her name. She used to call him a lot, and sometimes he would have to go back to work at night if she needed his help with a patient. I thought she was nice, and I remember that she made me think maybe I wanted to be a doctor someday.

It was almost a year after they got separated when I first found out. I was packing my things for the weekend. We had worked out a pretty regular routine—I had dinner with my dad on Tuesdays and I stayed over at his apartment every other weekend. My room at his place finally felt like it was mine, and not some boring guest room. We'd gone to Florida a couple of months before, and that was pretty fun. I don't know who decided that that was what all the divorced dads were supposed to do for February break, but it seemed like Ft. Lauderdale was filled with overly enthusiastic men alone with kids whose hair hadn't been properly brushed.

I could tell right away after my mom answered the phone that something big was happening.

"And this is how you tell me? At 7:30 in the morning? What do you expect me to do—congratulate you? Wish you and your lover good luck?"

I stopped what I was doing.

"Do I have to remind you that we agreed we wouldn't introduce her to anyone unless it was serious? Dr. Walters said that it can be very confusing for a child— Yes, thank you. I think I know how old my daughter is."

Wait, a girlfriend? That was interesting. I looked at the clock to see how much time I had before I was going to have to leave for school.

"So you're saying it's serious? How long have you been seeing her? We've only been separated a few months."

A few months is like three or four. It had actually been more like nine. I wondered if he corrected her.

"Who is she? Before I send my daughter off to spend a weekend with some strange woman I think I am entitled to know something about her. Where did you meet?"

Crap. I had to go or I was going to be late. I walked out of my room with my backpack and my stuff for the weekend.

"Hold on." She put her hand over the talking part of the receiver and said to me, "Don't leave."

"But I'll be late."

"I'll write you a note. Stay."

Stay. Like I'm a dog or something. I went back into my room and stood by the door, listening.

"So, it's Deirdre. Well, I should have seen that one coming. You are truly unbelievable. Do you want to tell me when it really started? Because if you think for a second that I believe—"

Deirdre. Okay. That's okay. She's pretty and nice.

"Oh, honestly. I really don't want to hear it. But you can forget about seeing Jenna this weekend. My daughter will not be a party to your—".

She didn't finish. He said something and she hung up the phone. Or maybe he hung up on her and it took her a minute before she hung up. Either way, that was it.

I didn't see him at all for a while after that. And then, later, when I did, I never saw Deirdre. It was weird. I mean, I could tell she was around. Her stuff was there. I could smell her perfume. One time there was a box of tampons on the back of the toilet. But he didn't say anything, so neither did I. I guess I felt like, he's the adult. If someone is going to bring it up, it should be him, not me. Neither of us ever mentioned her.

Mom sure did, though. Whenever I got home from seeing him, "Is he still with her?" "Do they live together?" "Do they know about them at the hospital?" I wished she wouldn't ask me, but I never asked her to stop. I was just glad to be able to tell her, "I don't know."

From then on, instead of complaining about our shitty apartment, she bitched constantly, to me and to anyone else who would listen, about how he'd lied to her, cheated on her. Stuff I really didn't want to hear. That he'd stolen the best years of her life. She'd been the best wife, and he'd betrayed her. She thought they had been happy, but now she knows it was all a lie. She acted like she was the first woman whose ex-husband ever got a new girlfriend.

Deirdre

CHAPTER 2

August 4, 1981

She wanted to kill him. "Are you kidding me? You said you'd come home first, so we could go together. Come on. You're going to make me walk in alone?"

"Dee, don't get nuts about it. It's just dinner. You'll be gorgeous. She's going to love you."

"It is not just dinner," she said into the phone. "It's your daughter. And who said anything about being gorgeous? I don't even want to be gorgeous. I want to be appropriate. But relatable. Do you really not understand that? I want her to look at me and think—" Stop, she told herself. Grow up and stop it. "Fine. I will meet you there. But you can't be late. Andrew? Tell me what time you will be there, and if you are even one minute late I get to smack you really hard. And you don't get to complain. Promise me."

"Sure, honey. Okay."

She could tell he wasn't listening. She heard people talking in the background.

"Sorry, Dee. I have some people in my office. I've got to go. Gio's at 7. You love me."

"You love me, too," she said, but he was already gone.

She smiled as she hung up the phone. As irritating as it was that he wasn't going to meet her before, that they wouldn't be walking in together, as a couple, she knew it really wasn't that big a deal. She was just glad that she had already planned to get dressed here, and not at his place. *Our* place, she imagined him correcting her.

As she went into the kitchen, she looked at her watch. 5:15, plenty of time. She kneeled down and reached into the cabinet under the sink and pulled out the box of steel wool from the back. She took out the cigarettes and the lighter, and left the empty box next to the sink. Then, with one knee on the counter, she pulled herself up so she could reach the ashtray at the back in the cabinet over the refrigerator. She went into the living room, opened the window, pointed the fan to blow out and switched it on. She turned the chair to face the window, sat down and lit a cigarette.

Three left. And then that's it. She'll be done, and she's not buying any more. Because really, how stupid is it? Andrew would kill her if he caught her, and he'd be totally right. She knew, as well as anyone, what smoking can do. She'd seen enough patients die, from emphysema, heart disease, cancer. She'd watched her own mother die from cancer. But she also knew that her mother's cancer wasn't caused by smoking. She'd read the studies. She'd co-written a paper on it. But just try telling anyone that. That surgeon general's warning may not have gotten smokers to quit, but it sure gave non-smokers something to be smug about. She looked again at her watch. Okay. Just enough time for a quick call with Mickey.

The phone rang four times and she was about to hang up when he answered.

"Soul Survival Gallery. Michael Schein speaking."

"Deirdre Schein speaking. You're Michael now?"

"Oh, I don't know. I thought I'd try it out. I'm also spelling Schein S-H-I-N-E. But I don't think it's going to stick."

"How've you been? Are you feeling okay?"

"Oh, is it Doctor Deirdre calling? I thought for a minute it was Sister Deirdre."

"It's both. Dad said he hasn't heard from you in a while."

"Jesus, I'm fine. Busy. Am I allowed to be busy?"

"Can you give him a break? Just call him. He worries about you."

"So he calls you in New York instead of picking up the phone and calling me? Just tell him— Never mind. I'll go over there. I'll stop by on my way home tonight."

"Thanks. But seriously, are you feeling okay?"

"Yes, doctor. I'm fine. I'm taking my meds, I'm going to meetings. It's just my back. I must have pulled a muscle or something. It's killing me."

"That's so strange. I woke up yesterday with a sore back. And I never have back pain."

"Uh oh. It's that spooky twin thing."

"Oh, please. That's a load of crap. I must have just slept funny." She looked at her watch. "Shoot. I've got to go. We're having dinner tonight with Jenna. Andrew's daughter? I have to get in the shower."

"Whoa. What changed?"

"What do you mean?"

"After all this time, he finally decided you get to meet her?"

"He didn't— It was her idea."

"Hmmm. Interesting. Just make sure you don't sit with your back to the door."

"What? Why?"

"Forget it. What are you going to wear?"

"I don't know. Pants and a shirt? I don't want it to seem like I'm making a big deal about it, you know?"

"It's a big deal. He's had you hiding under the bed for the past, oh, hundred years? So if this is the big reveal, you've got to dress for it."

"Really? So what should I wear then? Shit, Mick. I'm at my place. Half of my stuff is at Andrew's."

"Calm down. Mickey is here to fix it. All you need to do is dress like a woman. Not like a doctor. And not like some utilitarian worker for the cause. Put on a pair of heels, and something silky on top. And some lipstick and earrings. You are her daddy's lover, not his roommate. Make sure she understands that."

"Great. Now you're making me nervous. I really have to go or I'm going to be late."

"Break a leg."

She hung up the phone, took the last cigarette out of the pack, lit it and leaned back in her chair. Relax, she told herself. It's going to be fine. Better than fine. She's finally going to be acknowledged, to get the status she has been waiting for, to be introduced, included and recognized.

As what, Andrew's girlfriend? Jesus, she thought. That's what she's been waiting for? For this teenager to acknowledge her existence as Daddy's girlfriend? That's pathetic. And yet, somehow, it is this, this recognition of her place in Andrew's life, in his family, that she needs to feel legitimate, like a grown-up.

As she pushed open the door, she could see Jenna sitting alone at the bar, writing in a notebook. Deirdre took a deep breath, forced a smile and walked toward her.

"Is your father unbelievable or what? I knew he'd be late. I swear, I should have put money on it. Look, it's ten after and I still beat him here."

Jenna closed her notebook and slowly turned to look up at her. Deirdre saw her eyes narrow, and then widen in recognition.

"Why are *you* here?"

"Why am I—? Umm, dinner? The three of us?"

Jenna stared at her.

"Wasn't this—? Didn't you say that—? I'm sorry. I thought this was your idea. For the three of us to have dinner? Your dad—"

"My idea? I don't even know what you're talking about. My dad and I come here practically every Tuesday."

"Yeah, of course. I mean, I know that. I just thought— He told me—" She turned to look at the door. "He really should be here by now."

"He could have at least told me you were coming. I mean, God, this is so awkward."

Giovanni walked over to where they were talking. "Excuse me. Dr. Kessler just called and asked me to tell you that he's had an emergency and he is going to be late." He looked down at the paper he was holding. "He says that you should please eat without him. He will get something at the hospital and then he will join you here for dessert." He looked up and smiled.

Deirdre looked at him, then at the piece of paper in his hand.

"Jenna, I think we've been set up."

"Oh my God. Did he really do this on purpose? My dad is so weird."

"Yeah. No kidding. I'm going to kill him. Can I count on you to help?"
Jenna stared at her, expressionless.

Deirdre forced herself to smile. *Come on,* she thought. *If I can do this, you can, too. I'll be the grown up. I just need you to play along.* "But if we're going to kill him, I really think we should eat first. Will you join me for dinner?"

They both ordered without looking at the menu.

"So this is your regular Tuesday spot?"

"Yep."

"Your dad and I come here a lot, too. He's a real creature of habit."

"Mm hmm."

"And I bet he always orders the same thing, right? The seafood fra diavolo?"

"I don't know. I mean, yeah, I guess."

Jesus, Deirdre thought. Give me a break. She picked up her wineglass and then put it back down without drinking. *Slow down,* she told herself. You do *not* want to get drunk. "Have you been enjoying your summer?"

"It's okay."

"You must be looking forward to starting school. Columbia, right? It's so exciting."

"I guess."

"When does school start? Or, I mean, when do you have to be there?"

"The 26th."

Deirdre picked up her glass, and leaned back. That's it, she thought. I'm done. We can just sit here and not say a word.

"That's the day the freshmen move in."

Deirdre gave her what she meant as an encouraging nod.

"Orientation goes until the 29th. Which is when the other kids arrive. I mean the upper classmen. And I register for classes on the 31st."

"Sounds like it's going to be a busy few days."

"Yeah. So, I was looking at the course catalogue this morning? I can't decide if I should try to get most of the requirements out of the way first semester, or if I should spread them out."

"Don't you first need to know what you're majoring in to know what classes are required? Or I guess you already know your major. Creative writing?"

"There are these requirements that everyone has to take. It's called the Gen Ed curriculum. A math class, an english class, some kind of science, I guess. I don't pick a major until next year. The creative writing thing is just who gave me a scholarship."

The waiter brought their food, and they started to eat.

"So, do you know where you'll be living?"

"I saw my dorm when I went to this thing they had for accepted students. It's okay. And my roommate and I have been writing to each other. Her name is Elena. Oh, and we talked on the phone once. She's from Miami, and she seems really nice. She's bringing a TV and I said I'd bring my stereo. And we decided we'd both get pink and gray sheets and pillows and towels and stuff, so our room will be, like, you know, coordinated? But I haven't gone shopping yet."

"Well, you've been busy, right? Didn't your dad say you're working in an ice cream store?"

"No. I mean, yeah I was. At Haagen-Dazs. But then I quit because I got a job at Fiorucci. You know, the clothes store? It's really cool, and I get a discount. This shirt is from there. But anyway, Friday is going to be my last day. I didn't even tell my dad yet, but the people I babysit for? They're going on vacation to Italy, and they asked me to come with. To be their, like, mother's helper or something. You know, to help with Chloe. So we're leaving on Sunday. It's just for ten days. And then when I get back it's only like a week until school starts."

"Ten days in Italy—how wonderful," Deirdre said. "And these are the same people who helped you with the book?"

"The dad, yeah. But he didn't really help me. I mean, I wrote it myself. God, I don't get why everybody thinks someone had to help me."

"No, no. I'm sorry. That's not what I meant. I was just asking if it was the same guy."

"Yeah. Whatever."

"I don't think anyone really thinks you had help."

Jenna shrugged.

"It's such a sweet story. Your dad showed me the, what do you call it, the galley copy? Anyway, it seems so— I don't know. It seems so *you.*"

"How do you know? You don't even know me."

"That's true. I mean, it feels like I know you, maybe because of how your father talks about you."

"So, like, you two just sit around and talk about me? That's weird."

"No. But he's really proud of you. And he tells me stuff. I also remember you from a long time ago. But you probably don't."

"I remember. From when my mom used to bring me to the hospital to see my dad sometimes, when he was working. She would always say it was the only way he ever had a chance to see me awake. So, yeah, I remember you from then. But your hair is different."

"Oh, that's right." Deirdre ran her fingers through her hair, pushing it back from her face. "It's been a couple of years already. I just decided one day that I was ready for a change."

"I don't like it."

"Oh. Okay."

"It looked better when it was long."

Deirdre looked at her watch. She really was going to kill him.

"Are you and my dad going to get married?"

"I don't— Actually, that's not something—"

"My mom says you probably won't, because you're too old to have a baby."

"Well, maybe your mom should—"

"She says that you were my dad's midlife crisis. And that if he didn't marry you already, he's never going to. She said she's pretty sure you probably can't get pregnant, because if you could you would have, and that way he would have had to marry you."

"Well, you can tell you mother—" Deirdre stopped herself. She caught the waiter's attention from across the room, picked up her empty glass and nodded.

"How about this? Let's not talk about what your mom has to say about your dad and me, okay? I'm thinking your dad arranged this whole thing tonight because he wanted us to get to know each other. So maybe let's just try to stick with that."

"Fine. I have a question. Where do you go when I stay at my dad's?"

"I have an apartment. On 73rd Street."

"But you live with him, right? I'm not an idiot. Like, if it was supposed to be a secret? It wasn't."

The waiter brought her wine and cleared their plates. Where the hell is he? She tried to imagine what he would say if he was here. And then she realized that it didn't matter what he would say. He's not here, and she is.

"Look. Your father isn't perfect. And sometimes when imperfect people try to do the right thing, it ends up being the wrong thing. It wasn't ever supposed to be a secret. Or, I don't know. I guess maybe it was. But I think your dad was just trying to give you some time. To get used to it."

"To get used to what? Your coat being in the front closet? Besides, my dad would never buy Fresca."

"I know. It never really made sense to me. But I think he just wanted to keep your time together special for the two of you."

"It was disrespectful."

"Well, I agree with you. And thank you for saying so. But you know what? I just kept telling myself— Oh, you mean it was disrespectful to you? Because I think it was disrespectful to me. But, yeah. I guess maybe to both of us. You do know that he meant well, right? And that he loves you? More than anything."

"Yeah, right. More than you?"

And suddenly, finally, there he was.

"Hey, kiddo." Andrew leaned over and kissed Jenna on the top of her head. "Sorry I'm late. Did you eat?"

He sat down, turned to Deirdre, mouthed "sorry" and patted her arm.

"What was that?"

"What was what?"

"That . . . arm pat? That's how you say hello? Sweetie, she knows."

Deirdre leaned over and kissed him on the mouth. Out of the corner of her eye she saw Jenna smile and look away.

While Andrew was looking across the room, trying to get the waiter's attention, Deirdre punched him, as hard as she could.

"Ouch!" Andrew rubbed his shoulder. "That really hurt."

"Hey. No complaining. We had a deal."

Andrew smiled and turned to Jenna. "Don't ask."

The waiter brought over a piece of cheesecake with three forks. While Andrew and Jenna ate, Deirdre sat back and drank her wine. She listened to Jenna and Andrew talk—about her job, Italy, the roommate and the courses she planned to register for. Then she stopped listening, and just watched. It felt like a family.

They walked south together on Third Avenue, and as they approached 73rd Street, Deirdre stopped and turned to Jenna.

"Thank you for joining me for dinner. I enjoyed it. And we'll figure out how to deal with him another time."

"You're not coming with us to my dad's? It's really okay. I can handle it. I swear."

"I'm sure you can. But I have some stuff I need to do at my place. Maybe next time."

"Sweetie, are you sure?" Andrew asked, reaching for her hand. "I figured we'd all stay at the apartment tonight."

"Nope. I'm sure. You guys go do your thing, and I'm going to go home. Goodnight. You love me."

"You love me, too."

She gave him a quick kiss and ran across Third Avenue just as the light was changing. She stopped on the other side of the street, turned and watched Andrew and Jenna walk around the corner onto 72nd Street, out of sight. Then she went into the deli, wondering, while she waited her turn, how she would ever be able to give up her Tuesdays at home.

"Can I help you?"

She turned and looked through the glass door, across Third Avenue. Just to make sure they were really gone.

"Yeah. Marlboro box, please."

Jenna

CHAPTER 3

August 14, 1981

It had been my favorite day of the trip so far. It was sunny and breezy and cool, after it had been so hot and muggy the day before. Chloe and I were on our own while John and Mara were going to some more museums or churches or something. I got the restaurant guys at the hotel to pack us up some bread and cheese and stuff, and we went back to that place Mara found with the good pastries. We spent the whole day in the park at the Borghese Villa. We went to the zoo, had our picnic and ate gelato. We got someone to take our picture in front of the Seahorse Fountain. We met some hippie-ish Americans who'd been traveling all summer, and we hung out with them for a while. They were playing this game, where they stood in a circle and kicked a little beanbag thing up in the air. They made it look easy, but it wasn't.

We met Mara and John back at the hotel and the plan for after dinner was that Chloe and I were going to stay in while John and Mara went out. She'd signed them up for a nighttime city tour, but then she said she had a headache, that I should go with John, since it was already booked and paid for. The only time it felt awkward was when I saw that the sign in the window of the little tour bus said "Romantic Rome".

It was great. I mean, it was Rome at night, so obviously it was great. But we really had fun. The other people were pretty lame, mostly fat Midwesterners, so we pretty much kept ourselves separate from the rest of the group. They couldn't understand a word that the tour guide said, and kept asking him to repeat himself over and over, which totally cracked us up.

He told me how glad he was that I had come. Not that night, but with them to Rome. It had been Mara's idea originally, and he thought it wasn't necessary, but he said that he knew he'd been wrong because of how great it was to see Chloe having such a great time.

When we all got off the bus by the Trevi Fountain, John and I walked around to the other side, away from the crowd of people posing for pictures.

"Here," he said, handing me some coins. "They say it's good luck."

"Thanks." I turned around, my back to the fountain. "You're supposed to throw them in with your right hand over your left shoulder."

"Now, how do you know that?"

"Oh, I just umm . . . I did some research. At home, before we left."

"Research?"

"Yeah. About the fountains." I remembered standing at the copy machine in the library. It felt so dumb, so high school. "I thought we could, you know, that it would be a fun thing for Chloe. Collecting fountains."

"Collecting fountains." He looked at me, nodding a little, like he was really listening, thinking hard about that.

"When I was first thinking about things for me and Chloe to do here, I found out that there are fourteen fountains in Rome. Well, fourteen notable fountains. I made a list, and then I copied pictures of each one out of the encyclopedia. And we said we would try to collect all of them."

"Fantastic."

"We've been to nine so far. And we got someone to take our picture at each one."

"That's really terrific. And Chloe never said a word about it."

"That's weird. I mean, it's not that big a deal. But I would have thought for sure she'd mentioned it."

"She's always been a funny kid that way. She likes to keep secrets."

We realized that the people from our group weren't by the fountain any more, so I tossed my coins over my left shoulder and we ran back to the bus.

At the end of the tour, Paolo dropped us off back at the hotel but instead of going up to our rooms, we went to the bar at the hotel across the street. I ordered a Campari and soda, which I'd seen someone order at lunch the day before. I felt like an adult, beautiful and sophisticated, like what I said was important and interesting. Like we were a couple. Like he might reach over and take my hand and tell me that he knew what I was thinking, how I was feeling, and that he felt the same way.

"Did you make a wish?"

I panicked for a second, thinking maybe I'd said something out loud.

"At the fountain. Did you make a wish?"

"Oh, shoot. Was I supposed to? Or is it just for general good luck?"

"Don't ask me. You're the one who did the research. Actually, it was probably invented for the movie."

"There's a movie? Oh, yeah. I think I remember. But it's in black and white, right? I hate black and white movies." I was messing with him. I knew he was a big movie guy and that he probably thought all the good movies were made before there was color.

"Oh my God. Are you kidding me? What do they teach you in—? You are kidding. Didn't anyone ever tell you that nobody likes a smartass?"

"Yeah, actually. My dad says that exact same thing to me all the time."

That made us both laugh, but then I wished I hadn't said it. It kind of creeped me out to think of him and my dad at the same time, and to realize that they are alike in lots of ways, and how if they knew each other, they'd probably be friends.

He talked a little bit about his relationship with his sons, and how even though he's really glad that they get along so well with their stepdad, sometimes he feels like he isn't as a big part of their lives as he should be. I talked a little bit about my dad, too, and how I was still really mad at him for leaving, and leaving me with my mom who is so crazy and unhappy all the time, and how she made me feel like if things with me and my dad were good, it would not be okay with her. He asked me why I was mad at my dad and not at my mom, and I couldn't really say. But it definitely made me think.

After that, he told me this terrible story. About how when his sister was sixteen, she visited him at college during winter break. It was right when he'd first started dating the girl who ended up being his first wife. The three of them had hung out the whole time, making dinner together at his apartment, going to some tiny club where Bob Dylan performed before anyone had heard of him. I interrupted to ask "Who's Bob Dylan?", just to see his reaction. Her last day there, they went ice skating, and he was so caught up in this new relationship that he hadn't really paid too much attention when she fell and hit her head. It turns out she had a concussion, or internal bleeding or something that he should have noticed, but didn't. So later that same day, she was on the bus going home, and she went into a coma and never woke up.

"It's figured into everything I've done since," he said. "Her death. Every decision I've made."

I didn't know what to say. I'd mostly just been nodding and listening the whole time he was telling me.

"My marriage to Vivian never really had a chance. I think I married her to prove that it was real, and not just some schoolboy crush. As if that somehow balanced out what happened." He was staring into his glass, like he didn't even remember that I was sitting there. "But I blamed Viv, almost as much as I blamed myself."

"It wasn't your fault. How could you have known?"

"Yeah. Says you and more therapists than I can count. What we're working on now is correcting the mistaken belief that love and pain are connected to one another, love and death. That love kills."

Neither of us said anything after that for a long time. We just sat there, drinking our drinks. I wondered if he was thinking about us. If he was thinking the same thing I was, that the reason we aren't together is because of the pain it would cause. Because of the mistaken belief that love causes pain. Or death.

"Well," he said, "that took a dark turn, didn't it? I hope that you will forgive me. You are delightful company, and I had a wonderful time tonight."

He put some money on the table under his empty glass.

"Shall we?" he asked, standing up.

"Thank you." I tried to smile, wishing I could come up with better words to say what I was feeling. "Thank you so much. For everything." I wondered if he could hear the tremble in my voice. All of a sudden, it felt like I was going to start to cry, so I picked up my bag and rushed outside and across the street to our hotel.

December 19, 1981

Beth and Kristen were both home for winter break. It was our first time getting together since we'd all started college. Which also meant they would be there on Monday for the launch party that the publicist was having for The Adventures of Peanut Girl. I was nervous. I really wasn't comfortable being the center of attention, and I still felt pretty self-conscious about the book. So I was glad that they would be there. Plus, some of my friends from Columbia. And my old art teacher. And, of course, Chloe and John and Mara.

Monday was going be the first time that Beth and Kristen were going to meet them, and I really needed to come clean. They were my best friends, and it was stupid that I'd lied to them. It had been gnawing at me for months. Plus, John had been so nice to me. It would be horrible if anyone ever found out what I'd said about him. That I'd basically called him a cheater. The other thing was that I had a boyfriend. An actual real life, heterosexual boyfriend—someone I liked, who totally seemed to like me too. I didn't need a pretend married boyfriend anymore.

On my way to the bar, I thought about what I would say. It had started as a goof, a prank, just to see if they would fall for it. I had always planned to tell them that it wasn't true. And then it just started to feel so dumb. And the more time passed, the more embarrassing it was that I hadn't told them sooner. I hoped that they would understand.

They were already at a table when I got to First Base, the noisy bar in the East Village with the grumpy old bartender who'd been serving us pitchers of beer since we were barely sixteen.

"Author, author!" Beth shouted as I walked toward them.

Kristen handed me a waiting shot and we all raised our glasses. "To half birthdays!"

We all talked at once, about Beth's roommate the debutante, and the sorority that Kristen was rushing, and finals, and football games, and majors and meal plans. I really meant to tell them the truth about the John thing, but by the time we were halfway through the second pitcher it was easier to just tell them it was over. That I'd cut way back on the babysitting when school started, and that eventually it had just sort of faded. I told them that I still talk to him, mostly about book stuff, and that he and Mara and Chloe would be at the party on Monday. No, I said, it really wasn't weird. I told them what he'd said—"We're all adults. And this is business." Then I told them about Jeff, and that he would be there on Monday, too, and that I really liked him and couldn't wait for them to meet him. And that was it.

I was pretty drunk when I got home, but I had one more thing I needed to do before Monday. I went into my mom's room where she was in bed watching some old movie on TV.

"Hey, mom. Can I talk to you for a second?"

"Sure, honey. How were the Birthday Girls?"

"It was really fun. They're good. They're both coming on Monday."

"That's nice. I'm glad they'll be there. So what's up?"

"You know that Dad's going to be there Monday, right?"

"I understand that you want him there. And that he's proud of you, like I am. I wouldn't miss it for anything, and I know he wouldn't either. As long as I don't have to talk to him, I am sure it will be fine."

"Okay, good. I mean, thanks. But the thing is . . . umm, so Deirdre's going to be there, too."

"Deirdre?" She looked at me like I had just spun my head all the way around like in the Exorcist.

"I asked her to come."

"How did you—? When did—? You see her?"

"Yeah, so I've actually been spending some time with her. With her and Dad. We still have our Tuesday dinners and a couple months ago, I told Dad he should bring her."

Okay, so that wasn't exactly true. I wished it was. It would have been such a mature thing for me to have done. And it definitely made for a better story. I figured if my mom would realize that everyone else had moved on, maybe she would, too. Mom just stared at me, so I kept going.

"It just seemed weird to keep pretending that she's not around. I mean, it's been a really long time. And we're all adults, right?" That line again. It was really coming in handy. "I just felt like I should get to know her."

She looked at me like she was waiting, like she was expecting me to say that I was just kidding.

"So now it's usually the three of us for Tuesday dinner. It's not that big a deal. Really, it's just dinner." Still staring. "What? She's nice."

"Nice? You think so? I don't think you know what that word even means. Was it nice that she fucked a married man?"

Now I was the one staring. I could feel my eyes open wider. My mom had been bitching about Deirdre forever, but I never heard her talk like that.

"Do you think it was nice that she destroyed our family? And took my husband from me? And now that whore wants to take you, too?"

"What are you talking about? No one's taking anyone. Mom, God. Whatever happened, it was a long time ago."

Now she wouldn't even look at me.

"Mom, seriously. It's been years. You need to get over it."

"Don't you dare tell me to get over it. Do you think this is something that you get over? That just goes away? That if enough time passes it won't matter anymore what he did?"

"Actually, Mom, yeah. That's exactly what I think. That's how it works."

"I honestly can't believe that you thought this would be acceptable. Go, right now, and call your father. Tell him that he is not to bring her."

"Mommy, don't do this. Please? You're being totally unfair. This is my thing, not yours. I invited her, as my guest."

"I will not be in the same room with that woman."

"Are you really doing this? I don't even—"

"If she's going to be there, I'm not coming."

"Please don't say that. You're—"

"I'm what? I will not go if she's going to be there."

I couldn't believe it. Was she really going to do this?

"Fine. Do whatever you want. I really don't care."

*   *   *

Two days later, Jeff and I took a cab together to the book party. I was afraid we'd be late, so we got there almost half an hour early. It was in a really cool loft, a wide open space, all white with twinkling white lights and waiters dressed in black. Copies of the book were everywhere. Someone handed me a glass of wine.

The first people to arrive after us were the publicist, and some of the Little, Brown people. Then two of my Columbia friends came in at the same time as my dad and Deirdre. Roger introduced me to his wife, Vivian, and I saw Mr. Tartaglio, my high school art teacher, walk in with Kevin. Beth and Kristen came in with a ridiculous bouquet of roses, like I'd just won the Kentucky Derby. I saw John, Mara and Chloe arrive. Mara went straight into the kitchen, where I knew she was checking with the caterer to make sure the food was safe. Chloe ran up to giant poster of the book cover, where she posed with her arms folded in front of her and her head tilted back. I could tell that she was hoping people would see the resemblance.

John walked over to me with a big smile, and gave me a hug. And then I felt his hand on my ass. And he gave it a little squeeze. Wait, what? Did that just happen? I looked up at him. He raised his eyebrows, like maybe he was as surprised as I was, and followed it with a wink.

That wink again. It totally saved it. It said, in a fraction of a second, *yeah, I know. Me, too.* I smiled at him.

That's really how it began.

Jenna

CHAPTER 4

January 18, 1983

I absolutely loved having my own apartment. It used to be Deirdre's, and she let me stay here that first winter break when I was so mad at my mom because of the book party. And then when I found out that my roommate wasn't coming back for the second semester, and that they were assigning me some transfer student, I moved in for real.

Even though she never said anything about it, I sometimes think that Deirdre must have somehow known about me and John, and that she gave me her apartment so we would have someplace to go. I mean, I know it sounds crazy, but hey, she had been a married guy's secret girlfriend, right? So maybe she felt like she was doing her part, passing the baton to the next generation of sluts. Okay, it is weird and gross to even think that, and I do not actually think of myself as a slut. I am way less slutty than most of my friends. But do I like to tease John sometimes about how this has damaged me, and destroyed my self esteem, and ruined me for normal healthy relationships. Anyway, the reality is that John and I probably wouldn't ever have gotten together if it wasn't for Deirdre. I mean, where would we have gone?

Because seriously, even once it started, it started really slow. It was nothing like when I started going out with Jeff. With Jeff, we met one night at a party and liked each other enough for me to go back to his room with him. And then we just kept hanging out together after that. I mean, we never actually talked about it. It just became a thing. Which happens to be exactly how it ended, too. But it was totally different with John. In the beginning, it seems like all we did was talk about it. Partly, I think, because we both felt so guilty. "We can't." "We shouldn't." "We're bad people." "We don't deserve this." "We need to stop." "Never again." And it was like we were taking turns. If he wasn't the one saying it was over, I was.

Anyway, college was completely different once we started seeing each other. I just sort of checked out of the whole social thing, and I treated it like it was my job. I would go in the morning, whether or not I had an early class, and I would stay until at least 4 or 4:30. I usually got all of my work done between classes, which was good because that way I had my nights and weekends free. If John wasn't stuck at work and didn't have to be home, he'd come over and we would hang out for a while. Every once in a while we would go out for dinner, but mostly we stayed in.

I decided to quit the creative writing program at the end of my freshman year. It was okay, and I wrote a couple of things that I thought maybe weren't too bad. But after a while it seemed like it was this totally self-indulgent pursuit for overly confident college kids who had been told their whole lives how clever they were. Everyone took themselves so seriously, as if anything these 18 and 19 year olds had to say might actually matter.

Part of what we did in class was to sit around and critique each other's work. One day I got so frustrated with the way people were talking about this thing I'd written, telling me I wasn't going deep enough, that I was avoiding the truth, that I needed to be honest and get real. I wanted to scream, *This is fiction, people. Creative writing, get it? It's not therapy.* I had first started telling stories to my dad, thinking that if I had good enough stories to tell him maybe he would stay at home more. Like the problem was that my mom and I somehow weren't interesting enough to hold his attention. So I would take something that I'd heard about, something that happened to someone else, and I'd tell my dad the story, but I'd make it about me instead. Or sometimes I'd take something that had happened to me, but I'd embellish it, add to it, give it some conflict, or a better ending. I'd always have a bunch of stories ready to tell my dad whenever he was around. I really didn't get the point of just telling my own life story.

Another reason I quit was that I realized I didn't want the life of a struggling artist. I would picture myself sitting in a tiny walk-up apartment, broke and alone, drinking a cup of coffee that had gone cold while I sat staring at a blank sheet of paper in the typewriter. At some point, I realized that I could choose not to be that, that it was actually up to me to decide what kind of life I wanted. So I would think about the women I knew, and what their lives were like. And I knew that I would rather be like Deirdre, a doctor with her own life and career and money, and not like my mom, or Mara, sitting there waiting for her husband to come home. Wondering if he would.

Mara

CHAPTER 5

March 16, 1985

The waiter brought them their drinks, took their order and left them in silence. She knew John had something on his mind, that this was no casual dinner. They'd been married for fourteen years and this was the first time he'd surprised her this way. He first told her at 6 that they had a 7:30 reservation. She'd barely had time to get dressed. Sign of the Dove on a Saturday night? He must have made the reservation weeks ago. He cleared his throat and drank. No toast, she thought. So it's not a celebration.

"I'm so glad you thought of this. It was a good idea. I can't even remember the last time we were here. Was it that time with Debra and Phil? I forget what they were in town for. Or wait. Didn't we come here with your parents? When was that—do you remember?"

"I don't know. I've been here other times. With clients, I guess."

"Well, it's really lovely. Honestly? I'd forgotten how nice it is. We should do this more often, you know? Now that Chloe is old enough stay home alone. Don't you think? Maybe we should toast to that."

Silence.

"John. What is it? Is something wrong?"

"I'm sorry. I can't— I really don't— Look, I think you know that I haven't been happy lately. That we haven't been happy."

She squeezed the lime, stirred her drink and took a sip. She gave him an encouraging smile.

"We deserve to be happy." He cleared his throat. "I work too hard, *we* work too hard, not to be."

"Happy? Yes, of course. What do you—? I'm not sure I understand."

"There are things in life that we can control, and things we can't. I just think we owe it to ourselves to take responsibility for the things we can control. We can't keep just riding this tide. When something isn't working, you fix it, right? Even if that means taking it apart and starting over again. Do you know what I mean?"

"John, I'm sorry. I want to help, I really do. But I don't understand what you're talking about. Did something happen at the firm?"

"No. It's not work. Everything is fine at work. I mean, work is work. It's demanding, and the Datsun case is a pain in the ass. Those calls with Japan in the middle of the night are killing me. But it's fine. It's good even. It's everything else."

"Sweetheart, you're not making sense. Please just tell me what you need. Should we plan to go away someplace? Take a long weekend? Maybe we can rent a place at the beach this summer. Like we talked about that time? I can call that broker. A place with a pool, maybe. Or a tennis court. You used to love tennis. We haven't played in years."

"Mara, just stop. Can you see what you're doing? This is what you always do. You're just talking and not hearing me. Don't you want more than this? I'm not talking about a weekend at the beach. I mean more than this. Something real. Don't we owe it to ourselves? To Chloe? To give her a better—?"

The waiter brought their salads.

"Do not bring Chloe into this." She lowered her voice. "Whatever this is, it has nothing to do with her."

John looked to his left and then to his right, and then he leaned forward. "I'm sorry. I don't mean to hurt you. But I'm seeing someone." He spoke softly. "Someone I want to be with. I don't want to be married anymore."

She put down her fork and touched the corner of her mouth with her napkin, careful not to ruin her lipstick. She took a roll from the basket, and put it down on her bread plate. She looked at the butter sitting in a crystal bowl filled with tiny ice cubes—perfectly round pale yellow disks, each impressed with a simple outline of a dove. She wondered whose job it was to stamp the doves into the butter. Her heart was pounding. Minutes went by before the buzzing in her head quieted enough so that she could again hear the muffled conversations on either side of her, the clinking of silverware against plates, the laughter coming from over John's shoulder. She finished her drink before she looked up at him and smiled.

"This really isn't a good time. Let's not do this now, okay?

"Not now, tonight? Do you mean not now, not here, at the restaurant? Because what I am trying to say, what I am telling you, is that I want to— I want us to not be together anymore."

"Yes. I heard you say that. And I am saying that now is not a good time. You are very busy at work. You said yourself that the Datsun case has been difficult. And this has not been an easy year for Chloe. It is hard enough being thirteen years old, and now to be starting high school in the fall? She doesn't need to deal with your— With this— With your drama. Oh look, I think this is us."

She smiled at the two waiters as they approached the table, one for each of them. They put down the plates and removed the silver cloches simultaneously. It was perfect. Like ballet.

Jenna

CHAPTER 6

June 9, 1985

I reached around and caught the door just before it slammed. I closed it gently behind me, pushing on it with my shoulder until I heard it click shut. I kicked off my flip flops and put down the bags on the counter in the kitchen. I turned on the coffee maker and put out cups and plates and napkins.

We'd been out late the night before, celebrating our 22nd birthdays. Even though I'd taken some aspirin and drank a big glass of water before I went to sleep, I was still feeling pretty awful. It seemed like the harder I tried to be quiet, the more noise I was making. Just the sound the paper bag made when I took out the bagels was making my head pound. I was pouring myself some coffee when I heard Kristen from the living room.

"I swear to God, I'm never drinking again." She sat up on the edge of the sofabed.

"Shhhh, don't talk," Beth said, her head under the comforter. "I think my brain might be bleeding."

I brought them each a cup of coffee. "Well, at least no one threw up. Cheers to that, ladies."

We felt almost human after we ate and had coffee, so we put on baseball hats and sunglasses and went to our usual spot in the park, down by the Bethesda Fountain. They were talking about last night, how cool it was that so many of our friends had come out for our birthdays, and how much some of our friends had changed. Kristen kept talking about how cute and funny the bartender was. Beth was saying that she thought Connie might be anorexic, but Kristen said that she looked amazing, and that Beth was just jealous.

"Guys. Want to hear something? That I barely told anyone?" I always knew how to get their attention. "I'm going to law school. NYU. In September."

"Really?" Beth asked, looking skeptical "Law school? How did—?"

"Oh, no! Don't do that. That makes me so sad."

"It makes you sad? Kristen, that is so weird. Why would it make you sad? I swear to God, you sound like my mother."

"Because you're a writer. You're supposed to be the—"

"Oh, cut it out. I am not a writer. It was just that one thing."

"Slow down," said Beth. "I need to understand this. First, what did your mother say? Joanne is sad that you're going to law school?"

"Jenna, seriously," Kristen said, "You should tell your mother that I totally get it. It really does make me sad. Lawyers are so— I don't know. You were going to be the famous author. And Beth is going to move to Los Angeles and become some Hollywood bigshot, and I'll be the one who just gets married and has kids. But then you'll both realize that sometimes happiness—"

"Jenna, don't even listen to her. She thinks we are going to be the 1980s version of the Valley of the Dolls or something. But seriously. Tell me what she said."

"My mother? I don't even know. She's all bent out of shape that I managed to get through college without settling down—her words. By which she means without having a serious boyfriend. I swear, lately it's like she thinks it's the same as it was when she was our age. And somehow, going to law school is a bad thing. Because really, what boy would ever want to marry a lawyer, right?"

"Well, it's good to know that Joanne is still crazy. But law school . . . ? That just seems so out of the blue. I mean, what made you even—? Oh oh oh. Wait a second. Okay. I think I've got it. This was Mr. P's idea, right?"

"Oh my God, would you please stop calling him that? And no. It wasn't his idea. I didn't even tell him until after I applied."

"This is so cute," Beth said. "He must be so proud of you—his little girl is finally growing up."

"You didn't tell him? That's weird." Kristen asked. "I mean, he's a lawyer. So why wouldn't you—?"

"I didn't tell anyone. I mean, it was never like a big rest-of-my-life decision. I took the LSATs and I did okay, so I decided to apply to a few places. I didn't know if I'd get in, or if I'd decide to go. But I did, so I am. I have to do something, right? I mean, come on. My professional experience is babysitting, scooping ice cream and folding sweaters. So, fine, whatever. I'm going to law school. Jesus, why doesn't anyone just say 'wow, good for you'? Actually, you know what? It's getting late. I've got to go." I couldn't believe that we were having this conversation. I just wanted to go home. I started to get up.

"Jen, wait. Don't be mad. Kristen was being a jerk."

"Me? You were the one who—"

"I'm kidding. God, would you please chill out? Jen, I'm sorry. I was being a jerk. I guess I was still hoping you'd come to LA with me. I thought we'd—"

"I keep telling you, I'm not moving to LA. My life is here, okay?"

"You mean because he's here."

"Well, yeah, partly. So?"

"So, that's it. You're just going to sit here hoping he's going to leave his wife someday?"

"Just sit here? Are you kidding? I'm going to law school. I'm sorry if that isn't what you had planned for me." Beth just wanted me to go with her to keep her company while she followed her dream. She couldn't possibly think that it would be better for me to get some bullshit job in California.

"Come on, guys. Don't fight. She didn't mean it like that. Right Beth? Tell her. We're just afraid sometimes that you're, like, I don't know, missing out. Like, you know, that maybe you're not fully experiencing— Come on. You know what I'm trying to say."

I looked at Kristen, and then at Beth. They really should look in the mirror and stop worrying about me. "This is what you guys talk about?

You've got to be kidding me. Beth, do you even remember making out with that idiot Jack Gorman last night? And Kristen, that bartender? He was gross. Is that what you think I'm missing?"

"I actually thought Jack Gorman looked pretty good. Didn't he? But oh my God. Talking to him? He is as big a moron today as he was in tenth grade. No lie. When I told him I'm going to drive out to LA he asked if I am going to do the drive all in one day. Look, I'm sorry. I really am. I just want to make sure you're okay. And happy. And I swear to God. If that peanut dad hurts you I will personally fucking kill him. Okay?"

I know they mean well. And they worry about me because they love me. But I'm really fine. Better than fine.

"Yeah, okay. I'll be sure to tell him you said so."

John

CHAPTER 7

March 28, 1987

He'd gotten to the restaurant early, on purpose, so he would have time for a drink before Roger got there. He told the hostess he'd wait at the bar. Once he had his scotch in front of him, he allowed himself, for the first time, to try to figure out what this was about, why his ex-wife's husband wanted to buy him dinner. Maybe one of the boys was having a problem in school. But, no. That was the kind of thing Vivian would call him about. It had to be something bigger than that. A money thing? Can't be. Roger's not the one paying three kids' tuition, and besides, he makes plenty of money. Maybe it's Viv. If she's sick? Christ, he thought, that would be terrible. But that's got to be it. It seemed like he'd been hearing more and more lately about women in their forties getting cancer. Or Alzheimer's. There was that thing he'd seen on TV about younger people getting Alzheimer's. That would be some kind of kick in the ass, huh? Tragic. And not just for her. Imagine poor Roger and the boys having to—

"Hey, man. Sorry I'm late," Roger said, patting him on the shoulder. "She says our table's ready and that they'll move your tab."

He finished his drink in a single swallow and followed Roger and the hostess to their table.

The waiter brought their drinks, and they looked over the menu. They ordered steaks, onion rings and a side of creamed spinach.

"So what's Providence going to do tomorrow? Do you think Pitino can take them all the way?"

"Oh, basketball?" John hadn't watched any of the games, but he made a point of paying attention to the results just for conversations like this one. "I think he already took them farther than anyone would have guessed. My money's on UNLV."

"Yeah? I have Syracuse going all the way. But watch, it'll be some kid in the mailroom who wins the pool. I think its something like five hundred bucks in my office."

"I let Chloe make my picks. We were out after the first round."

Roger took a long drink, put down his glass and cleared his throat.

"So, listen. There was something I wanted to talk to you about." Roger took a quick look around the room and leaned forward.

Here it comes. He looked into the amber liquid in his glass, and braced himself for what was coming.

"I'm leaving Coleman McBride."

John looked up. "You're what?"

"I know. It's crazy, right? I've been there 21 years. I tell you, I can't believe I'm doing it. It doesn't seem real to me," Roger said, shaking his head. "I mean, when do you ever hear about a partner leaving one firm to go to another?"

"Oh, I don't know. It's not completely unheard of these days. We've had a couple guys leave to go to other firms."

"I don't know. When I made partner at Coleman, I thought that meant that I'd be there forever. I mean, you know how it is."

"Well, yeah. That's great, though, Roger, really. Congratulations." John raised his half-empty glass.

"But let me tell you, it was the toughest decision I ever had to make. And who was I going to talk to about it? I obviously can't talk to any of my partners. I mean, it's been all these secret meetings, cloak and dagger stuff. Viv is great. You know how she is. But what's she going to say about it? 'Sure, honey. Sounds fine. Whatever you decide.' So, anyway, she's the one who suggested I call you. She thought that maybe you and I could get together, that I should talk to you. I hope you don't mind."

"Mind? No, of course not. Anyway, is it official?"

"I should have something in writing from them by Tuesday or Wednesday, and I figure I'll tell the guys at Coleman on Friday." Roger picked up his glass, and took a long swallow. "Honestly, though, I don't even know how I'm supposed to do it. Quit, I mean. I guess I just walk in and tell the chairman, right? That's going to be tough, though. After 21 years? It'd be like telling your wife you're leaving her."

They looked at each other, then both looked away.

"You haven't even told me where you're going."

"I know. I feel like an idiot. But I'm afraid I'll jinx it if I say it out loud. Porter & Gray."

"Hey, good for you. That's a great firm. I know a couple of the IP guys over there. Good guys. Really, Roger, that's terrific. Porter & Gray, that's funny. Wait until I tell Jenna. Small world . . ."

"Jenna. You mean Chloe's Jenna? The author? I didn't know she's still around."

"Oh, yeah. She's still— Umm, yeah. We still hear from her sometimes. She and Chloe—"

"What's she up to? Did she ever do anything else after that—? What was it, Peanut Girl? I don't think I've heard a thing about her. It's got to be five years already. Six?"

"Yeah. Going on six. She's in her second year at NYU. Law school. And she's doing great. Really great. Like, way up at the top of her class. As a matter of fact, she has a job at Porter & Gray for the summer. She's going to be a Summer Associate there."

"No kidding. Well, that's great. Good for her. She was a nice kid. I'll be sure to say hello."

That could have been it. If he'd just kept his mouth shut, that would have been it. A couple of guys, a couple of steaks, no big deal. But he'd been worried that he said too much. That something he said would get back to Mara.

"Nice night," Roger said as they walked out onto the street.

"Huh? Oh, yeah, it is. Nice. So, umm, listen. I'm not going to say anything about your plans, right? To anyone. I mean, until it's announced. I'm just going to keep it to myself."

"Sure, thanks. It's probably just a week, but yeah, I appreciate that."

"Because you wouldn't want— I mean, you'd hate for—" John stopped and looked around, getting his bearings. "Hey, do you feel like a cigar? There's that place over on 52nd. You know that cigar place?"

Sitting in the dark smoky room with a fresh drink in front of him, John said what he'd been trying to say out on the street. "I need you to do me a favor. Can you not mention to Vivian that I said anything about Jenna? Or to Sam or Ricky? Look, I know it's dumb, but I'd hate for it to get back to Mara. You know, through Chloe or something."

"Sure. Whatever you want," said Roger. "I can't really see how it would even come up. But, yeah. Okay."

What kind of idiot am I? John wondered. He shouldn't have said anything. Of course it wouldn't come up. *Jesus,* he thought. *I need to just stop talking.*

"You're right, of course. Why would it even come up? It wouldn't. It's just that— I was just thinking how I'd hate for Mara to hear something. Something perfectly innocent, but you know how she is. Or, I guess maybe you don't. Look, it's no big deal. Really. But it's just that I'd hate to give her a reason to think there was anything going on between me and—"

What am I doing? he thought. *Why don't I stop talking? Why is he looking at me that way?*

He started at the beginning, and he told Roger everything. It was the first time he ever said any of it out loud. It seemed important that he get it right, and he struggled to find the right words. He wanted Roger to understand that it wasn't just sex, that it wasn't just a thing he had going on the side. That he loves Jenna, that he's in love with her. But that he can't leave right now. Because Mara isn't like Viv. He'd always known Vivian would be fine. Mara can be unstable, unpredictable. And Chloe's the one who would suffer the most. He won't do that to her. But he wanted Roger to know that he'd always been straight with Jenna. He never lied to her, and he never asked her to wait for him. He told Roger that he knows Jenna might not be around when he's ready, and that he encourages her to date, to go out with other people, to live her life, even though it kills him just to say it. He mostly wanted Roger to know that he's not a bad guy.

March 29, 1987

He looked at his watch, 7:10, and he started to run. He figured he could get a full six miles in and be home in time to have breakfast with Chloe before she went off to do whatever it is she does these days. He'd stop on the way home and pick up croissants from that new place Mara told him about.

The morning was cool and damp. It was just what he needed to clear his head. He breathed deeply, and felt his lungs clear, replacing last night's cigar smoke with the new day's air.

He'd started out too fast, and he could feel it after only a few minutes. He should have stretched. He slowed down to a jog, and tried to breathe through the pain in his side. Maybe if he stopped for a minute. He stepped onto the grass, out of the way of the other runners behind him, and bent forward, stretching his hands toward the ground. He stood up, and raised his arms over his head, first reaching up, then leaning to the right and then to the left. He dodged the bike and jogger traffic to cross to the benches on the other side.

He sat down, stretched his legs in front of him, leaned his head back and closed his eyes. The sun was warm on his face, and it felt good to sweat out the booze. Just a couple minutes, and he'd get back to it.

What he'd wanted Roger to know was that this thing with Jenna isn't the same as when he and Mara got together. Not even close.

Mara had been assigned to him to replace his secretary when she retired. She was young and pretty. And smart. She had a great attitude. The guys were always finding reasons to come by his office, hanging around her desk. But Mara either didn't notice, or didn't care. She just wanted to help him. "My job is to make your job easier," she'd say. There wasn't anything she wouldn't do for him.

It was the year he was up for partner, and he was working his ass off. There was a brief due on a Monday, and he'd needed her to come to the office on Saturday to help him get it done. They somehow managed to finish earlier than he'd expected, and she suggested that maybe they could grab a quick bite, if he wasn't in too much of a hurry to get home. Over dinner, she told him about having lost her parents, and how she'd been on her own ever since. He thought about how there would be sixteen of them at his parents' place for Thanksgiving next week, and he pictured her, by herself, watching the parade on TV. He called Viv and told her it was taking longer than he'd thought it would, that he'd be late and that she shouldn't wait up. Then he went with Mara to her apartment in Jackson Heights, so that, at least for a few hours, she wouldn't be alone.

It got pretty intense pretty fast after that first night. She said she hadn't meant for anything to happen. That she'd never wanted to break up his marriage. That she loved Vivian and the boys. Looking back, though, it seems that she knew exactly what she was doing. It was like she'd written the script, but she only gave him a couple of pages at a time. He was up for partner, and screwing his secretary behind his wife's back, with two little boys at home. If it got out, it could ruin his career. "Think about what you would tell a client to do," she'd said to him. "You have to get in front of the story." And of course she was right.

He rented an apartment, told Vivian and moved out. A few weeks later, Mara quit her job and a couple weeks after that she moved in with him. She was pregnant before his divorce was even final. They got married before she started to show.

That was fifteen years ago. He had no regrets. What could have been a total disaster had turned out okay. Better than okay. Chloe was a terrific kid. Vivian and the boys survived, thrived even. Look at them now, living happily ever after. He'd made partner, right on schedule, and he and Mara had a good marriage, a good life. So what the hell was he doing with Jenna?

He'd seen her grow up. She was what, about 13 or 14 when she first started sitting for Chloe? He remembered thinking she was a great kid right from the start. She was smart and funny, and responsible—mature. Granted, she was a couple years older than Sam and Ricky, but it was like she was a different species, the way she would look you in the eye and actually engage in conversation. Of course Chloe loved her. And Mara trusted her, which was practically a miracle. When Jenna came into their lives, it was like a cloud of anxiety had been lifted.

Maybe he'll skip the run, he thought. Give Jenna a call, see what she's up to today. If Chloe isn't going to be around anyway, he can tell Mara he's going in to the office for a couple of hours. She should be up by now. He made his way out of the park, and over to Columbus Avenue, looking for a payphone.

Chloe

CHAPTER 8

September 23, 1989

Chloe stood under the big arrivals and departures board by the escalators, waiting, imagining reasons Jessica might not show up, trying to figure out what to wish for. She stopped herself from considering a train crash. She didn't want Jess dead. Or even hurt. And she definitely didn't want to involve a train full of strangers. Maybe she never got on the train. Maybe she got a phone call just as she was leaving her house. There'd been a death in the family. But it would have to be someone who was already old. And sick. No, that's a terrible thing to wish for. Car trouble. Okay, yeah. That's good. Please, please, please, let her have missed the train because her car broke down on the way to— And there she was, dropping her bag and kissing her on the mouth.

"What are you doing?" Chloe took a step back, looking around. "God, we're right in the middle of Penn Station. What if someone—?"

"Lighten up. Didn't you miss me?"

They'd met in July. Chloe, sitting alone on the bed her mother had made with brand new extra long twin-sized sheets, had just returned to her dorm room after waving goodbye as her parents drove away. She'd left the door open, like her mother said she should, to make it easier to meet people. She thought about unpacking, but decided to wait a while since she wouldn't have anything to do once it was done.

"It's summer school, not the fucking army."

It sounded like it was coming from right outside the door, but from where she was sitting, Chloe couldn't see who was speaking.

"Jesus, Mom. Just go."

A door slammed. Chloe sat still, waiting for the mother's response. There was nothing. No sound of the door being opened. No knock. No urgent whispered "let me in", like she would expect from her own mother. Was that it? Did she really leave? Chloe leaned forward, trying to see out into the hall. She stood up and walked tentatively toward the doorway just as a girl pushed past her into the room and threw herself onto Chloe's bed.

Jessica was from Annapolis. She dressed all in black, her short hair was tinted maroon, and she wore heavy eye liner and black nail polish. Like Chloe, she had just finished her junior year in high school and was attending Cornell's pre-college program at her mother's suggestion, because it would look good on her college applications. They discovered that they liked the same music, they'd read some of the same books, and they were planning to take two of the same classes.

They were together from that point forward. It was as if Jessica had decided that the first girl she saw after her mother left would be "the one".

Mara wasn't home when they got there, so Chloe went along with it when Jess said they should just hang out for a while, rather than go sightseeing, as Chloe had planned. She'd figured out over the summer that there really wasn't any point in trying to change Jessica's mind.

"What do you think about Georgetown?" Jessica was sitting at Chloe's desk, looking through her copy of the Insider's Guide to the Colleges. "As a reach school?" Jessica opened the desk drawer. "Where's a pen?"

"Sure, okay." Chloe, lying on her bed, closed her eyes. She had already decided to apply to other schools, that she would keep her real list a secret. But she was letting Jessica think that they would apply to the same places, that they would go to college together, like they'd talked about.

Jessica got up and took a large book from her bag and sat down on the bed next to Chloe.

"Look. I made an album of all of my pictures from the summer. Move over."

She stretched out down next to Chloe. After they'd looked at the photo album, Chloe reached across her and picked up the Insider's Guide.

"What does it mean that it's Jesuit?"

"Mm, I don't know. I'm sure we can skip the churchy parts." Jessica took Chloe's hand in hers.

"Yeah, but do you think it's super catholic? Will we be the only—? Like, what if everyone is walking around in plaid skirts and blouses with peter pan collars? I just want to— Hey, what are you doing?" Chloe pulled her arm away and saw that Jessica had printed the words "I'M GAY" on the palm of her hand. "What did you—? What's the matter with you?" She sat up and snatched at a tissue from the bedside table, wetting it with her tongue.

"It's not going to come off. I used a Sharpie."

"Why did you do that? God, you're such a jerk."

Jessica followed her into the bathroom. "I'm trying to help. Isn't it time you told them already? I really don't think it's—"

"It doesn't matter what you think. It has nothing to do with you."

"Of course it does. How can you—? Do you even know how you made me feel at the train station? When you shoved me away like that?"

"I didn't— We were in a public place. I didn't want to make a scene. Is that such a big deal?"

"And I just want to help you tell your parents. Is *that* such a big deal?"

"Yeah, Jess. It is. It really is."

"Well, don't be mad at me." Jessica stuck out her bottom lip in an exaggerated pout.

Chloe stared at her, wondering how she would get through the next twenty-four hours. "Come on. Let's get out of here before my mother gets home."

"Does everyone have everything they need? Here Chloe, have some of these green beans. I made them the way you like." Mara turned to Jessica. "Chloe says you live in Maryland?"

"Mom. I don't want any—"

"That's right. Annapolis."

"Beautiful city," said John. "I was there with Sam a few years ago. Or was it Rick? I can't remember which one. We were visiting colleges."

"Did you look at the Naval Academy?"

"We did the whole DC, Maryland, Virginia tour, but the Naval Academy wasn't on anyone's radar. Good school, though."

"Oh, for sure. My dad's an instructor there. But it's definitely not for everybody."

"Have you decided where you'll be applying?"

"Well, yeah. I mean, me and Chloe are—"

"Dad, please. I am begging you."

"What?" He looked first at Chloe, then at Jessica. "What did I do now?"

"Can we please just have a conversation that isn't about college? I swear, it's all anyone ever—"

"I guess we're sort of all talked out about college right now. We spent the whole afternoon going over our list. Right Chloe?" asked Jessica. Nobody spoke "This chicken is really delicious. Chloe said you were a good cook, Mrs. Toberman, but this is better than a restaurant. What do you call this?"

God, thought Chloe, she is such a suck up.

"It's just a dijonnaise. Chloe, honey, don't you want one of these rolls?"

"If I wanted one, don't you think I would—?" Chloe stopped, leaning back in her chair.

"Why are you behaving this—?"

"Mara, let it go. She's okay," John said. "She'll take one if she wants it. Right, Peanut? You're not shy."

"Oh my God, Chloe. People call you Peanut? Why didn't tell ever me? That is adorable."

"They don't. Not really. It's just my dad." Chloe tried to cut a piece of chicken with the side of her fork, the table shaking from the effort. "Can you pass the rolls?"

"What's wrong with your hand?"

"Yeah, Peanut. What's wrong with your hand?" Jessica asked with a smile.

"What? Nothing." Under the table, she unclenched her fist and slid her hand onto the seat of her chair, under her thigh.

"Your hand. Did you hurt yourself?"

"It's fine. Can you all please just leave me alone?"

Jessica and John did most of the talking for the rest of the meal, with Chloe trying to avoid her mother's inquiring and concerned looks, eyebrows raised, lips pursed, from across the table. As soon as there was a lull in the conversation she announced that she and Jessica were going out and would be back later.

"Call me if you'll be late," Mara said as Chloe closed the apartment door behind them.

September 29, 1989

Chloe and John stood on the corner, waiting for the light to change. They hadn't spoken since leaving the apartment, riding silently down in the elevator, walking through the lobby and out onto the street, and heading toward Broadway. She'd been waiting all week for a chance to be alone with him, an opportunity for them to talk, just the two of them. And she had a feeling that he had too. She knew that he was patient, that he'd wait for her, give her the chance to start the conversation that she wanted to have when she wanted to have it. Not knowing how to begin, she reached over and took his hand. The light turned, and they crossed the avenue, holding hands, and continued walking east.

"What do you need to pick up? Something for school?"

"Nothing really. It's a nice night, and I guess I just wanted to get out of the house. Besides, you're always in the mood to go to a bookstore, so I figured you'd want to come." She looked up in time to see him smile, pleased to know that she'd intended for him to join her, that he'd interpreted it correctly.

"Did I ever tell you about SallyAnn? She was my first love. This was before Vivian even, when I was still living at home. I thought that she was the most beautiful girl I'd ever seen. I'd had a crush on her for years, and she wouldn't give me the time of day. And then one day, out of the blue—"

"Mom told you, right? About how she walked in on me and Jessica?"

"Yeah. She did."

"Was she, like, completely freaking out?"

"She was pretty upset about it."

"*She* was upset? It's not her thing to be upset about. Why can't anything ever just be mine?"

"Hey, easy. She was upset with herself. For not knocking. And not respecting your privacy."

"Oh."

"It's hard for her to let go of you. To give you some room to be who you are. It's like when you were a baby, and she never wanted to put you down. Even when you took a nap, she'd sit there for hours with you asleep in her arms. I didn't see how you'd ever learn to walk."

"Sometimes I think she wishes she could still carry me around all the time."

They'd passed the bookstore without going inside. When they got to Central Park West, John nodded toward a bench. "Want to sit?"

"What else did she say? About when she came into my room."

"Really just that she felt bad that she'd violated your privacy. She was afraid that she'd embarrassed you. And that you would be upset with her."

"That's it?"

"Uh, yeah. I think so."

"So, she didn't say anything about what we were doing? When she came in?"

"You mean that you were in bed?"

"With Jessica. Yeah, that."

"Not really. I figured it out. From the way she was carrying on about how you're not a child anymore, and that we need to better respect your privacy."

"Oh. Okay. I guess I would have expected her to freak out about it. About me. You know? Me being . . . with a girl?"

"Nah. She didn't really say anything about that." A leaf fluttered to the bench next to him and John picked it up. "This time of year always feels like a new beginning to me. I guess it's still that back to school feeling. You never really outgrow it."

"What about you?" She turned and looked up at John. "You're okay about me being with a girl?"

"None of my business, really. As long as nobody's getting hurt? If you're okay, I'm okay."

"Yeah, I'm good."

"Good. Me, too And Jessica seems, umm, okay."

"Seriously? She's horrible. We broke up."

"Oh, that's good. I actually thought she was kind of a jerk. Let's go buy some books."

Jenna

CHAPTER 9

July 8, 1991

The doorman opened the taxi door for me as the driver reached around to hand me the receipt. We ran through our usual routine while I walked through the lobby, got my mail and waited for the elevator—"You're home early. What's this, a half day for you?" "Oh, you know me. Slacking off again." I swear, after almost three years as a lawyer, the worst part is coming home so late from work and having to have these idiotic conversations.

Riding up in the elevator, looking through the bills and catalogues, I saw a letter from Beth. No return address, but I would recognize her handwriting anywhere. Weird that she would write me a letter. I got upstairs, let myself in, put the mail down on the table by the door, and went into my bedroom to change. After I took out my contacts and washed my face, I went into the kitchen to consider my options. I looked at the clock—too late to make pasta. I checked the expiration date on the yogurt and tossed it in the trash. I took the box of Wheat Thins into the living room, sat down on the couch and turned on the TV in time to catch the end of Johnny Carson.

I don't know what made me remember the letter. Maybe something in Letterman's monologue. I went and got it, sat back down on the couch and opened it.

Neil asked me to marry him.
Do you see how crazy that looks? That's why I had to write a letter.
Because if we were on the phone you would be screaming and I would

get totally caught up in the excitement and I would never be able to tell you that I think I don't want to get married. That's not even true. I definitely want to get married. I think I don't want to get married to him.

You don't have to tell me that he's great. I know he's great. He's really cute and he's pretty smart, even though he says really dumb shit sometimes.

Having dinner with you and John that night was so fun, but I swear, it totally messed me up. I'm really sorry for every bad thing I ever said about him. And for every bad thing I ever thought about him. I should have known you wouldn't be with a creep. He's totally awesome. And he is so into you. Do you even notice anymore how he looks at you? And how he listens to every word you say, like he thinks you are the most interesting person in the world? Watching the two of you, there's no question that you are perfect together.

So the next day after we had dinner that night I came back here, and Neil picked me up at the airport. I kept waiting for him to look at me the way John looks at you. Just for a second. And he never did. I don't look at him that way either. It made me wonder if he and I would even be together if it wasn't so easy. Do you know what I mean? You and John have had to sneak around. You've been waiting forever. You've been listening to me for years telling you to stop. And you know that, best case, someday a whole bunch of people are totally going to be totally judgmental of you, and at least a few people are going to be really pissed. But you're together anyway.

By the way, I said yes. I figure there is plenty of time for us to come up with a way to get me out of this.

Here's why I don't want to marry him:

1. *I have always hated the name Neil. Remember that kid, Neil Hemmings? The one who used to bring a hot dog in a thermos to school for lunch? That's what I think of every time I hear the name Neil.*
2. *He's from New York. Which I know on paper looks like a good thing. He's already talking about how we'll move back before the*

wedding. But when I came out here it was supposed to be to expand my universe, not to find a guy who we totally could have met at a high school party. Shit, if I'd just stayed on 84th Street I probably would have met him eventually.

3. *I don't know how to cook, and I feel like I am going to be expected to throw dinner parties. I keep picturing myself freaking out in the kitchen while there is a bunch of hungry strangers sitting around my dining room table.*

I know this doesn't make sense.
Call me.
PS—my ring is gorgeous!

I read it three times in a row, and then I called her. And she was right. We screamed and got totally caught up in the excitement, interrupting each other, talking about a million things—how he proposed, dresses and hairstyles, how many bridesmaids, the Plaza or the Pierre.

We decided that I would go visit her in LA as soon as I could get a few days off from work.

August 1, 1991

I didn't know how some of my colleagues did it, with husbands or wives, and kids and dogs at home. I couldn't have kept a cactus alive if I tried. When I was busy at work, all I did was work. I didn't buy groceries, I didn't do laundry, I didn't open my mail. I worked, slept, showered and went back to work. I just kept going, telling myself that that was why they were paying me so much money, and that I wouldn't do it forever.

I'd ended up joining the Real Estate Department, and while it wasn't exactly a passion, it was okay. I learned a lot. I worked on some big deals, I got good bonuses, and I was starting to have some client contact, which was nice. This particular deal, though, was a killer. If it didn't get done by July 31st, fortunes would be lost, heads would explode, stars would fall from the sky. Whatever. I had worked 34 days straight, without a day off. A few of us ended up pulling an all-nighter that last night before the closing, and we somehow got it done. John came over that night and we ordered a pizza, smoked a joint and hung out for a while. I woke up when he got into the shower, and then again when he kissed me goodbye. I got up the next morning, threw a pair of jeans and some t-shirts into a suitcase and got a cab to the airport.

When the stewardess started doing the safety thing, I took out my Walkman, put on my headphones and reread Beth's letter, this time through John's eyes. I'd shown it to him and wanted to see again what he'd read, what she'd said about him, about us.

I kept thinking about something she'd said that night on the phone. That she was afraid she didn't love him. Or that she didn't love him enough, as much as she was supposed to. It made me think of this time in high school when Beth was sleeping over my house after a party. We were really high and I picked up the color wheel I had made for my art class, and said something about how isn't it weird that you can't know if what you call blue looks the same to you as how what someone else calls blue looks to them. She totally understood what I meant, and we went on and on about how you learn from the time you're a little kid that the sky is blue. And blueberries are blue. And this is a blue crayon. And that's your blue dress. So we know that everything that looks like that should be called blue, but we don't know what blue actually looks like to anyone else. We thought we were making some huge philosophical breakthrough and then the next morning we were like "who cares?"

People act like love is some objective thing. "Do you love him?" "Are you in love with him?" But I think it's like the color blue. You can't know if what you are feeling is what anyone else would call love.

If someone asked me what I love about John, what would I say? There's the obvious stuff—he's smart and handsome and kind. And he is always really interested in what I have to say. He says he loves the way my mind works. He's a good dad. Whenever he talks about Chloe or Ricky or Sam, it is with this combination of love and pure pride—you could only hope that your dad talked about you that way. He has an unbelievable memory. It seems like he remembers every goofy story I ever told him. He knows a million old jokes and old stories and songs and movies, and can always come up with exactly the right one to make a point. And he is a problem solver. It's unbelievable—whatever you need, he can hook you up. Your vacuum cleaner is broken? He knows where to take it. You need a painter, or a guy to take your old couch away? He's got the guy. He collects people and saves them, so that when someone needs something, anything, he can make a call and get you what you need.

He respects my opinions, and calms me down when I get overwhelmed and start talking myself out of things, which I totally have a tendency to do. Like when my building went co-op and I said I thought maybe I should buy my apartment. I thought about it and we talked about it, and he agreed that it was a good deal and it made a lot of sense. Then, when it started to feel like it was too complicated, like I didn't have the time, he introduced me to a mortgage guy and helped me put all the papers together. And then when I told him less than a year later that I was thinking I might buy a new place and rent out the old one, he didn't tell me I was crazy to think I could be a landlord. He helped me find a tenant for the Peanut Palace. And now I get a rent check every month that covers my mortgage.

Here's why I love John. I had just landed, back in New York. On my way to the taxi line, I walked toward the crowd of limo drivers, holding up their little signs printed with the names of the people they were there to meet. I found myself glancing from card to card, looking for my name, even though I hadn't made any arrangements to be picked up. The names didn't even register, until one caught my eye. I looked at it, and looked away. I kept walking, and then I looked at it again. Neil Hemmings. The kid who brought a hot dog to school in a thermos? No way, that's too weird. I took one more step, and then I stopped and turned, and looked again. John looked down at the name on the sign he was holding, looked up at me, shrugged and smiled. And then he drove us home.

August 15, 1991

Since I'd been so busy at work leading right up until I left for LA, I'd known it was going to take some effort to get my life put back together after I got home, so I'd already planned to take an extra day off before I was going back to work. I went through a pile of unopened mail and threw away about a million catalogs. I put in a load of laundry, and dropped off a mountain of dry cleaning. I went to the store to buy some food and other stuff I'd run out of, and I stopped at the drugstore to pick up the prescription I'd called in to refill but forgot to pick up before I left for LA. I'd missed a couple days, so I took two pills, Sunday, Monday, right there in the store, ignoring the pharmacist's weird look. I figured I'd just double up for a couple of days until I was caught up.

It was strange, but while I was running around doing errands, busy and productive, I felt myself getting mad at John. It wasn't anything he'd said or done. Nothing had happened. I don't know, I guess it was all the wedding talk with Beth. Or maybe it was the hormones. But I started getting really pissed that he was still with Mara. It was ridiculous already. What was he waiting for? He'd never said so, but I always assumed that when Chloe went to college, he'd move out. I mean, it was certainly a reasonable assumption. And now she'd just gone back for her sophomore year. Which meant that for all of last year, while Chloe was away at school, and I was alone, they were together, having a marriage. What am I, a fucking idiot? He can just swing by when he has some free time, when Mara doesn't have anything she needs him to do? Anyplace she needs him to be?

I went home to drop off my groceries, and then I went out again. I didn't want to just sit at home. I needed to keep moving. It was like I was having the fight with him in my head. I imagined what I would say to him and what he would say back to me. That was the thing, though—he was kind of a mean fighter. I mean, he fought to win. Somehow, even if it started because I was pissed off about something, I usually ended up crying and apologizing. Which I guess is why I pretty much never said anything to John about him leaving. That, and because it was a conversation I really couldn't stand to have. It just felt too gross. Like I was some problem he was going to have to figure out how to solve. Plus, I wanted him to choose me. Not to leave her just to shut me up. Or because he owed it to me, for waiting so long. *In recognition of your years of service, we thank you.*

But seriously. I am twenty-eight years old. When does it get to be my turn? Who says I can't have what other people have? Maybe I want a diamond ring and a black tie wedding at the Pierre. To be someone's wife. Or even just to be part of a couple. But then I remind myself, like I always do, that it's not about a ring or a party. I really don't care about that stuff. It's him. It's us. And it's being together. It's not like I would choose to be with someone else, just because they are available, because I might get a diamond ring. And I had to admit, this sort of worked for me right now.

We usually saw each other at least once a week, sometimes twice, and we pretty much talked every day. And actually, that usually felt like enough. I always imagined that he would someday get his own place for a while, and we could sort of start from the beginning. Well, not really from the beginning. But I don't think he's ever lived on his own. Like, he went from college to marrying Vivian, to moving in with Mara. I thought it would be good for him to have his own place for a while, to be on his own. And plus, maybe that way we could sort of ease Chloe into what was going on with him and me. I guess in retrospect I thought my dad and Deirdre had gotten it right.

I got over it, like I always do. We did have a conversation, and John pretty much said that Mara had been acting really weird lately, weirder than usual, and he was afraid she'd do something really crazy if he tried to leave right now. He told me that he'd tried before, told her he was leaving, that there was someone else, more than once, which I hadn't even known was happening at the time. I guess it made me happy to know he'd tried. But anyway, he said she just didn't accept it. Which, I didn't actually understand. What does that even mean? He's a guy who gets things done, who makes things happen.

September 24, 1991

Things were really slow at work the whole month of August, and it had just started to pick up a little after Labor Day. I was in my office, reading a Credit Agreement when my secretary buzzed in, "Mr. Berman is here to see you. Alright if I send him in?"

Roger? That was weird. I hardly ever saw him. His office was on a different floor and my work had nothing to do with what he does. When I did see him, like in the elevator or at a firm event, he was always really friendly, but he'd never come to my office before. I pushed the intercom button on my phone. "Yeah, sure. Thanks."

I noticed when he walked in that he had a weird look on his face. Like his mouth was smiling but his eyes were sad. I wondered for a second if I was getting fired. But that didn't make any sense. If they were firing me, they definitely would have sent one of the guys I actually worked for.

"Hi, Roger. Good to see you. What's up?" I gave him a big smile.

He closed the door behind him, moved my bag off the guest chair and sat down.

"How's real estate? I hear you guys have been busy."

"Yeah, things were kind of crazy down here until about a month ago. But then August was pretty dead. How about you? You're looking tan and fit. Did you have a good summer?"

"I did, thanks. I've taken up golf. I'm pretty terrible, but it gets you outside."

He looked at me, again with that sad smile. I smiled back, but I wasn't sure why.

"There's something that I need to talk to you about. Something you should know. I'm sorry to do it like this, but I didn't think it should wait."

What could it be? Was it because my timesheets were late?

"It's John. John is dead."

I noticed that his shirt collar wasn't buttoned down on one side. At first I thought he'd lost the button but then I saw that it was there. It just wasn't buttoned. I wondered if maybe I should tell him.

"Jenna? Are you okay? Do you need me to get you something?"

"Like what? I mean, what would you get me?" I could hear my voice but it didn't sound like it was coming from me.

"A glass of water maybe? Here, let me—" He started to stand up, but then sat back down.

I couldn't look away from his collar with its empty buttonhole, curling away from the button. I knew I was acting weird. There was something I should be saying or doing, but I didn't know what.

"No, I'm fine, thank you. Thank you for coming by. And for telling me."

"Of course. It's a terrible thing. Just a terrible shock. But I wanted—"

"I'm sorry. Would you tell me again? What you said? I think maybe I didn't hear you right." I stared at his mouth, watching the words come out, so there would be no mistake.

"It's John. He had a heart attack. He's gone."

"Okay. Thank you. That was what I thought you said." I rolled my chair back, leaned over and pulled the trashcan out from under my desk. And then I vomited into it.

"Jenna—"

"Oh my God." I grabbed a tissue from the box on my desk. "That was disgusting. I am so sorry. I don't even— I'm sorry. Hang on. I will be right back."

I picked up the trashcan and walked fast down the hall. I left it inside the door to the freight elevator lobby, next to some bags of garbage and flattened cardboard boxes. I stopped in the ladies' room, and rinsed my mouth.

I went back to my office, closed the door and sat down. "I am so sorry about that. I can't really— I must have eaten something that—"

"It's okay, Jenna. I know. About the two of you, you and John. I know how close you and he were."

No. That's not possible. He's lying. He can't know. John never told anyone. Was this some kind of a trap? Did Mara set this up to see what I would admit to? To try to catch us? No, that doesn't make sense either.

"Where's Chloe? Is she okay?"

"She's on her way home. Sam is picking her up and they'll drive home this evening. They'll stop in Connecticut and get Ricky on the way. It's good, I think, that they will all be together. But right now I'm worried about you. I know that this must be very difficult for you. He was a special guy, and I know that you were very important to him."

"How do you—? What did he tell you?"

"It was a few years ago. Before you started working here."

"Oh my God, is that why I got this job? Did he ask you to hire me? He promised me—"

"No, no. Not at all. I wasn't even here yet. You got here all by yourself. He was so proud of you."

I felt my eyes fill with tears. I'd already puked in front of the guy, I wasn't going to start crying too.

"I can't do this. I can't be here right now." I picked up my bag from where he'd put it on the floor, and I walked out. I heard my secretary call my name, but I just kept going, with my head down, until I was out on the street.

I walked for hours, without paying any attention to where I was going. At one point, when my shoes were starting to kill me, I went into a store and bought a pair of flip flops. I threw out my work shoes in a garbage can on the street. Eventually, I ended up at my dad and Deirdre's. I didn't have anyplace else to go. When the doorman told me they weren't home, I told him that I'd wait. I sat down on the couch in the lobby, closed my eyes, and tried not to cry.

I ended up falling asleep. I couldn't believe the doorman let me just sit there. It must have been because he knew me. Maybe he even would have let me in to their apartment if I'd asked, but I was afraid that if I opened my mouth to speak I might throw up again. I heard people come and go, getting home from work, walking their dogs, telling the doorman good-night, but I didn't look up. At one point he came out from behind the desk, put his hand on my shoulder, and asked me if I was okay. I nodded yes, and closed my eyes. I woke up when Deirdre sat down next to me. I didn't know how long I'd been there, or what the doorman had said to her. All she said was "Come on," and I followed her to the elevator.

It was late, after midnight. She'd been out with some girlfriends, and my dad was in Atlanta for some conference. She asked me if she should call him, and I shook my head no. She asked me what was wrong, but I couldn't tell her. I couldn't say it out loud. I couldn't say anything. She asked if something had happened to my mom. I shook my head. If I was sick or had been hurt? No. Was I in trouble, or had something happened at work? It started to feel silly, her asking and me shaking my head no each time. Her guesses were going to get weird, and I was afraid I might start laughing. I wasn't ready to laugh, so I told her.

"John died. John Toberman? You know, the guy whose kid I used to babysit for? He died today. I just found out."

"Oh, Jenna, no. Oh, Sweetie, I'm so sorry. Well, of course you're upset. My God, you must be devastated. I know how much he meant to you."

I walked right into it.

"Oh my God, you knew too? Did everybody know about us? It is unbelievable. Why did we even bother sneaking around for all those years if everybody already knew that we were together?"

She looked at me, eyebrows slightly raised, with a small smile on her face.

"Oh, shit. You didn't know."

"No. Or, I don't know, now that you mention it, maybe I did. You know, how you sometimes get a vibe? Just from the way you sometimes talked about him? But it doesn't matter. To me. I mean, of course it matters. I honestly can't— What happened?"

She was right, it didn't matter. There was no reason to keep it a secret anymore, and no reason to ever tell anyone about it now. It was over. It was this huge important thing that for ten years had affected everything about me, every single day, and then, in one second, it was gone.

I never knew before that night what people meant when they described someone as a good listener. But Deirdre turned out to be a really good listener. She listened, and paid attention, smiling at the good parts and looking sorry at the sad parts, acting like she was following what I was saying, even when I wasn't making sense. She sat with me and let me talk until I fell asleep. When I woke up in the morning, she told me that she'd made some calls, and had found out that the funeral was going to be that day. She said she thought I would regret it if I didn't go, and that I shouldn't go alone. We got there late, and stood way in the back. We left as soon as it was over.

Mara

CHAPTER 10

September 25, 1991

"Mom, wait," Chloe said. "Don't throw all that away. Someone spent a fortune on it. I won't eat any. It's fine."

"There are sesame seeds all over them. I specifically asked people not to send bagels. Anyone who knows us at all knows that you're allergic. I even called Zabars this morning to tell them not to send anything with nuts or seeds."

"Jesus, Mom. I am nineteen years old. Seriously, I know what not to eat."

"It's okay," Mara said. "I stopped on my way home and picked up some of that challah that's safe. Here, watch out. I'll just get rid of this."

Chloe watched her tilt the tray, spilling the pile of bagels into the open garbage can. "Oh my God. Mom, would you stop for a minute? What is wrong with you? Seriously, what is the matter with you? Can you please just show some fucking emotion?"

She didn't know what to say. Chloe had never spoken to her that way. She was just trying to make sure everything was going to be nice. Chloe followed her out of the kitchen and watched her move the flowers from the table to the piano.

"Forget the flowers. It's shiva, not a party. Would you please just come and sit down with me?"

"I'll be right there. I just want to check one thing in—"

"Mom, stop. It's fine. People will be here soon. Sam and Ricky said they'd come early."

"How early? We said five o'clock."

"Just forget it. Oh my God, I seriously can't deal with you. You're being totally crazy." Chloe stood up and started to leave the room, then stopped and turned. "They are my brothers. He was their father, too. You get that, right?"

"Half brothers," she corrected, and immediately wished she hadn't.

"I can't believe you." Chloe slammed her bedroom door. Hard. Mara could hear her crying.

He'd had a massive heart attack, and died immediately. That was what the doctor said. Massive, and immediate. At the club while he was changing for racquetball. Someone, she already couldn't remember who it was, told her that one minute he'd been telling a story and the next minute he was dead.

Ricky and Sam had each spoken at the service. Nice, handsome boys. Men, really. Ricky looked just like his father, Sam more like Vivian. They were good boys, always polite. You could tell that they'd been well-raised. She had to hand it to Vivian. Watching them today, she realized that she'd never really gotten to know them that well, that she'd never had much of a relationship with them. She was their father's wife, Chloe's mom. But sometimes she forgot that she was also their stepmother. She wondered what would happen now. They'd always been close to John, and they were very sweet with Chloe, treating her like a little sister. Which, she supposed, she still was.

She looked around the crowded room and thought that maybe she should turn up the air conditioner. She was afraid that it might get warm with so many people there. All in all, she was feeling pretty good. It had been a beautiful service, standing room only. They'd gotten lucky with the weather after all that rain. And Campbell's certainly knew how to do a funeral. They had a good turn out for shiva. A nice steady stream of people in and out. Even Jenna, Chloe's old babysitter who John had been so fond of, stopped by. She wondered who'd called her. So many of his colleagues from the firm were there, all with such lovely things to say. She felt like it reflected well on her that he was so well-liked and respected. And it didn't hurt that the apartment looked good, and there was plenty of food. You couldn't exactly invite people to come at dinner-time and then not feed them.

Looking across the room at the crowd of young lawyers, she asked John's secretary to tell her who was who. She thought maybe she would be able to figure out which one was the girlfriend. She was certain it was someone from work. It was always someone from work, wasn't it?

It didn't matter, though. She'd won. She was the grieving widow, not the invisible girlfriend, whichever one she was. She was glad they'd stayed together. He'd tried to tell her, more than once, that there was someone else. Probably thinking that she'd tell him to leave. Maybe even hoping she would. But no. She'd kept her cool and come out on top. Looking back, she realized that of all the things she'd ever done, she was most proud of how she'd conducted herself. With dignity. And grace.

Jenna

CHAPTER 11

October 23, 1991

I never actually let myself cry about it. About John dying, I mean. I felt like I didn't have the right. Like part of the price you pay for being the girl in the affair is that you have no claim to the tragedy. It doesn't belong to you. He was never really mine, and his dying didn't change that.

I guess that from the outside, it looked like I bounced back pretty quick. I did the only thing I could do. I kept moving, and waited to start feeling normal again. But I didn't feel normal. I showed up every morning, just like before. I read my documents and wrote my memos, and sat in on meetings and conference calls. I was fine, except that I wasn't. It was like time had slowed, and I felt the passage of every second, every minute. My mind was blank, and it felt like my ears were stuffed with cotton. I couldn't eat. I was nauseous all the time. And I was exhausted. If I wasn't at work, I was sleeping. I felt empty, like a ghost, like I was becoming invisible.

It wasn't until the middle of October that I realized that I hadn't gotten my period in a long time, like not since July, before I went to California. I never really paid much attention to it. I had been on the pill forever, but I'd missed a few when I was away, and then I just stopped taking it the day he died. I was sure it was just stress, but Beth convinced me to do one of those in-home tests. She stayed on the phone with me while I peed on the stick and waited. She cried when I told her that it was positive, but to me it was just another thing to get through. She offered to come home, so she could go with me to the doctor, but I told her I'd be okay, that I just wanted to get rid of it. Besides, she'd be home in a couple of weeks for the party.

When I made the appointment, the lady on the phone said I would need to have someone come with me, or meet me there, that I wouldn't be allowed to leave without a companion. I asked Deirdre. It felt like this was the last piece of saying goodbye to John, and she'd been there from that first night. I knew she wouldn't be judgmental. I valued her opinions, but mostly I appreciated that she would keep them to herself unless I asked.

I spent the next four days before the appointment rethinking my decision. I changed my mind a million times about what to do. Was I meant to have this baby? Maybe it was to be John's legacy. Or was it just an accident, a weird, fucked up biological twist of fate? Or maybe God is real and this was my punishment. Like, some kind of cosmic payback had caused John's heart to explode in his chest, and then put this alien creature, this manifestation of our sin, inside of me. Or maybe this thing, this future baby, this son or daughter, was a way for me and John to continue to be together, for our relationship to keep going. A way for us to be a family, even without him here. But then I would think about my job, and what my life was like, and what it would be like to raise a baby alone. And what would I tell people when it started to show? Who would I say was the father?

I went to bed the night before my appointment, knowing that I couldn't go through with it. That I had to keep the baby. I would quit my job and figure out something else to do for money, something more flexible, with better hours. Maybe my mom could help. I picked up the phone to call Deirdre to tell her I was going to cancel the appointment, but then I saw what time it was, and I decided I would wait and let her know first thing in the morning.

I woke up in the morning, really mad at John. How could he have done this to me? He promised he would never leave me. He never promised that he would leave Mara, or that we would ever be together. But he promised that *he* would never leave *me*. And he did. He fucking left me. And he didn't even just leave me. He left me with this huge fucking problem to solve. How was I supposed to know what to do? For my entire adult life, I hadn't made a decision without talking it through with him. And now, because of him, I had to make the biggest, most irrevocable decision of my life, without him. All by myself. I knew then that I couldn't do it. There was no way I could raise a child alone. I could barely take care of myself.

Sitting in the waiting room, still thinking I might change my mind and leave, Deirdre asked me what I thought would have happened if John hadn't died. I didn't understand what she was asking at first, I guess because I somehow felt like I only got pregnant after he was gone.

"I wouldn't have told him. I mean, I would have eventually. But I would have gotten an abortion first, and then told him about it after."

"You wouldn't have wanted him to know? To be a part of the decision? It seems like it would be easier if it didn't feel like a choice you had to make alone."

"That's true. If I didn't tell him, I would have blamed him for not being part of the decision. And I would have hated him for it. But if I told him, there wouldn't have been any right answer. Do you know what I mean?"

"I don't— I'm not sure."

"If I told him about it before, and he said I should keep it, that he would leave Mara and we would be together? That would have meant that he would leave her for a baby, when he wouldn't leave her for just me." I could see that Deirdre was really thinking about what I was saying. She wasn't just making conversation while we waited.

"But if I told him about it and he said that I should get an abortion? That would have been a huge rejection, the ultimate fuck you. Like it was a mistake and he was telling me to erase it, undo it, make it invisible."

"But you know what would have been even worse?" Deirdre asked. "If he told you that it was your decision. That it was up to you."

"Yeah. You're right." I could feel myself wince. Just imagining it felt like a punch in the stomach. "Because that would be telling me I'm on my own. That I've always been on my own." I realized then that I really didn't know very much about her and my dad's relationship. I was pretty sure that she and my dad were together for a while before he and my mom split up, but I had no idea what it had been like for her. "I think getting pregnant would have ended it either way. If he hadn't died I mean. Whatever he did, I think I never would have been able to forgive him for it."

"Oh, I don't know. Love lets you forgive a lot."

When the nurse finally called my name, I was certain, really for the first time, that I was doing the right thing.

November 23, 1991

It was late, and I should have taken a taxi, but I didn't want to risk getting stuck with a chatty driver. I was all talked out. It had been a lovely party. Beth seemed very comfortable in her role as bride-to-be. And it was nice to see her and Neil so happy, and to watch their families interact. But I was done. All I wanted was to be home, alone. When I got on the subway, the car was weirdly empty. It was later than I'd thought. I looked around, thinking how if this was one of those disaster movies, like Long Walk to Daylight or whatever that was, these were the people I would have to rely on to make it all the way to the end. There was a tiny Chinese lady and an older couple sitting at one end of the car, and three black guys—younger than me, teenagers, or early 20s maybe—toward the other end. They were pretty rowdy, talking too loud, popping up and down, in and out of their seats, sort of play fighting with each other. I thought about the Central Park Jogger and tried to make myself invisible, hoping they wouldn't pay any attention to me. When the Chinese lady and the couple got off to switch to the express, it was just me and them. Great. In case of emergency, these are my people? Where is James Brolin when you need him?

Even looking down at the floor, I noticed them notice me. They came over to where I was sitting. One of them sat next to me and the other two sat across from us. They were talking about partying, the party they were going to or maybe the party they were coming from. I tried to tune them out. The one next to me told me I was pretty, but that I needed to smile. The train pulled into a station and the doors opened, but I didn't even look up. He was sitting way too close to me. He just kept talking. I could feel his breath on my cheek. He asked me where I was going all dressed up, why was such a pretty girl alone on a Saturday night, why wouldn't I smile for him. I don't know why I didn't get up. I just ignored him, hoping he would stop. He touched me under my chin with his finger.

"Hey, back off." I shifted in my seat, turning away from him.

"Aww, come on now. Don't be like that."

"Oh, snap," said one of the friends.

"Damn girl, you prejudiced?" said the other one.

He touched me again, this time taking my chin more firmly in his hand, turning my head to face him. I pulled away.

"Hey! The lady said back off."

I looked up and saw a well-dressed guy with glasses, maybe early 30s, walking toward us from the end of the car. One of the friends stood up.

"Yo, Clark. Who are you talking to?"

He got right up in the kid's face.

"I'm talking to your buddy, and I'm telling him to BACK THE FUCK OFF."

He gave the kid a hard shove, two hands to the chest, just as the train was coming to a stop. The kid stumbled and fell backwards, sitting down hard on the floor. When the doors opened, nobody moved for a few seconds. Then he grabbed me by the wrist and pulled me up out of my seat, off the train, and onto the platform, just as the doors closed behind us.

We both stood there and watched the train pull away.

"Holy shit." He turned to face me. "Did you see the way he went down? That was fucking awesome. And how the other two just sat there?"

Awesome? Was this guy serious?

"What?" he asked. "Why are you looking at me like that?"

"Are you kidding? You think that was awesome?"

"Yeah, actually. It feels pretty awesome to not be dead right now, don't you think?"

"You just— You didn't have to do that. Everything was fine."

"Really? It didn't look fine. It looked like three assholes who were about to get out of hand while you just sat there and let it happen."

I had nothing to say to that. I looked down at the subway track.

"Those guys were huge. They could have killed us both."

They really weren't that big, but I managed to stop myself from saying so. I looked at him while he was looking away, and I saw that he was cute, in that mild mannered reporter for a great metropolitan newspaper sort of way. "Clark Kent. I get it." I smiled.

"What?"

"The guy. When he called you Clark? He meant like Clark Kent. It's funny."

"What is wrong with you?" he asked, looking at me like he thought I might be insane.

"Nothing. Jesus. Look, I didn't ask to be rescued, okay? I can take care of myself."

"Yeah, great. I'm sure you can. And next time, maybe you should. Instead of just sitting there like some kind of—"

"You're right. I'm sorry."

"Sure," he said. "Whatever."

We stood next to each other, both facing straight ahead.

After a few minutes, I stepped forward and looked up the track into the tunnel to see if a train was coming. "You know what? I think I'm just going to walk from here."

He looked at his watch. "Good idea. Let's go."

I apologized again when we got up onto the street, figuring we'd go our separate ways. But when I started walking, he walked with me.

We walked in silence until we were about a block from my building. I apologized for what felt like the tenth time, and I thanked him. When we got to my front door, I stuck out my hand and said "Lois."

"Excuse me?"

"My name is Lois. Lois Lane." That got him to smile.

"I'm Matt." He shook my hand. "Okay, Lois. You have a good night."

"You, too. And thank you for rescuing me."

I went inside and walked through the lobby, knowing that I'd acted like an idiot. It took a minute for the elevator to arrive. I got in, turned around and pressed the button for my floor. I looked out, across the lobby and through the front door, and there he was, Matt, still standing on the street, looking in at me. Then the elevator door slid shut.

December 7, 1991

Matt was in the kitchen, helping Annie with the dishes, when she asked if he was seeing anyone. It seemed that his friends, mostly his friends' wives, were not going to rest until he got himself married. It was almost two years since he and Shira broke up and it seemed like they still weren't over it.

Was he seeing anyone? The answer to that was obviously no, he was here alone, wasn't he? But there were a couple of ways he could respond. He could tell her about some of the dates he'd been on recently. With a little effort, he could make it sound like he was having too much fun to even think about settling down. Or he could tell her some of his latest horror stories. They always went over well with married people, who would laugh and look at their spouses thinking "thank God we don't have to do that anymore". Or he could just tell her no, and turn the conversation to other things—her job, her family, the ski house she and Chuck had a share in.

"No, not really. I've been dating some, but nothing— It hasn't— You know what? There's this girl. Who I can't stop thinking about."

"Oh, so that's good." Annie turned closed the dishwasher, dried her hands and sat down. "Who is she?"

"That's the thing, I don't know her. I don't really know anything about her."

"Okay, start at the beginning."

"It was nothing. I don't know. She was just this sad girl in a party dress."

"Who is she? Where'd you meet her?"

"Her name is Jenna. We met on the subway, when I almost got myself killed getting these thugs to leave her alone. Then she and I got into an argument about it. And I walked her home."

"Yeah? And then what happened?"

"That's it. Nothing."

"When was this?"

"Two weeks ago."

"So call her. What are you waiting for?"

Chuck called to them from the living room, "Hey, come back out here. Jay and Carla have something they want to tell us."

"Oh, great", she whispered. "Now we get to pretend to be surprised. Like we didn't notice her fat ass and that she's not drinking. Hon," she called to Chuck, "we'll be in in a minute. I just want to finish in here first."

"Matty, come on out. Let her finish. You don't need to help. She loves cleaning up."

Annie rolled her eyes and smiled.

"That's okay," he said. "We're almost done. We'll be there in a minute." He turned back to Annie. "I don't have her number."

"Oh my God, are you kidding? Matthew, please don't be pathetic. Look it up. It's really not that complicated."

"I don't know her last name. I only know her name is Jenna because I went in and asked her doorman after she went upstairs."

"Okay, let's think. Wait, I know. Here's what you do. Obviously. Leave her a note. You said she has a doorman? Oh my God, you know what? This is going to be so good. Seriously, I love this. A note, written in your perfect handwriting, that says you can't stop thinking about her? That's so great. I'm not kidding. She's going to totally die."

"I don't know. I'm not sure how she'll react. She doesn't really seem like other girls."

"Trust me. With something like this? We're all the same."

Beth said I should wait until Thursday to call him. He'd waited two weeks to drop off the card, so she said it was appropriate that I should wait at least four days to call him. And then, she said, I shouldn't make a date with him before a week from Saturday. I only made it until Tuesday, and I asked him if he would meet me for a drink after work on Thursday. I knew that there was a chance that he'd turn out to be a jerk, but I felt like I needed to show him that I was not a total weirdo.

We had a really nice time. I learned a lot about him. He's an architect and works for a small firm in SoHo. He lives in Chelsea. He grew up outside Philadelphia. His parents are still married to each other, and he has two younger brothers. He went to UPenn, both undergrad and for architect school. He's never been married, although he was close to getting engaged a couple of years ago. Instead, he said, he broke up with her when he realized that the only reason he was even thinking about proposing to her was because everyone expected it.

I told him about myself, the easy stuff. It felt good. After being off for so long, spaced out, disconnected, lost in my thoughts, I was on that night. Chatty, clever, funny. Everything I wasn't the first night we met. When I told him that I'm a lawyer, I surprised myself by saying out loud that I was thinking of making a change, but that I don't know what I want to be when I grow up. He said he thought I should host a talk show, interviewing people I thought were interesting. That made me feel good, like maybe he could see who I really am, even better than I can. I told him that the only thing I'd been able to come up with was opening a fancy cupcake store, but then I had to confess that I don't actually like cupcakes. Which he said he was pretty sure was one of the top five traits exhibited by psychopaths.

We had two drinks and then he walked me home, even though it was pretty cold out. I apologized again for that night on the subway, and explained that I'd had a rough couple of weeks and that it all sort of came to a head that night. I said that it was a long story and I'd tell him about it another time. He asked if I wanted to get dinner on Saturday, and I said yes even though I knew Beth would say I shouldn't be available on such short notice. I gave him a quick kiss on the cheek and went inside. This time, I didn't look out from the elevator to see if he was looking in.

It wasn't until I was inside my apartment that I realized how nervous I'd been, how afraid I'd been that I wouldn't be able to get through it, and how relieved I was that I'd been able to act like a normal person. I sat down on the couch and looked around. I'd bought the apartment thinking that John and I would live there together someday. He'd hooked me up with a decorator he knew, and she'd helped me pick out every piece of furniture. Every single thing was the right size, the right color, the right texture. It was like a place you'd see in a magazine. I imagined that Matt the architect would approve.

Mara

CHAPTER 12

April 19, 1993

Sitting alone in the windowless room, not much more than a wide closet, really, all she could think was that none of this would have happened if Chloe had moved back to New York instead of staying in Boston after graduation. The problem was that she was alone, that she had too much time on her hands. If Chloe were here, they'd be doing things together, going out for lunch, seeing a show.

She took a deep breath and tried to take stock of her feelings. Like they said in that book she'd read, Getting Lucky—Ten Steps to Finding Your Sparkle. It had all made sense when she read it. So who knows, maybe it really would work if she did what they said. It couldn't hurt, and she certainly could use some help finding her sparkle. Own your feelings. Be present. Make a list. She turned to a clean page in her Filofax and wrote the date and the words "How I'm Feeling Right Now" at the top. Number one would have to be embarrassed. She was more embarrassed than anything else. And humiliated. Had it really been necessary for them to have made such a spectacle? Thank God she wasn't going to have to explain this to John. She looked at the clock. Three fifteen. Embarrassed, humiliated and inconvenienced. And it was bad enough that they were making her wait, but in this depressing little room? With this scuffed metal table and that buzzing fluorescent light? Not at all what you would expect at Saks. She wondered if this was where the salesgirls normally took their breaks. Or do they go out for lunch? It must be hard for them in this neighborhood—everything is so crowded and expensive. Punching in and out for what, five or six dollars an hour? She was lucky she'd never had to live like that. Embarrassed, humiliated, inconvenienced and, she supposed, lucky.

All things considered, they had been very kind. Moreso, she imagined, after someone had had the good sense to look up her account. See that? She smiled. Being such a good customer for all these years had paid off. God, she loved this store. The way it looked. The sounds and the smells. The way the escalators passed each other, so the shoppers could see each other coming and going, some heading up, just getting started, some heading down, successful, shopping bags in hand. Even the way the doorman welcomed you as you came in from the street. Just being in that store, you felt like you had something to be proud of. It was too bad that she wouldn't be coming back. No. Not after the way that one man had taken her by the arm, the way he'd spoken to her. Not now that she'd seen this room. These things have consequences. And Saks had just lost itself a very good cust—

"Mrs. Toberman?"

"Yes, please come in. Are we done?" It was him again. That red faced man with the badge. She slid the pen back into its leather loop, snapped the book closed and looked at her watch. "I actually have someplace I need to be."

He raised his eyebrows and turned to look over his shoulder at the woman standing behind him.

"Mrs. Toberman. I am Bernadette Watson, the store manager." She stepped past the red faced man and into the small room. "I am sorry this has taken so long. We've determined that we can handle this as a private matter, that there is no need to involve any third parties. So yes, we are done. Let me help you with your things, and I can see you out."

Now, this was the way she was used to being treated at Saks. She wondered if she should ask Bernadette to arrange to have her packages delivered so she wouldn't have to wrestle them into a cab.

"Just one thing, Mrs. Toberman. Did you want us to ring up the bag for you?"

"The bag?"

"Yes. The umm, the Fendi. With the—"

"For Christ's sake, lady. The bag you tried to steal."

"Thank you, Mr. Davis. That's enough. I'll take care of it from here."

She didn't think of it as stealing. Taking, maybe. That certainly sounded better than stealing. Like she was simply taking what was hers. Or what should have been hers. She'd lost so much. It really didn't feel like she was doing anything wrong. In fact, it felt like she was making things right.

In the beginning, she only took small things, and it only happened once in a while. It was really only the past couple of years, since she'd been alone, that it was happening so much more often.

The first time it had been an accident. God, it must be eight years ago now. She remembered that Chloe had just started high school and it seemed like every day she had a new list of school supplies to buy. Mara went to Woolworth's for the notebooks Chloe needed, and while she was there, she picked up a nail polish, some kitty litter and a box of laundry detergent. She'd put the nail polish in her coat pocket while she was shopping because everything else she was holding was so bulky and she hadn't taken a cart. It wasn't until she got home and reached into her pocket for her keys that she found it. She'd gasped. What a thrill. It was like she'd been given a little gift, some small compensation for all that had been taken from her. Besides, no one got hurt. It was a victimless crime. No, not even a crime, really. An accident.

That first time, there had been no reason keep it a secret. She had nothing to hide. And besides, if she told people, it proved that it was an accident.

"Chloe, honey. You'll never guess what I did today. I stole a nail polish. I mean, not really. It was an accident. It was just that I had so much to carry. I meant to take it out of my pocket when I got up to the register, but then I forgot. Can you believe it? I didn't even realize—"

"Sorry, Mom." Chloe took off her headphones. "What did you say?"

"I stole a nail polish. From Woolworth. It was an accident."

"Oh. Okay. So are you going to take it back? Pay for it?"

"What? No, I don't think so. I mean, I wasn't— Do you think I should?"
"No. I don't know. Whatever." Chloe put her headphones back on.

When she finally got home after that ordeal at Saks, she found herself much more pressed for time than she would have liked. The reservation was for eight o'clock, and she had to rush to get showered and dressed, hair and makeup done, and then a cab back to midtown. Not quite the leisurely day of shopping she'd planned.

The maitre d' was charming, a real professional, calling her by name and asking, as he walked her to her table in the Pool Room, if she had dined at The Four Seasons before. She said she had, a few years ago, and that she was sure her husband would be there soon.

She sipped her drink slowly, thinking she ought to try to make it last, and looked around the room. How wonderful, she thought, to be out, here, among these beautiful people. It was as if that little mix up at Saks today hadn't happened at all. There would be no record of it. No one who knew her had been there, had seen it. Of course, she would never mention it, and no one would ever know. But it was important that she learn from the experience. She could not afford make those same mistakes again.

She was glad that she resisted the pressure to buy the Fendi bag. It was expensive, and she didn't even really like it very much. If she'd bought it, it would have just been to shut up that smug security guard. Mr. Davis, Bernadette had called him. She should write that down. Just in case she someday had an opportunity to get him fired.

It obviously made sense that the larger, pricier things were more of a challenge. But interestingly, as far as the department stores went? The nicer the store, the less security they tended to have. There were exceptions, of course. But until today, she'd never had a problem at Saks or Bergdorf's. Whereas, at Macys, they treated you like you were a criminal, counting how many items you took in and out of the dressing room. Supermarkets were the easiest. But she found that taking food was depressing, it always made her think of poor people, who couldn't afford to buy food for themselves. And when she took food, she always threw it away. In fact, she threw away most of what she took. She knew it was odd, but it was the taking that felt so good, not the having. She had plenty of money. She could afford just about whatever she wanted. So if she wanted something, she bought it. Like this dinner tonight. She could afford it. Why shouldn't she take herself someplace special? It was like she'd read in that book. Treat yourself the way you wish to be treated. Give yourself the gifts you deserve. Find your sparkle.

She watched the people around her, at tables for two or four, eating and drinking and laughing. And talking. She strained to listen to their conversations, but she could only pick up bits here and there. She tried to remember what people talk about over dinner.

It felt like the waiter was starting to hover, so she ordered another drink. When he brought it to her, she told him that she and her husband were celebrating, that it was their wedding anniversary, twenty-two years. She said that she was sure that he was just stuck at work, probably tied up on a call. That he was a lawyer, and that he had a very demanding job. He was lead counsel on the Datsun case. Then she remembered that the Datsun case had been years ago. She didn't even know if Datsun was still around. But it didn't matter. He was just a waiter—how would he know either way? She told him she'd like to take a look at the menu while she waited.

She took her time reading the menu, imagining what John would order if he were here, thinking about the preparation, the ingredients, and considering, as she always did, what would be safe for Chloe.

Chloe. She couldn't understand why things were different, what had changed. They'd always been so close, best friends, really. She thought that losing John would have brought them even closer. But it was like it had the opposite effect. Chloe always seemed to be angry with her. Impatient, frustrated. Honestly? It felt like a slap in the face. Whenever she called, if Chloe answered at all, she would say that it was a bad time, that she was running late, that she had one foot out the door. Mara understood that she was busy, she knows what law firms are like. Chloe was working as a paralegal, trying to decide if she wanted to go to law school. But Mara couldn't understand why she'd decided to stay in Boston, when they had so many law firm connections here in New York, where she could have moved back home and lived rent-free.

She ordered another drink, and told the waiter she'd have the oysters, "just to tide me over until he gets here." When he came back with her drink, he brought a telephone and asked if perhaps she'd like to make a call. She realized then that she hadn't fully thought through how this evening was going to end. She picked up the phone, pressed "talk", and started to dial his number at the firm. When the waiter turned and walked away, she pressed "end", and put the phone down. She looked at her watch. It was already 9:40. She looked around the room. Plates were being cleared, desserts and coffee were being served, checks were being paid.

When the waiter returned, she was feeling the effects of the vodka. She looked down at the oysters he put in front of her, cold and wet, glistening in their shells. What had she been thinking? She looked up at the waiter.

"He's not coming."

"Ah, there's been a change in plans then. Well, these things happen. Will you stay for dinner? Or shall we bring you the check?"

"He's dead. He's not coming because he's dead." She bit her lip and tried not to cry.

"Oh my goodness. I am so terribly sorry, Miss. How did—? How might we—?"

"It's okay. Really." He seemed so devastated by the news. She smiled. "It was two years ago." When she felt the sob rising up inside her, she pushed past him and hurried to the ladies room, head down, knowing that people were watching.

She thought she might stay in this room forever. She sat down on the couch, a fainting couch she thought it was called. She'd always assumed they were for breastfeeding mothers, or for women overcome by menstrual cramps. But now she understood that it was for women like her. Women who had lost everything. Who had nothing left. She slipped out of her shoes and laid down. How was it that, for the second time in one day, she was alone, in a room without windows, taking stock of her feelings? Embarrassed, yes. Embarrassed and humiliated. And alone, with absolutely no chance in the world that Bernadette Watson would come in and apologize for the inconvenience, and offer to help her with her packages. There was no one to rescue her. She closed her eyes.

She woke up to a young woman with a Russian accent leaning over her. She said her name was Lena, that she was the coat check girl. Lena said that the restaurant would be closing soon, and that the maitre d' had sent her in to get the phone number of someone they could call, someone who could come and get her. When Mara said no, that there was no one, the Russian girl whispered that if she didn't give him a phone number he would call the cops. Fine. She sat up and gave her Chloe's telephone number in Boston. Good luck, she thought. Let the two of them figure it out.

Lena came back in, and left a cup of coffee and a plate of cookies on a silver tray. And then she was alone again. She drank the coffee and took a bite of a cookie, and then stepped back into her shoes, and stood up. Whatever was going to happen next, she knew that she needed to compose herself. Best case, she was going to have to get into a taxi, and then walk past her doorman and through the lobby of her building. She looked in the mirror. So much for finding her sparkle. She splashed water on her face, and was trying to wipe the mascara trails off her cheeks when the door pushed open. It was Jenna, Chloe's old babysitter.

"Hey, Mara. It's me. How are you doing? Is everything okay?

"Jenna? What are you doing here? How did you—?"

Jenna sat down on the couch.

"Chloe called me. She said she thought maybe you could use some help. Why don't you come and sit with me for a minute? And then let's get you home."

Deirdre

CHAPTER 13

October 26, 1995

Deirdre woke up disoriented in an unfamiliar bed. Hungry. She'd been looking forward to the complimentary breakfast since she checked in the night before. She imagined the buffet, a bright spot in what promised to be a shitty day. *Damn it, Mickey. What did you do?* She showered and dressed quickly, repacked the few things she'd taken out, zipped her bag shut and left it on the bed. She said good morning to the woman who was waiting for the elevator, and smiled at the boy with her, figuring he must be about six or seven. The entire ride down she watched him scratching at a rash on his neck. Eczema, she thought, trying to get a peak inside the collar of his tee shirt, thinking she'd like to take a look at the backs of his knees. Totally treatable, but only if you take him to the doctor. She wondered if the mother had even noticed. Then she reminded herself, "Not my problem. I've got my own shit to deal with today."

She lifted the lid of the warming tray, saw the watery eggs, and decided that she would just have some toast or a muffin. Then, after watching Elevator Boy paw through the bread basket, she picked out the least green banana and put it in her bag. She poured coffee and milk into a Styrofoam cup and took it outside to the parking lot. It was hot, already humid, and not even nine o'clock. She found a spot in the shadow of a minivan and sat down on the curb. She lit a cigarette and inhaled deeply.

She'll drink her coffee, she thought, and then she'll stop at the desk to remind them that she was waiting for a Fed Ex envelope. If he remembered to mark it for early morning delivery, the package should arrive by nine. It was pretty remarkable, she supposed, that her father had even had an extra key, that he could find it. She ran through the plan one more time. When the package arrives, she'll check out and get a cab to the tow pound. Hopefully, they will give her the car without too much of a hassle. It looked like it would be about a 20-minute drive to the hospital, and they said that the doctor would be able to speak with her at eleven. She was hoping they'd be on the road by one at the latest. If they could split the driving, they could do it in two days, but she had no idea what kind of shape Mickey would be in. She didn't even know what he was doing in Houston.

She lit another cigarette and closed her eyes. One more reason to be pissed at him. Add it to the list. It had been more than four years since she'd finally quit for real. Four fucking years. And it took all of fifteen minutes after her father's call before she was outside in the rain, smoking under an awning.

She remembered that the phone had been ringing as she'd walked in from work, her shoes wet, umbrella dripping. Jesus, was that just the day before yesterday? She'd spoken to her father twice since Mickey'd been gone, and both times he'd let her chatter on about who knows what while he didn't say a word about it. He only told her after he'd gotten the call about the car. It had been almost two weeks, by then, since Mickey had disappeared. And now he's in a hospital in Houston. What the fuck?

She looked up as the Fed Ex truck pulled around to the hotel entrance. Okay, she thought, picking up the cigarette butts and dropping them into her empty coffee cup. Let's do this thing.

After she and the doctor had talked for about 15 minutes, the nurse brought Mickey in to join them. He walked in, pirouetted twice, sat down in the chair next to hers and crossed his long legs, Indian style, on the seat.

She leaned over and kissed him on the cheek. "Hey, Mick. You okay?"

"I'm fine. But what about you? Jesus, what happened?"

"What? Nothing, why? What do you mean?" She ran her fingers through her hair, wishing she'd put on lipstick.

"I don't know. I mean— I don't even know what it is. You just look so, I don't know, different. It's like you— You got so fucking old."

She felt her face redden before he threw his head back and laughed.

"Oh honey, I'm kidding. You should have seen the look on your face just now. I swear, I wish I had a camera."

She turned to the doctor and their eyes met.

"Oh, both of you, cut it out. Deirdre, don't be mad at me. Honey, if you're old, I'm old. There is no escaping the twindom." He turned toward the doctor. "Don't we look alike?" he asked, batting his eyes. "It's okay, I've always been the pretty one. She's used to it."

Maybe she was imagining it, but the doctor seemed relieved to sign the discharge papers and send them on their way.

She'd been driving for almost two hours when she asked him why he'd gone to Houston.

"I'll tell you," he said. "But you have to promise not to give me a hard time about it. Seriously. Because even I know now that it sounds crazy, but it made a lot of sense at the time."

"Okay, yeah. I promise."

"I felt like I needed to be here for the trial. To make sure it happened. The Yolanda trial? I was afraid that if I wasn't here, it wasn't going to happen. That she'd somehow get away with it."

"What trial? What are you talking about?"

"Are you kidding? It's only like the trial of the century. Girl, you've got to start paying attention. Don't they have the news in New York? Yolanda. Yolanda Saldivar?"

"I swear to God, Mick. I have no idea who that is."

"Selena's killer. Selena? Oh, you poor thing. We have got to get Young Dr. Kildare to let you out of your cage once in a while. God only knows what else you've missed."

"It's Kessler, not Kildare. Oh, duh. I got it. That's from that old show, right? Can't you please just call him Andrew? Anyway, go back. Who is

Selena, and why did Silvana kill her? Oh, wait. Is this from a TV show, too?"

"Not Silvana. Yolanda Saldivar. Jesus. Okay, I'll go slow. Pay attention. Selena was a singer. Hugely popular. The queen of Tejano music. Okay? The fucking queen. And she was—"

"Would I know any of her songs?"

"You? Definitely not. So, anyway, she was this huge star, and just getting started in the fashion business, when she was murdered by Yolanda Saldivar, who worked for her, but was about to be fired. For stealing. She was the president of her fan club. Selena confronted her about it in a hotel and Yolanda shot her. But only after she told her some crazy story about being raped in Mexico. They just had the trial. She was sentenced to life in prison."

"Because you were there."

"Did we not just agree that you wouldn't make fun of me? Look, I don't know. It just felt like it was important for me to be there, okay?"

"Yeah, so when did you stop taking your meds?"

"What's that? La la la. I'm sorry. I can't hear you. Did you say something? Shush, I'm sleeping now. Wake me up when the lecture is over."

"Fine. Just tell me how you ended up in the hospital."

"It was a misunderstanding. I'm there, right? At the courthouse, every day. And I wasn't the only one. There was a whole group of us, and we—"

"I'm guessing you were the only 50 year old Jewish guy who traveled down from Cleveland?"

"Not really sure why that's relevant. May I continue?"

"Please do."

"So they pretty much left us alone, the cops, and the reporters would come over during the breaks and tell us what was going on inside. I would sleep in the car, parked at night at this warehouse, and come back in the morning. But I guess one day I left the car in a bad spot and it got towed. So I bought some speed off this guy, because it seemed safer to stay up. You know what I mean? Better than sleeping on the street. But you know how you get after speeding for a few days? No, you probably don't. Trust me. Things start to get really intense. So I guess I was saying how we, the whole group of us who were out there, should just, like, overpower the security guys and push our way into the courthouse so we could be inside for the verdict. Like, I don't know, to bear witness. I didn't even really mean it, but I guess I went on and on. A couple of the girls told one of the guards that I was saying some scary shit. So, all of a sudden, I'm the crazy one. Like, they're not? We'd all been standing there outside the courthouse together, for more than a week at that point, and now they are afraid of me. Next thing, I woke up in the hospital, clean and in a bed, pumped full of my anti-crazies. How did they know to call you?"

"They called Dad. The car place called. From the registration, I guess."

"Shit. That's bad. I was really hoping he wouldn't find out. He gets so—"

"Are you serious? Mick, you stole his car. And you thought maybe he wouldn't notice?"

"It's called borrowing if you intend to give it back. Besides, I left him my car to use while I was gone. I wasn't going to leave the guy without a car."

"Why didn't you just take your own car? If you didn't want him to know?"

"It's on a lease."

She turned to him eyebrows raised.

"What? Don't give me that look. I would have gotten absolutely killed on miles."

Mickey was asleep when she pulled off the highway for gas. Even asleep, he was restless, twitchy, agitated. She parked and got out, closing the door gently. She used the ladies' room and bought a coffee for herself and a vanilla milkshake for Mickey. She had just come outside, sat down at a picnic table and lit a cigarette when she saw Mickey walking toward her. God, he is beautiful, she thought. The way he moves, like liquid, like heavy silk charmeuse fluttering in the breeze. Even sitting still, she felt clumsy watching him glide across the parking lot.

"Here. I got this for you."

He put down the cup without taking a sip.

"We're smoking? Deirdre, you naughty girl. I'm afraid we're going to have to report this. Hand me the lighter." He pulled in deeply and exhales. "Well, this road trip just got a whole lot better."

"Shut up. I don't even really smoke. I'm not kidding, I don't. I quit, for like years. This is your fault."

"My fault? Oh, please. You've got to lighten up. Besides, this falls clearly within a recognized exception to the rule."

"What are you—?"

"The no smoking rule. What? I'm serious. Everyone knows this. You are allowed to smoke if you are in jail, in the event of the death of a member of your immediate family or if you have to bust your favorite brother out of the nuthouse."

"Great. Just please don't say anything to Dad. Or Andrew. Ever. I mean it. He thinks I quit like twelve years ago."

"It really warms the heart to know that you kids have such an open and honest relationship. What's the deal with that guy anyway—he still won't marry you?"

"You know what, Mickey? Fuck you. What makes you think that I even want to get married?"

"Yeah, right."

"God, I hate you."

"No, you love me."

"No, I hate you."

"No. You love me."

"Okay, fine. You love me, too."

She woke up when he turned off the car. "Wow, I was really asleep." She looked at her watch. "Jesus, Mick. It's after two in the morning. What did you do? We should have been here by midnight." She looked out at the

Rodeway Inn sign, half of its lights out. "Wait, where are we? We were supposed to stop in Memphis."

"Would you relax? Memphis is nothing but tourists standing in line. We are in Hurricane Mills. Home of the Loretta Lynn Ranch and Museum. Trust me. This is going to be so much better than Graceland."

"Who said anything about going to Graceland?"

"You're kidding, right? You can't go to Memphis and not go to Graceland. But forget Graceland. We're here now. We'll go to the Ranch first thing in the morning. I think a couple hours should be enough. And then we can get on the road after that."

She put down her bag on the floor outside his room, and knocked. Yesterday had actually gone much better than she'd expected. He seemed okay. Too thin, and still kind of manic. She guessed it was going to take some time for him to stabilize, now that he was back on his meds. Issues with impulse control, was what Dr. Roman had said. Yeah, she thought. No kidding.

She remembered the first time he'd gone nuts. His nervous breakdown, they'd called it. It was when their mother's cancer had first come back, when they knew it was bad. She had managed in the years since to block out most of the details, but she would never forget the feeling when Mickey, wearing Mom's wig and her muumuu from Hawaii, ran out onto the football field in the middle of a game. She spent the rest of high school trying to be invisible, dreaming of the day she would leave for college, where she wouldn't be known as Mickey's twin.

She knocked a second time, louder. I'm going to fucking kill him, she thought. He opened the door, holding a towel around his waist, a toothbrush in his mouth.

"We said eight thirty," she said.

"And it's what, like ten to nine? That's totally within the margin of error. Go downstairs and check us out. I'll be ten minutes, tops."

She held the door open and watched him turn around and walk into the bathroom.

She told herself that she wouldn't say anything, that she would wait, that sooner or later he would tell her. But once they were back in the car and she'd pulled out of the parking lot onto the highway, she couldn't stop herself.

"Have you been to a doctor about the spot on your forehead?"

"What, this?" He slid open the visor mirror. "It's nothing. You can't even see it."

"Upstairs I could. Before you covered it up. And on your leg, too. You need to go to a doctor."

"I've been to the doctor. I've got it under control. Can we please talk about something else?"

"What did the doctor say?"

"Do we really have to do this? You know what he said. Just like I knew what he was going to say before he said it."

"KS?"

"KS. Kaposi's. It doesn't matter what you call it, right? Still means the same thing."

"Yeah? What's that? I mean, I know what it means, but what do you think it means?"

"Kaposi's sarcoma is an AIDS-defining illness," he recited, sounding bored. "Which means that I've graduated from being HIV positive to being officially diagnosed with AIDS. That's what he said, that it's official. And you, my fair twin, can be the first to congratulate me. It's going to be this left."

"How long have you known?"

"It looks like it should be about a mile and a half on this, and then it's a right onto Old Highway 13."

"There are treatments now, you know. They've had a lot of success with the anti-virals. It's not a death sentence."

"Stop. I've been on anti-virals. And now you see how well they worked for me. Don't tell me it's not a death sentence. I have seen too many people die for you to say what is or is not a death sentence. You know what? This conversation is over."

"Fine. But Mick, you can't—"

"Stop. I mean it. You are at the home of Ms. Loretta Lynn, the coalminer's fucking daughter, so you need to show some respect. Don't you dare sully this experience with talk of unpleasant things. Look, you can pull in right up there."

That was the kind of thing he did that pissed her off the most. He was impossible, the way he manipulated everything to turn it into an adventure. You couldn't even stay mad at him, because even though everything had to be his way, his way was always better, richer, more fun. She'd expected that this whole thing was going to be a nightmare. She'd prepared herself for it. Flying at the last minute to Houston, fighting to get the car, finding him in God knows what kind of shape and wrestling him out of the psych ward, and driving more than 1,300 miles back to Cleveland. But, Goddamn him. She was having fun.

"You're awake? You slept for a long time. We should be at Dad's in less than an hour. What time did you tell him we'd be there? Oh, also will you remind me to call Andrew when we get there? I haven't spoken to him since Houston."

"I wasn't asleep. Just thinking. Remembering something. Did you know that Mom asked him to help her die? And he wouldn't do it?"

"Who, Dad?" she asked.

"No, Andrew. What kind of stupid question is that? Yes, Dad. Honestly, for a smart girl you can be so fucking dumb."

"Don't be mean to me. I can't help it. It's like you're always half a conversation ahead of me."

"Well, Jesus. Try to keep up, would you?"

"How do you know?"

"Know what?" he asked, leaning over to change the radio station.

"That she asked him."

"She told me."

"When? Where was I?"

"I don't know. Probably studying for a test or something. It was just me and her, no one else was home. I was lying in her bed with her, talking."

"She told you that she asked him? And he said no?"

"He said he couldn't do it. Not just because of his license, and that oath they make you sign when they teach you the secret handshake, but—"

"The Hippocratic Oath. They don't actually—"

"Well, whatever. I guess he was worried about losing his license. That was definitely a part of it. But mostly, he said he couldn't do it because he loved her too much. He couldn't let her go. She told me that she begged him. They'd been talking about it for days. She said she told him that it would be an act of love."

"Oh my God. That must have been torture for him."

"For him? What about her? Deirdre, she was dying, in pain. You were there. Do you remember what it was like? It was fucking agony for her. She was begging for mercy. He never should have let it get to that point."

"When was it? Like, how long before she died? Do you remember?"

"Of course I remember. She died the next day."

"So then it didn't even matter that— Oh, wait. Did you—? Mickey, did you do it? You helped her? What did you do?"

"Let's just say that getting drugs has always been a talent of mine. I know, it's a gift. I went out that night and got some Seconal and the next day, when she was ready, I helped her take them."

They didn't speak. Deirdre leaned forward and turned off the radio.

"I remember when I got home that day. And she was gone. You and Dad were there, in her room, sitting with her. I could tell before I even came upstairs. It felt different. The house. Quieter."

"I called Dad, right after. And he came home."

"Do you think he knew?"

"What I did? I guess. I mean, probably. But you understand why, right? Why I did it? I mean, yeah, I did it for her. Because she asked me to. But I did it for him, too. It could have gone on like that for weeks and it was fucking killing him. Do you remember? It was killing all of us."

"I know. I just, I don't know. You're right though. I mean, yeah, I totally understand."

"Do you?"

"It was actually a very kind and brave thing you did for Mick. It's still so fucking sad, though, you know? God, even after so many years. Will you see if there's a tissue or something in the glove box?"

He handed her a napkin and they rode in silence. After a few minutes, she looked over at him. His eyes were closed and he was almost smiling. He looked like he was at peace for the first time since the hospital. Maybe for the first time in years.

"Hey, Mick?"

"Yeah?"

"What were we just talking about?"

He opened his eyes and turned to her.

"You weren't— We were talking about Mom, right?"

He smiled at her. "We have to stop at Angelo's. I told Dad we'd bring home a pizza."

Jenna

CHAPTER 14

July 20, 1996

The farther we got from the highway, the nicer the neighborhood was. I found myself studying the houses we drove past, looking up the driveways, catching quick glimpses into slivers of backyards, wondering who I would be if I lived there. I wasn't thinking about what it must have been like to grow up there. Although that actually would have made sense. I was imagining living there now, owning that house, planting those flowers next to that front door, driving home in that car, picking up the newspaper from that porch. It was weird. I turned in my seat to face forward.

"How much longer?"

"We're here. Practically. It's just down the next street on the left."

"Really? It's so nice here. Pretty."

"I told you it is. Remember? When you said how you were dreading this weekend and I told you that it's nice here? When you made me promise that we would have a nice time?"

"I didn't say that I was dreading it. Did I? I was just—"

"It's okay. It'll be good. They are going to love you."

"I know they will. What? Don't give me that look. I'm good with parents. Seriously. I wasn't worried that they aren't going to like me. Until now, anyway."

"Jenna, really. It's just dinner with my parents. We've had dinner with your mom. And with your dad and Deirdre, lots of times. No big deal. They've heard about you, and they want to meet you. That's all. And then, tomorrow we'll get up, have a bagel and hit the road. Okay?"

"Okay, fine. They are going to love me. I am going to love them. It'll be a lovefest." I looked at my watch. "You've got twenty-four hours, starting . . . right . . . now!"

He smiled as he turned back to face the road. He slowed the car and pulled into a driveway.

It was a nice house, on a nice block. Wide, even sidewalks. Tidy front lawns. Big, leafy trees. It was like what Hollywood imagines an affluent suburb to look like. I guess Hollywood actually gets it right. He turned off the car, got out and closed the door, opened and then closed the trunk, and came around to my side and opened my door. I was still sitting there, my seatbelt still on. Like I was waiting for something, a sign that this really was going to be okay.

"Come on. What are you doing?"

The front door opened and two dogs tumbled out, scrambling down the steps, across the lawn and around to my side of the car. Matt put down the bag he was holding and got down on his knees and the dogs were all over him, licking, panting, pushing each other out of the way. He lay down in the grass and let them have their way with him, a tangle of paws and noses and wagging tails.

I looked up and saw Matt's mother standing on the porch, smiling, holding a Frisbee.

"Fifi, Gigi, that's enough. Girls, hey! Over here." She tossed the Frisbee onto the grass and the dogs ran to it.

Matt got up, laughing, wiping his face, and turned to me. "Come on. They're harmless."

Matt's mother was wearing a pink t-shirt, gray pants and white Reeboks. I felt stupid in my silk blouse, like I was showing off.

"Hi, Mrs. Gardiner. I'm Jenna. It is so nice to meet you." I put out my hand to shake.

She leaned right in and wrapped me in a hug, my right hand mashed between us. She was soft and warm, and smelled like powder, and maybe a hint of onions. "Come on inside. We're so happy to have you here. But please, call me Louise."

"Oh my God, it's like Thanksgiving in July!" I was almost knocked over by the smell of roasting turkey. I imagined a cartoon drawing of pale blue clouds of deliciousness wafting in from the kitchen and curling up into my nose.

"You know what it is? I figured out that a turkey's the easiest thing to make for a crowd. I'm serious. It would have been more work to barbecue."

Behind her back, I looked at Matt and mouthed the words *a crowd?*

"Mom, what did you do? I thought it was going to be the four of us."

"Oh, shush. Go ahead and put that down by the stairs. You two will stay in your room. How was the drive?"

"Mom, seriously. Who's coming?"

"What? Nothing. It's just us. You two, me and Dad, Josh, and Jake and Susie. They wanted to meet Jenna. Oh, and Stevie and Kamala."

I knew that Josh and Jake were Matt's brothers. And Susie must be the girlfriend.

"Stevie's still around?"

"He's back. His mother couldn't— Well, it wasn't working out." She turned to me. "Stevie goes to Marty's school. He'll be a senior. There was some trouble at home, so they've been staying here for a little bit."

"I guess I forgot to tell Jenna about Dad's tendency to pick up strays. Who's Kamala?"

"Oh, now, be nice. Stevie's a good boy. Kamala is his sister. She stayed with family the last time. An aunt maybe? I don't remember. Whoever it was, they couldn't take her this time. Those poor kids. They haven't had an easy time of it. Besides, we've got plenty of room, and frankly, your dad and I could use the company."

"And Mr. Gardiner, Marty, is the principal? That's so nice of him. Of both of you. But are you even allowed to do that? Just, like, take in someone else's kids?"

"Well, who's going to object? They'd be on the street if it wasn't for us."

"Yeah, but isn't there some process you're supposed to go through? I mean, aren't you like, I don't know, circumventing the foster care system?"

"We're just helping out some kids. Giving them a safe place to stay. It's not like we're taking money for doing it."

"No, no. Of course. I'm sorry. I didn't mean— Oh my God, I'm sorry. That came out wrong."

"If they had anyplace else to go, or if there was anyone else who wanted to help them, it might be different. All Marty wants is to make sure they get through school and have a chance to go to college." She turned, her back to me, and opened the oven.

"I guess it's just hard for me to imagine my high school principal doing something like that."

"Jen, I seriously doubt that there were any high risk kids at Whitbern."

"Well, yeah. But still."

"Matt, honey", his mother said over her shoulder. "Why don't you show Jenna around while I finish up in here?"

The house was well-maintained, clean and comfortable, the tour ending in Matt's room. He closed the door and I threw myself face down onto the bed and pulled a pillow over my head.

"She fucking hates me."

"What? I can't hear a word you are saying." He pulled the pillow away. "What did you say?"

"I said she hates me. Did you see how she turned away? Like she couldn't even bear to look at me?"

"What are you talking about? Everything is fine. You're being ridiculous."

"Well, I basically just accused her of welfare fraud. Or foster care fraud, if there even is such a thing. What is wrong with me?"

"Would you please chill out? You asked her a question and she answered it. Really, it's fine."

"I swear to God. You have got to stop telling me it's fine. The more you say it, the less fine I know it is."

I felt him climb onto the bed and lay down on top of me. It felt good at first, safe, until it started to feel like he was crushing me.

"Get. Off. Can't. Breathe."

We went for a drive around the neighborhood. Matt showed me his high school, and where his old elementary school used to be. We drove past the hardware store, where he'd had his first job, and we parked for a minute in the very spot behind the supermarket where he got his first blowjob. I considered replacing his post-prom memory with a fresh one, but then I remembered that his mother was waiting for us at the house, and that she already hated me. We picked up some ice cream for dessert before heading back. When we got there, there were two cars in the driveway, so we parked on the street in front of the house.

We walked in to utter chaos, dogs barking, the oven timer going off, one of Matt's brothers and the pretty girlfriend setting the table, the other brother cleaning up a puddle of what must have been dog pee next to the front door, and the dad standing in the living room, waiving one arm in the air, shushing everyone, while he was talking on the phone.

When he hung up, he turned to me, smiled and said "Welcome to the circus. I'm Marty, and it is my pleasure to meet you." Then he held up his index finger and said, "Wait. Or I will forget. Louise," he shouted toward the kitchen. "That was Bonnie. She's stuck at work so we have two more for dinner." He turned back to me and said, "Now, count to ten."

"What, me? Oh, umm, sure, okay. One, two, three, four—"

The doorbell rang. He stepped around me and opened the door. Two young girls, maybe eight and ten years old, ducked under his arm and ran past me. They were halfway up the stairs when the second one turned around and asked "Where's Kamala?"

"Go on up. She's in her room getting changed." He turned to me. "That's Heather and Lily. They live next door. And you, I'm guessing, must be Jenna."

I realized then that Matt was no longer standing next to me. I saw him carrying two folding chairs into the dining room while the brother made room for two more places at the table.

"Have you met everyone? Well, other than Steve and Kamala. They'll be down in a minute. I just picked them up from tennis. Do you play?"

"Tennis? No, not really. A little bit at summer camp, but I was never any good at those kinds of sports."

"The kind with a racquet, you mean?"

"Pretty much the kind with a ball, actually."

"Well, that doesn't leave much, does it?"

"I can swim. That counts, right? And I used to do a little gymnastics. I mean, I wasn't any good, but that was the closest I came to ever really trying, you know? In a sport, I mean. I promised myself I would stick with it, at least until I could do an aerial. You know, a cartwheel where you don't put your hands down on the floor? I thought if I could do that, it would mean—I don't know, that I'd accomplished something."

Matt's mom shouted from the kitchen that dinner was ready, just as Stevie and Kamala came down the stairs, Heather and Lily right behind, and Matt walked over to where his dad and I were still standing by the front door.

"Hey, Dad. Sorry. I didn't even say hello."

They hugged, and did that clap on the back thing that men do, and then his dad held Matt by his shoulders, looked into his eyes, studying him, smiled and kissed him on the forehead.

"You look happy. That's good. Let's go." He directed me toward the dining room, his hand behind me, not quite touching my back. "So Jenna, did you ever do that aerial?"

What would it say about me if I told him the truth? That I'd lost interest, that I skipped practice one day and never went back. That I can't even remember deciding to quit.

"I did. Exactly three times. And the fourth time, I fell and broke my wrist, bringing an abrupt end to my career as a gymnast."

Where did that even come from? Why didn't I just say yes or no? Jesus. It's one thing to lie, it's a whole other thing to make up some stupid story that could totally come back to haunt me someday. Like, what if Matt someday says something to someone about my broken wrist? I can imagine my mom—Broken wrist? Jenna never broke her wrist. God, I'm such an idiot.

I sat between Matt and his mom. As the plates were being passed and people served themselves, Matt introduced me to everyone. People were talking and eating, refilling their glasses, teasing, laughing. Questions made their way to me, from across the table, ducking under one conversation, bending around another. I did my best to answer. "Real estate law." "Columbia undergraduate, and then NYU." "No, we're going back tomorrow." "Yep, New York City my whole life." I was having a hard time keeping up. Heated debates across the table, a whispered conversation between Josh and Jake, comments directed from one end of the table to the other, people reaching for seconds. There were at least four conversations taking place at all times, and it seemed like everyone was following all of them, so they could turn away from one to interject into another, and then go back to the first without missing a beat.

Susie said something to Matt about her new job, while either Heather or Lily told Kamala about passing the deep-water test at day camp, and Josh and Jake and Stevie were talking about the new Will Smith movie. I saw Marty beaming from the far end of the table and when I looked up at Louise, she was smiling back at him.

"Things tend to get pretty noisy here. It can take a little getting used to. I guess this wasn't what you were expecting?"

"It's nice. I mean, it's great, everyone getting together like this? It's like a party. I guess I'm just not really used to big family dinners." I looked around. The eating had slowed, but the conversations continued.

"Do you have any brothers and sisters?"

"Nope. Just me. My family is pretty much the opposite of this."

"Well, they say opposites attract, right?"

"Yeah. And after my parents split up, it was just me and my mom."

"You two must be very close, then. I always imagined that if we had a daughter she and I would be best friends." She stood up and picked up my plate and hers. I picked up an empty bowl from the middle of the table and followed her into the kitchen.

"Yeah. My mom didn't always— The divorce was— We're okay now."

I looked up when Stevie came in holding a stack of plates, and then I saw Matt and one of his brothers, with Marty right behind them, everyone carrying something from the table.

"Come on, let's go sit. They've got this."

"That's okay. I can—"

"This will give us a chance to get to know each other."

I followed her back to the dining room, which was now empty. Wow. It was like she'd choreographed it.

"So, just you and your mom. How old were you?"

"I was thirteen, I guess, when they got separated."

"So that must have been a lonely time for you."

"Lonely? Not really. I don't know. Maybe. I guess I never really saw it like that."

"Well, just different than this, I suppose."

"I mean, I had a lot of friends. And my dad was around. Him and his girlfriend. It really wasn't as bleak as I think I may have made it sound."

Kamala came in and sat down on Louise's other side.

"I actually think it was good for me. Spending so much time alone? I feel like it made me more independent, you know? Confident."

Kamala rolled her eyes. "Ugh. That sounds like when the guidance counselor says that thing about how if there's something that doesn't kill me, that it's going to make me stronger?"

"Something like that." Louise squeezed her hand and smiled, and then turned back to me. "But tell me what you mean. How do you think being on your own made you more confident?"

"I don't know. Maybe that's not even what I really mean. But it's like— I used to make up these stories. Just goofy stuff, kids' stories. But I knew that they came just from me, without any help. Like, it wasn't competitive. It wasn't collaborative. It was just me, do you know what I mean? So then, when my book got published, it was this amazing thing. I mean, I was a freshman in college and I had this book— What? Why are you—?"

"You had a book published when you were a freshman in college? That really is amazing. What is the book?"

"It was just this children's book. I first made it up as a bedtime story for a kid I babysat for. It's called The Adventures of Peanut Girl." I hadn't told anyone about it in a long time.

"Wait, what? You wrote Peanut Girl? No shit!" Kamala put her hand over her mouth. "Oops. Sorry, Louise. No way! I loved that book."

"Get out. You know it?"

"You get out. My mom used to read to me from that book like every night. It was my favorite bedtime story. I would always try to make myself have Peanut Girl dreams. I would go to sleep thinking of ways she could use her powers to help us. You know. Like, to get us out of trouble. Wait, I have to go to tell Stevie."

"That is really quite an accomplishment. I can certainly see how the experience of being a published author would give you confidence."

"That's not really what I meant. I mean, yeah, definitely. But I meant before then. Like I trusted my imagination enough to tell the story, and to write it down and draw the pictures. Does that make sense? I don't think I'm really—"

"Do you still write?"

"No. It was pretty much just that one thing. Besides keeping a journal. Well, that's actually not true. I wrote some stuff for school, short stories. But, I don't know. It started to feel too real, you know? Too honest or something. I mean, the stuff I was writing in college was like sort of intensely personal, which I guess kind of freaked me out. And then, law school just sort of crushed it, you know?"

"Matt. Why didn't you ever mention that Jenna is a published author?"

I looked up just as Heather or Lily pushed past Matt, who was standing in the doorway from the kitchen. She was pulling Marty by the hand.

"We'll be right back. Marty's taking me home to get Peanut Girl. Kamala said maybe Jenna will read it to us."

Matt was looking at me when he answered. "I guess it just seemed like it was Jenna's thing to tell."

We had a huge fight driving back from his parents' yesterday. It was the worst fight we ever had. Like, by a lot. God, it was so like him, not to say a word about it the whole time we were there, pretending everything was fine. And then once we got in the car, I'm like an idiot, telling him what a nice time I had and how much I like his family, and he basically tells me what an asshole I am. And how stupid it made him look that he first heard about Peanut Girl from Kamala, when she was telling Stevie about it. And how humiliating it was for him to find out about this whole part of my life that he didn't even know about. A part of me that he didn't even know.

I apologized. A hundred times in a hundred different ways. I told him it was nothing, a stupid little thing that turned into a big thing for like five minutes. That it was a long time ago, and I hadn't even thought about it in years. That I had no idea if kids still read it, or if you could even still buy it. I told him that he was crazy to feel humiliated. That it was never a secret. It wasn't a thing I was keeping from him. I tried to tell him that it was like his job at the hardware store, something from a long time ago, that didn't matter anymore, that he never told me about before that weekend because it didn't mean anything. He didn't buy it. He said that he watched me while I was talking to his mom that night at the dinner table, and he said he saw me light up in a way he hadn't seen before. It seemed like the worst thing was when she said she'd like to read my stories, the ones I wrote in college, and I said I'd send them to her.

So we fought. I yelled, I cried, I apologized. And then we rode in silence for what felt like forever. I finally told him that we needed to stop so I could pee. I didn't even really have to go, but I thought maybe it would end the fight. It didn't.

I spent the whole last half of the ride thinking about when he would come and get his stuff from my place, wondering if I should pack it up for him. How we would split up the stuff we'd gotten together? Like, just because he'd bought the rug in my living room, did that mean it was automatically his? Or was it a gift? Or was I going to have to pay him for it? I was glad he'd never fully given up his apartment. It would be so much harder if we really lived together. As we got closer to my place I started thinking about what I was going to say, how I was going to say goodbye.

We were about two blocks from my place when I took a deep breath and blew it out slowly.

"Look, I don't want to do this in front of the doorman, okay? So maybe we can just agree that we'll be fair. Can we do that?"

He pulled over, in front of a hydrant, shut off the car and turned to me. "What did you just say?"

"Just that we should, you know, be fair. Try not to hurt each other." He didn't say anything, so I kept going. "I'm really sorry that it didn't work out, you know? That I fucked it up. I never meant for— I mean, I'm not angry. It was good, you know? What we had? It was really good. I'll always— What?"

"Are you done?" he asked.

"What? Yeah, I guess. I just didn't want to, I don't know, say goodbye like it was nothing. It wasn't nothing to me."

"Jen, stop. We're having a fight, not breaking up. Okay? There's a difference."

"Oh. I just thought— I mean, you wouldn't answer me. You wouldn't even look at me. I never saw you get so mad before. I figured if you could—"

"Look, I probably overreacted, okay? I shouldn't have gotten so mad. It just felt like that thing you do, when you push me away, or hold yourself back from me. It feels like you're keeping secrets from me."

"I'm not. I mean, I don't mean to. It's just how— I don't know."

"I need you to trust me. And to trust us, what we have."

"I do. Trust you. I really—"

"Plus, you've got to understand who my mother is. She lives for this shit. Like how now she's going to think she knows you better than I do. I should have warned you—she will be so far up your ass, you won't be able to believe it. And if you really show her your stories? Forget it."

"So, we're not breaking up?" My eyes filled with tears, and my voice didn't sound like me. It was the voice of a little girl.

"Jenna, look at me. We're not breaking up. We're going to get married. Okay?"

"We are? I mean, okay. Yes. Did you just propose to me? I said yes. You got that, right?"

"Got it." He smiled, and leaned over and wiped my tears and snot with his hand, and then he wiped his hand on my jeans. "But I am going to ask you better, okay? So we'll have a better story to tell our kids someday about how I asked you to marry me."

That was two days ago, and when Matt got home from work today he gave me a laptop computer. I still don't know how I feel about it. I mean, I love it. It just seems like a really big present for no reason. But I guess I've been saying for a long time that I wanted to get a laptop, and I kept talking myself out of it, deciding that I didn't really need one. I don't know. Maybe he was just getting sick of hearing me talk about it.

He said his thinking was that maybe I wouldn't hate my job so much if I had more flexibility, like if I could leave the office at a normal hour and work from home if I had to. It mostly feels really great that he wants to help me figure out what to do, like we are partners, or a team or something, but I swear to God, sometimes I just want to scream at him to back off, that I didn't ask for his help. Like, just because I complain about something, it doesn't mean I need him to fix it.

I actually think that him giving me this computer was his way of showing me that he's really not mad at me, that we are good, and I guess to encourage me to write. Or at least to try to make it so writing isn't this awkward thing between us. It's weird though. It feels like the fight is still lingering, hanging over us. Like after you've had a really bad headache and it finally goes away. But it's like there's still a shadow of it, like you can still feel where it used to hurt.

Joanne

CHAPTER 15

April 10, 1997

Joanne looked up, disoriented, surprised to find herself walking into the park. She had no recollection of having finished and left, although it was easy enough to reconstruct what would have happened. Dr. Benheim would have glanced up at the clock, closed her notebook, and gently but firmly interrupted to tell her that they were out of time, that they would pick up there next week. She would have stood up, picked up her sweater and her bag, thanked Dr. Benheim and walked out of her office. Someone might have been sitting in the waiting room, or maybe not. So far, it hadn't been the same from week to week. So she may or may not have nodded and smiled at Dr. Benheim's next patient, and then she would have walked out, down the stairs, out the door and onto 63rd Street. She'd somehow come all the way from Lexington Avenue, crossing four busy streets, without any awareness of what she was doing. It was amazing she hadn't been hit by a bus.

She still couldn't quite shake herself out of what they'd been talking about. She'd tried to explain it in a way that made sense. So that Dr. Benheim would understand. But the more she'd talked about it, the less sense it made. What had she been so angry about? Had she gotten it all wrong? Could she have done things differently? She looked around to get her bearings, and decided to walk north, toward the reservoir. Oh, what was the point anyway? It was all so long ago, it was impossible to change any of it now.

It was so different with Dr. Benheim from how it had been with Alice.

She'd always left Alice's feeling good, energized, ready to take on the week ahead. With Dr. Benheim, it felt like work. Hard work. It was exhausting, as if she'd just spent 50 minutes wrestling to hold onto something that was being yanked away from her. Like something that was attached to her, a part of her, was being ripped away.

She was starting to think that Alice's having died might be the best thing that had ever happened, but then she felt terrible for thinking so. It was tragic, of course. And Joanne knew that she would miss her. She already missed her. You don't see someone every week for more than 16 years without developing a relationship. It felt more like a friendship than therapy.

Joanne had felt totally comfortable with Alice. She knew exactly how long it took to get to her office, when she had to leave the house to get there with enough time to flip through the latest People Magazine. Where to stop on the way to pick up a coffee, and a tea for Alice. She liked that the doorman knew her, and would always give her a smile and a slight nod of the head, directing her toward Alice's office, just through the lobby to the right. As if she needed to be reminded.

She even felt like she'd gotten to know the woman who, for the past couple of years, had the appointment before Joanne's, even though they had never exchanged a word. She missed her, too. That moment each week when the door opened, and she would look up as the woman came out of the inner office, her eyes sometimes red-rimmed, makeup smudged, before Joanne looked away, respecting the woman's privacy.

It was completely different with Dr. Benheim. First of all, she is a psychiatrist, and Alice was—what, a psychologist? A therapist? Joanne didn't mean to be a snob about higher education—she hadn't finished college herself—but she knew what it took to get through medical school. You had to respect that. She figured Dr. Benheim was about her age, maybe a couple of years older. Which meant she would have been in medical school in the sixties, the same as Andrew. She didn't wear a ring. Joanne wondered if she'd ever been married, if she had kids.

The thought of starting over with someone new had been overwhelming. Alice knew her whole story, who everyone was, everything that had happened. She could just pick up each week where she'd left off, telling Alice what was new since they last spoke. It turned out Dr. Benheim wasn't really interested in hearing about her week. That first day, she did something that Alice had never done. She asked Joanne why she was there, why she was in therapy. What was she hoping to get out of it, to learn, or change, or fix? It was a few weeks before she had an answer. Funny, it had been Jenna, or Matt really, who had helped her figure it out.

She'd met them at the Mexican place on Amsterdam. She'd assumed, when Jenna suggested dinner, that they were finally going to talk about the wedding. It was ridiculous already. They'd been engaged for months, and hadn't even set a date. What were they waiting for? At this rate, she would be lucky to have a grandchild at all, let alone more than one.

It seemed like they were going out of their way to avoid the subject. Matt went on and on over the chips and salsa about his brother's rehab after ACL surgery, and the exercises he was supposed to be doing. And then they'd talked about some movies they'd rented recently. Jenna had fallen asleep during The English Patient, and he'd liked it more than she did, which surprised them both. They'd enjoyed Ed Wood, which they hadn't gotten around to seeing in the theater. By the time the waiter brought them their entrees, she couldn't take it anymore.

"Oh, for Christ's sake. Are we ever going to talk about the goddamn wedding?"

They both looked at her, and she knew that it hadn't come out right.

"Mom, Jesus."

"I was kidding." She forced a smile, and attempted a giggle. "It's just that, there's so much to do. And I've been looking forward to it. Once we have the place booked, the rest can wait. But if we want to do it— You know, some places get booked more than a year in advance."

"Mom, there's not going to be a wedding."

Joanne looked across the table at Jenna's hand. She was still wearing her ring. She turned to Matt, then back to Jenna. "What are you talking about? Did something happen?"

"What Jenna's saying, Joanne, is that we've pretty much decided— We think we'll just go to Las Vegas. Over a long weekend or something. Beth and Neil will come out. And maybe my brothers and—"

"Jenna, no. You can't do that. I never had a real wedding. I always imagined that, you know. Ever since you were a little girl, I just figured—"

"Yeah, well, I figured too. But it's not going to work. So everyone is just going to have to get over it. Can we please talk about something else now?"

"Joanne, we knew you'd be disappointed." Matt reached over and took Jenna's hand, but she pulled it away. "Believe me, my folks are pretty upset too. But we just sort of realized that it was going to get too complicated, you know? With you, and Andrew and Deirdre. Just trying to figure out how we would . . ." He didn't finish his sentence.

"So you're saying this is my fault?" She turned to Jenna. "I don't suppose your father has anything to do with it. Jenna, he's the one who did this. You're not putting this on me. Things are the way they are because of him, not me."

"Oh my God. Mom, stop. I really can't have this conversation again."

"Again? This is the first time we're talking about the wedding since you got engaged. I don't understand. What's again?"

"We don't have the right kind of family for that kind of wedding. Okay? I mean, think about it. There'll be three people on the bride's side, except that they can't actually all be in the same room at the same time. It's not going to work. It's fine. Whatever. Please, just leave it. Really." She put her napkin on the table, and turned to Matt. "Now do you see? This is what I was talking about." She picked up her bag from the floor next to her chair. "I'll be back." Jenna got up and walked toward the ladies' room.

"Oh, I see. So he gets to live the life he wants, and what? Somehow that turns into it's my fault that she can't have a wedding?"

"No one's blaming anyone. It's just that she can't really deal with it, you know? It's hard for her. It's supposed to be this happy thing, but there is always this cloud there that she feels like she has to, like, maneuver around. This dark angry cloud."

"And that's me? I'm the dark angry cloud?"

"Every time we'd start to talk about, like, trying to make a guest list, to figure out how many people, how big a place we'd need? She'd just kind of shut down. She couldn't deal with it. I think she's afraid that we are going to plan this thing, this big day, right? And we're going to spend all this money on a dress and flowers and a band. And then, at the last minute, you'll— Look, I don't know. I'm the new guy here, right? I wasn't there. I didn't even know her then. But she told me about how you didn't go to her book thing that time? I guess because Deirdre was going to be there? I know it was a long time ago and everything, but it seems like it was a pretty big deal. To her. And I guess that's why she didn't go to her graduation."

"You mean her law school graduation? That was her idea. I would have gone. I wanted to go."

"She seems really tough sometimes, you know? Like she's this big bad lawyer, and confrontation doesn't scare her? But with some stuff, she'd rather just walk away. She'd be worried about you, being there alone. And with Andrew and Deirdre—"

"Why does it always have to be about them? I'm her mother. The mother of the bride."

"They're her family, too. Joanne, I'm sorry. I'm overstepping my bounds here, I know that. And whatever went down with you and Andrew and Deirdre, it was way before my time. It just seems like you're all sort of stuck in this bad pattern, you know? Where everyone keeps doing the same things and saying the same things, and acting the same way. Jenna doesn't want that. And I just want her to be happy."

The next time she saw Dr. Benheim, she told her about her conversation with Matt, which she couldn't stop thinking about. She could definitely see that she was stuck. That she'd been stuck for a long time. And that was what she wanted to get from therapy, to get unstuck. To stop being the dark angry cloud. She didn't necessarily agree that she was "depressed". And she had been a little put off, frankly, when Dr. Benheim had first suggested Prozac. But it had been more than two months since she'd started on it and she had to admit, she really was feeling better.

*   *   *

She hadn't been paying attention, and didn't know how many times she'd circled the reservoir. The sun felt good, and she didn't feel like going home yet, so she kept walking. Her appointments with Dr. Benheim had been pretty intense the past few weeks. They'd already covered the basics of her history. That her mother had died when she was thirteen. And that her father and Marjorie had gotten married pretty soon after that. That she'd dropped out of college and left home when she and Andrew got married. But now they were "digging deeper", as Dr. Benheim put it.

She hadn't had much to say about it at first. For God's sake, she was 55 years old. Why bother with ancient history? But there she was, last week and again today, talking about things she hadn't thought of in years.

At first, all she'd remembered was loneliness. How she'd never felt like she was a part of her father's new family. That Brenda was spoiled, and her father and Marjorie had been more than willing to give her the attention she'd demanded. She remembered noticing that Marjorie didn't keep house like her mother had, that she'd been certain her father had noticed too. She'd decided one day that she ought to make herself useful, cooking and straightening up, making things more like her father was used to. She'd thought her father would see what she was doing, and that he would appreciate that she was doing it for him, but instead she'd ended up feeling like the hired help. Yes, she supposed, it had been her choice. But she'd really just wanted to be noticed.

She told Dr. Benheim about the morning of the wedding. How she'd pretended that she was still asleep when her father came in to her room. She'd been hoping they would have a special day together, their last special day. She'd imagined that they would go to the cemetery to leave flowers at her mother's grave, and then they'd go out for breakfast, just the two of them. Her eyes closed, she'd sensed him standing next to her bed, and she heard him put something down on her bedside table. She opened her eyes as he walked out, gently pulling the door shut behind him. Back out in the hall, he knocked twice and said that it was time to get up, that they had a big day ahead of them. She looked at the velvet pouch that her father had left, her mother's pearls, and understood that he meant for her to wear them that day.

She could still remember every detail from the wedding. She and Brenda had worn matching dresses in pale yellow with a wide satin ribbon at the waist, a fat bow at the back. They held bouquets of pink and white peonies. She'd worn her first high heels, dyed to match. Brenda wore patent leather maryjanes, little girl shoes. Marjorie had helped her with her makeup, blue eye shadow, and a hint of lipstick. She could still remember that *floof* sound the flash made when the photographer took that picture of the four of them. She didn't wear the necklace, sparing her mother that one last indignity. Her father didn't mention it.

They'd moved right after the wedding, the summer before she started high school, to a house in a town that was new to all of them. This would be better, her father had said, than if they'd moved into Marjorie's house, or if Marjorie and Brenda had moved into theirs. It would be a fresh start, he'd promised. A chance for her to reinvent herself. A school filled with new friends. It turned out that no one was particularly interested in the new girl, and the cliques were impenetrable. She spent most of her time alone, upstairs in her room, doing homework, reading, daydreaming, wishing that everything had stayed the same, that anything had stayed the same.

She'd wanted to make friends, but when Marjorie started showing so soon after the wedding, Joanne was too self-conscious. It was embarrassing. Her mother had been gone for less than a year, and her father was already remarried with a baby on the way.

And it wasn't just the baby. It was like her father became a different person, someone she could barely recognize. He started dressing differently, and he grew out his sideburns. He came home one day with a television. A television! She didn't know anyone who had a television. He was like a stranger to her. She remembered one time when she was doing homework at the kitchen table. He'd stepped out of his shoes in the hall and tiptoed into the room, holding his finger in front of his mouth, silently shushing her, and snuck up on Marjorie while she was doing the dishes, hugging her from behind, kissing her neck and rubbing her swollen belly. It was disgusting.

She'd never understood how her father could have been so happy so fast. Like he didn't even miss her mother, the family they used to be. Had any of that meant anything if he could move on so quickly, so completely? It was as if he'd brushed off his hands, taken two steps to the right and started a new life. It was the same way Andrew had been with Deirdre. He hadn't even stopped to reflect on the past before he moved on, and then he never looked back. And now they've been together for more than 20 years. Living happily ever after.

She wrapped her sweater around her and crossed her arms. The sun was setting and it was getting chilly. Her legs ached. She looked at her watch. She'd been walking for more than three hours. Living happily ever after. Obviously, that was the point, right? That was what Matt had said too, about Jenna. That he just wanted her to be happy. That was it. The goal. What they were all supposed to be looking for, working toward. Had she missed it? Had she somehow not known what everyone else knew? That she was supposed to want what everyone else wanted? Could it really be that simple?

When she got home, she changed her clothes and broiled a couple of lamb chops for dinner. While she was eating, she thought that she ought to call Marjorie, to see how her father is doing. It had been a few weeks since they'd spoken. She didn't think he would be able to make the trip, but maybe Marjorie would come to the wedding without him. And even if they couldn't be there, Brenda and Steven would probably come. And Kimmie and Jay, too. Jenna is their cousin. People travel to a cousin's wedding all the time. She should probably tell them to invite Joe, too. Funny, he'll be turning 40 this year and she still thinks of him as Marjorie's baby.

She picked up the phone and dialed Jenna's number. Maybe it wasn't too late to fix things.

Jenna

CHAPTER 16

May 3, 1999

Matt picked up on the second ring. "Hello?"

"It's me. Beth's not here yet, but I still think I'll be home by 9. She just called me to say she'll be here in a few minutes."

"See that? I told you having a phone would be a good thing."

"I hate this thing. I honestly don't think I've ever actually managed to answer a call."

"But she left you a message?" He was amused by my struggles with technology.

"Yeah, but I can never remember how to listen to it. It showed me that it was her so I just called her back."

"You'll get the hang of it."

"I don't know. I still feel like a dick talking on the phone in public."

"Maybe try not saying dick in public."

"I'm in the ladies' room. Did you really think I was sitting in the middle of a restaurant talking on the phone? That would be seriously dickish."

"Whatever you say. Tell her I say hi, and I'll see you—"

"Wait. How's Hermione?"

"She's fine. She misses you."

"Everything was okay at daycare?"

"Yeah."

"Because she cried when I dropped her off this morning."

"They said she did fine."

"Okay. Did she poop?"

"Jesus, Jenna."

"What? I'm just asking."

"Yeah, she pooped on the walk home. And I fed her, and now she's asleep under the table. Go have dinner and call me when you're on your way back."

"Okay. Bye."

I snapped my phone closed and dropped it into my bag. Someone was in one of the stalls, so I washed my hands even though all I'd done in the bathroom was talk on the phone. Walking back to the table, I saw Beth coming in the front door.

She was wearing a v-neck t-shirt and jeans, and she looked fantastic. Like she always did. It made me wish I'd stopped at home to change, although it wouldn't really have made a difference. She was the girl, she had always been the girl, whose white t-shirt was whiter than yours. Whose jeans fit better, and were faded to just the right color, in just the right places. She had two kids at home, and she still had the body of a sixteen year old. A sixteen year old with a really good body. I swear to God, if she wasn't my best friend, I'd seriously hate her.

She was already talking, before she was even halfway to the table.

"I'm sorry I'm late. Have you been here long? Traffic was totally stupid. But oh my God, it is so nice out. Were you outside at all today?"

"That's okay. I know, right? I ended up walking here because—"

She leaned over and gave me a kiss on the cheek, rubbing my sleeve with her hand.

"I like that. Is it silk? Red is such a good color on you. Where's it from?"

"Thanks. I can't remember. I've had it for a—"

"Excuse me, Ladies. Sorry to interrupt. My name is Anthony, and I will be your server this evening." He handed us menus. "What can I bring you to drink?"

"Let's get a bottle, don't you think? Sancerre? Or do you want red? I think I'm more in the mood— Wait. You're not pregnant, are you?"

"I'm not pregnant. But hey, thanks for asking."

"What? That's not a bad question. I mean, your ovaries are almost 36 years old. Plus, it's not like I said you *look* pregnant. But seriously, what are you waiting for?"

I turned to the waiter and smiled. "You know what? A bottle of Sancerre would be great."

"You got it. I'll be right back."

"Seriously, though. Have you been trying? Because with Mallory, it took me all of like 15 minutes to get pregnant after I went off the pill. It took longer with Wes, but actually not that much. That's why I made Neil get snipped. I told him that was the only way he'd ever have sex with me again."

"We're sort of trying. I guess. I mean, we stopped using birth control. Does that count?" It felt weird to say we were trying. Trying would involve thinking about it more, or talking about it, or more consciously wanting it. "I feel like it's like dieting. Like, you can sort of start eating smart, right? Stop eating cookies and French fries? But you don't really lose weight until you get kind of obsessed about it. Like, you have to commit to it emotionally. Do you know what I mean? So I guess we're trying. But maybe not really trying hard enough. For now, we're just letting it happen when it's supposed to."

"Yeah, okay. First of all, getting pregnant is actually pretty much the opposite of dieting. But I will say, your approach is very—"

"Oh my God. I keep meaning to tell you. Guess who has a gentleman friend."

"A gentleman friend? Who? Wait, your mother? No way."

"I know, right? And he's this totally normal guy."

"Where'd she meet him? I cannot imagine Joanne with a boyfriend. It's like, I don't even know what. It goes against everything we have ever known to be true. It's like discovering that that parallel lines really do bisect at some point, or that the Pythagorean theorem was wrong."

"Really? The Pythagorean theorem?" That was such a Beth thing to say.

"Yeah. That's the one about triangles. A squared plus B squared equals—"

"Oh my God, you are so weird. But yeah. I guess I know what you mean."

The waiter was back with the wine. He opened the bottle and poured a little bit into Beth's glass. She totally overdid it, holding her glass up to the light, swirling it around, taking a long sniff, before finally taking a sip. I rolled my eyes.

"Delicious." She put her glass down. "Fill 'er up."

He poured us each a glass, put the bottle in an ice bucket and asked if we had any questions about the menu, or if we were ready to order.

"I'm sorry, Anthony," Beth said. "We didn't even look at it yet. You know what though? We haven't seen each other in like forever. And we have a *lot* to catch up on. So, we're not going anywhere any time soon. But don't worry. You'll be fine because we happen to be excellent tippers."

He smiled. "No problem. I'm not going anywhere either. Take your time."

"We haven't seen each other in like forever?" I asked. "You guys were just over a couple weeks ago. When we—"

"Whatever. He doesn't know that. He's new, isn't he? I don't think we've ever seen him before. So, go back. Who is the guy? Have you met him?"

"His name is Ted. He's a professor at NYU. Comparative Literature, or something like that. We had dinner with them last week. He seems nice, handsome. Like, way more handsome than you would expect a college professor to be. Matt really liked him."

"Where did she meet—? Wait, do you think they're having sex?"

"Gross. I don't know. But, yeah, I guess. I mean, don't you think?"

"Can you imagine what it must have been like for her? That first time? It has to have been 20 years, right? More." She sang, "Like a virgin, hey . . ."

"Okay. You really have to stop now. Let's please talk about something else. What's up with your kids?"

"They're fine. But hold on. First, where'd she meet him? Like, in a bar?"

"No. Some friend from her book club introduced them. I guess she's been seeing him for a few months. I know. It's nuts. They're going to Vermont this weekend. Can you believe it?"

"Holy shit. It's like she's a different person. Do you think maybe she got hit on the head or something?"

"It's the drugs. They totally fixed her. I told you, didn't I? That she started taking Prozac? Hey, did you read that book? Prozac Nation? By Elizabeth something."

"Wurtzel I think, right? Neil's sister went to camp with her. I forget which one. It was one of those Jewish camps that everyone who went there totally loved and then still talked about for years and years after they stopped going. Anyway, I didn't read it."

"Me neither. And I know what you mean though, about those camp kids. Like, sleepaway camp was their most defining life event. It's weird. But maybe we should read it."

"Fuck that. Maybe we should *take* it."

"Yeah, right? I'm sure I told you. Think about it. We never could have had that wedding before Prozac."

"Maybe you did. But you're totally right. I mean—"

When she stopped talking, I saw her look over my shoulder and shake her head no. I turned to see our waiter shrug and turn toward the kitchen.

"I mean, she was actually really good at your wedding. And it must have been— Oh, shit. What time is it? I forgot to tell you. Kristen's coming. We have to order. She said we should eat without her. Where's the waiter?"

"Kristen's coming here? Now? How did that happen?"

"She called me. She's here to see her dad. He's sick, I think. Like, bad sick. Anyway, I told her we were having dinner and she said she'd come by."

"That's too weird. It's been years since I've spoken to her. Seriously. And she hates me."

"She obviously doesn't hate you if she's coming here, knowing you'll be here. Tell me again why she was so mad at you?"

"Come on. You know this."

"Yeah, but it's so good when you tell it."

"Because when she told me that she was marrying that guy, Russ, right? I told her—"

"Not like that. Tell me the story of what happened. Start at the beginning. From when you met him."

"Fine. So it was my last year in law school and I went to visit her over my spring break. They had just started going out, and she wanted to hang out with him the whole time. Which was fine, or it would have been, except he was so awful. And so different from her, from us. Do you remember? He drove this shitty pickup truck. Which is also fine. I mean, it's not like I was offended by his choice of car. But there was all this garbage on the floor, like fast food bags and soda cans. Which he just sort of kicked out of the way to make room for me. And he was a total mullet head, playing really bad music. He mispronounced some word, I can't remember what it was, but it was horrifying. And Kristen would just sort of giggle and say 'Oh, Russ.'"

"What about the part about when you were at her apartment?"

"You mean when we made dinner? I barely remember."

"Come on. It's the best part."

"It was somehow decided that he'd come over for dinner, and she and I are going to cook. We go to like four different stores and buy all this food and wine and flowers. And then we spend the whole afternoon cooking and cleaning and putting candles in candleholders. It's like she's expecting the Queen for dinner. When he gets there he's like 'gross, what's that smell?', talking about the food we'd just literally spent the whole day cooking, and she acts like he was teasing her, but he wasn't. What killed me though was the cocktail thing. Do you remember that? When he got there she was like 'let me fix you a drink.' I think she might have even said 'it's five o'clock somewhere,' which would have made no sense because it was definitely after five o'clock, but that's how ridiculous she was being. And meanwhile, he was all, like, slapping her on the ass and calling her his woman. Anyway, she makes him a rum and coke which, if that's what he drinks, fine, you know? But he so clearly would have rather had a beer. Which would also have been fine. I mean, we were like 25 years old. Anyway, the whole thing was super weird, like she thought she channeling a sitcom wife from the 1950s."

"Too bad you barely remember."

"But then the freakiest part was when she left the room for some reason and he poured his drink into the sink and, quick, refilled his glass with just coke. Like, he didn't even want the stupid drink.

I refilled each of our glasses, and Beth waved over the waiter.

"So, what can I get for you?"

"The usual?" I nodded. She turned to him. "We'll have a Caesar salad with grilled shrimp, and a margherita pizza with olives on half. And we're sharing, so you can bring them both at once. With extra plates."

"You got it."

"Oh, and Anthony? We're going to be one more person, but she won't be eating. But we will need a glass for her. Oh, and some bread."

"And olive oil."

"And balsamic vinegar."

"Anything else?"

"Mmm, nope. We're good." She waited until he was about three steps away before saying, "He's adorable. Do you think he got all that? I really hope so. It drives Neil crazy when waiters don't write down your order. If he was here, he would have been like, aren't you going to write that down? Which always kind of makes me feel like I need to be on the side of the waiter. And then I'm so relieved if they get it right. Like, yay, we did it. Anyway, keep going, before she gets here."

"Really? You know the rest."

"Just tell me."

"When she told me they were getting married, I was literally speechless. I remember talking to John about it. I wonder why I didn't I call you. You must have been away or something. Anyway, I was completely freaking out. Like, she was clearly making a huge mistake. Not just because he was awful. But it was like they were both pretending that this relationship was something it wasn't. And they weren't even pretending it was the same thing. Do you know what I mean? It was like he was imagining that they were going to be jumping into this icy cold mountain lake and she was pretending they were about to jump into the warm blue Caribbean ocean, when in reality, there they were going be, sitting knee to knee in this shitty fiberglass hot tub. There was no way they weren't both going to be disappointed. And I just thought, what kind of friend would I be if I didn't say something. She was one of my best friends. I couldn't just sit there and watch her ruin her life and say nothing. So I called her back that night and I told her that. But in a totally nice way."

"And what did she say?"

"That she was very sorry that I felt that way. And that was it. Seriously. That was the last time I spoke to her. Eleven years ago? Jesus."

"Well, if it helps, you were right. You know that they got divorced, right? After less than two years I think."

"I think that actually makes it worse. I can't believe she never moved back. What is she even still doing in Florida?"

"She's not still in Florida. She lives in Israel. For like years. And she's married and has a ton of kids. I never told you that?"

"Whoa, whoa, whoa. Hold up. First of all, no you never told me. I would definitely remember. And how many is a ton of kids?"

"After she got divorced, her parents gave her some money and she went to Israel. I don't know, to live on a kibbutz or something. And she met this guy with three little kids, whose wife had died. I forget why she died. Probably a bomb on a bus, right? Or a bomb in a shopping center? Seriously, why would anyone live in Israel? Anyway, she married him. And then they had some more kids. Two more, maybe three? A ton."

"And you've been in touch with her this whole time? I can't believe you never said anything."

A busboy put a bread basket down on the table and refilled our water glasses. The waiter was right behind him, with bottles of oil and vinegar. Beth told him that we are going to need another bottle of wine.

"I talk to her maybe a couple of times a year. Seriously, that's it. I wasn't keeping it a secret. You never asked."

"Well, how was I supposed to know to ask? I just sort of assumed she was mad at you, too. Oh, shit. So she doesn't even know about John?"

"Of course she does. I mean, I wasn't going to not tell her that the guy died. She should have called you or sent a letter or something. I'm actually surprised she didn't. I mean, she felt terrible about it. But anyway, she knows everything about you. That you got married, that Matt is awesome, and that you're this totally big-time partner in a big old fancy law firm. She's happy for you."

"This is so fucked up. I don't even— Am I supposed to apologize to her? Or are we going to just pretend I never said anything and she was never mad at me? Come on, help me. We need to figure this out before she gets here."

"Whatever. Just be normal. I really don't think— Here comes our food. How much do you want to bet he got something wrong?"

We had just finished eating, but our plates were still on the table, when Kristen arrived. It was kind of weird at first, awkward. She looked different. Like the past ten years had been harder for her than they were for us, which was probably true. She didn't look bad, just kind of tired. Maybe a little faded. Like she'd been through the wash too many time, and left out too long in the sun. She told us about her husband, Gabriel, a teacher, and showed us pictures of their kids. Beth had some pictures of her kids, but they were from a couple years ago, when Wes was still a baby. I decided not to take out pictures of our dog.

"Beth said your dad is sick?"

"Yeah. I came home for Mom. I mean, for him, too, to see him. But I'm more worried about her. He's always been the one who took care of everything."

"So it's bad, huh? I'm so sorry. He was always so nice to us," I remembered. "The way he talked to us? Like we were actual people, and not just idiotic girls."

"It's pretty bad. I mean, yeah, really bad. Pancreatic cancer. The doctor didn't tell me, but Mom said it'll probably only be— It won't be long. It's so strange, though. Knowing that he's dying? I mean, it's terrible. It's so much better, I think, when someone just like, boom, drops dead. Because then you just deal with it, you know? Like there's this moment of shock, you feel it and then you move on. None of this long, sad— Oh, shit. I'm sorry. I didn't mean— I should have called you. When I heard about John, I mean. I felt really bad, but I didn't know what to say. I was just sort of a wreck then."

"That's okay. I was, too. And I know what you mean. But I always thought it would have been good to have a chance . . . I don't know, to say . . . something. Goodbye? You think about the last conversation you had. Not thinking for a second that it would be the last one. And you wish it had been different. I'm not even really talking about me. But like, for Chloe? It was so—"

"Oh, I remember Chloe. Peanut girl. Do you still see her? God, she must be, what, like 30?"

"Yeah. She lives in Boston. She's a chef. The last time—"

"She's a lesbian," Beth said.

I looked over at her and realized that while Kristen and I had been talking, she had just about finished the second bottle of wine herself.

"Really? I still picture her as this tiny little girl dancing around on her tiptoes."

"Still tiny, but full-on lesbo. She brought her girlfriend to Jenna's wedding."

I looked at Kristen and rolled my eyes. "She and Waverly came to the wedding. We actually don't see them that much, especially since Mara, Chloe's mom, moved to Florida. She got remarried a couple of years ago."

"Well. Life goes on, I guess. I mean, look at us. Three married ladies."

We all just sort of sat there for a minute, taking that in, and the lull in conversation made me anxious. I was relieved when Kristen asked Beth where Mallory was going to school. It started a whole conversation about the process of applying to private schools in New York, and how competitive it is and how much it had all changed since we were in school. I knew that it could go on forever. I excused myself and went to the ladies' room. I saw that I'd missed two calls from Matt, and I never even heard the phone ring. I called to tell him I'd be late and that my battery was about to die.

I could tell even before I got back to the table that something had changed. Beth's back was to me, but I could see Kristen's face. She was listening, and nodding in a way that looked sympathetic. I slipped into my seat, careful not to interrupt whatever was going on.

"So he's never been cuddly, but then it's like one day he just stopped talking. A few months ago. At first, I didn't think much of it. I mean, for a while I didn't even notice. Mallory had started talking much younger than he did. But they say boys' language skills develop more slowly than girls', right? I mean, have you seen that with your kids?"

"Yeah,. I mean, I've heard that. But we speak Hebrew at home. And my kids speak it better than I do. So it's hard for me to—"

"Wait. You speak Hebrew at home? No way. Jen, did you know they speak Hebrew in Israel?"

"Well, yeah, I guess. I mean, I never really—"

"Everyone there speaks English, too. But we mostly speak Hebrew."

"Huh, I had no idea. Anyway, he started talking kind of late, I think, to begin with. And he was kind of a funny baby. I mean, just different. And I swear, it was like he was speaking a made up language. It was impossible to understand what he was saying. But he was improving. Or I don't know, maybe I was just getting better at guessing. And then one day I noticed that he'd pretty much stopped talking. And Mallory just talks all the time, right? I mean, she never shuts up. So I just thought that maybe Wes had figured out, like we all did, that it was easier just to let her talk and not to even try to get a word in. Plus, the quiet was such a relief for a while. I would drop Mallory at school and it was like Wes and I would just enjoy the silence. I would push him in his stroller and be so happy not to have to answer any questions for a while."

"Maybe you're overly sensitive to it because you're in it, you know? I mean, I'm sure it's just—"

"And now he doesn't make eye contact. It's like he won't connect at all. And it was my fucking mother who pointed that out. So what kind of mother am I that I didn't even notice?"

"What does Neil think?"

"Neil? He thinks that Wes is fine and my mother is crazy. And that if there is anything wrong with him, it's my fault. And I should fix it."

"I'm sure he'll be fine. Kids are funny. Gabriel's mother told me about this one time when Chava was little. She's the oldest. They were—"

"I'm taking him to a neurologist. I have an appointment next week. He's supposed to be the best guy for . . . you know, for developmental disorders. Fuck. I can't believe I even just said those words. How is this my life?"

"It's going to be okay. You're going to figure out what's wrong, and then you'll fix it. You can do this. Don't you think, Jenna?

"Definitely. You're a great mom, and he's a great kid. I'm sure it's just—"

"Okay, enough. New topic. It's almost our birthdays. Let's get dessert."

We ordered cheesecake, crème brulee and chocolate mousse, and three coffees.

"So, Jenna. Your turn. What about you?"

"Oh, umm, well, so you know I got married. The wedding was at my dad and Deirdre's place in Connecticut. Small. Pretty much just family."

"Oh my God, Kristen, it was gorgeous. It was outside. They have this big backyard. It was all green grass and white chairs and blue sky. It made my wedding seem so gaudy and fussy in comparison."

"Oh, stop. It was a nice day. We got lucky with the weather. Anyway, Matt's an architect. We live in Tribeca. We have a dog. Her name is Hermione. You know, like from Harry Potter?"

"You've got to see their apartment. It's in this sort of crappy industrial building that looks terrible on the outside and still has a giant freight elevator. But then you get inside and it's amazing."

"Wow. Sounds nice."

"We sort of lucked out. I knew the guys who owned the building, and they were converting it to condo, so we got a really good deal. And then Matt did the renovation. And I'm still a lawyer, but I kind of hate it. It's hard, though, to figure out something else to do instead. I've been doing this for ten years. It's the only thing I know how to do."

"So everything's good with you."

"I guess. I mean, yeah. My dad and Deirdre are good. Even my mom. I was just telling Beth, she's got a boyfriend, if you can believe that. So yeah, everything's really good."

"You know what's fucked up, though?"

Beth and I both looked at her.

"Mmm, no. What's fucked up?"

"There were never any consequences for you."

"Consequences? What do you mean?"

"I mean, how is it okay that you did what you did and got away with it?'

"Kristen. Don't—"

"No, Beth. Hold on. I'm serious. She spends all these years fucking this married guy. And God forbid you tell her you think it's wrong, right? Or that she's making a mistake? But that never stopped her from judging everyone else."

"What do you mean? I never—"

"They never got caught. No one ever found out. And then he died, which okay, is obviously tragic. But for who? For him, sure. And for his poor wife and kid. But for Jenna? Nope. Fifteen minutes later she meets the greatest guy ever. And the kid, that poor kid whose father you were screwing behind her and her mother's back all those years, she comes to your wedding? You really must have had a good laugh about that. And 'oh, boo hoo, poor me. I hate my job where they made me a partner and pay me tons of money.' We're all really sorry that your job isn't more fulfilling."

I just sat there for a minute, absorbing what she'd said. I felt like I needed to catch my breath.

"Wow. Okay. I umm, I guess I'm going to go. Beth, can you take care of the check and I'll pay you back?"

"No, don't. I'm leaving. I have to go take care of my father who is dying so my mother can get some sleep."

I watched her walk out, and turned to Beth, who was taking her wallet out of her bag. "What was that?"

"Whatever. Look, I'm sure she's just stressed out about her dad. Or jet-lagged, or something."

"That was horrible. I mean, she seriously hates me."

"She's just jealous of you. Of course she is, right? Think about it. In a million years, would you trade your life for hers? No way."

We split the check, rounding up so we wouldn't have to wait for change. When we got outside, there was a cab coming up the street, which she ran toward, calling over her shoulder, "Love you. Call me next week." She got in and closed the door. I was alone on the street.

Chloe

CHAPTER 17

September 14, 2001

Chloe stood in the kitchen. She couldn't see the TV in the living room but she could hear it. She hadn't turned it off since Tuesday, hadn't changed the channel. There were lots of things she hadn't done since Tuesday. She hadn't showered. Or left the house. She knew that she must have slept a little, curled up on the kitchen floor. She'd barely eaten, just some of the chickpea and avocado salad left over from Sunday. She'd made coffee at one point, but never poured a cup. She must have turned off the coffee maker, but she didn't remember. Maybe it turned itself off. She hadn't told anyone. Hadn't yet said it out loud.

Her mother had called her right after the second plane hit. She told her to put on the TV. They'd watched together, in silence, for more than an hour. When they saw the first tower collapse, Chloe told her she had to go, that she'd call her later.

Waverly had left that morning without saying goodbye. Or maybe she had. Chloe pictured her at the door, ready, with her suitcase in one hand her briefcase in the other, anxious to be outside, even though it would make her impatient, that she'd be checking her watch, looking up the street for the car she'd arranged the night before to take her to Logan. But then stopping, putting down her bags, turning around and going back upstairs and into the bedroom, leaning over the bed, brushing back Chloe's hair and kissing her gently on the forehead. Or better, kissing her gently on the mouth. Chloe imagined that she would have stirred a little, smiled in her sleep, maybe reached for her hand, without opening her eyes. Or had Waverly thought *ah, screw it*? Knowing that Chloe wouldn't wake up, wouldn't know one way or the other. Thinking that she didn't know what the traffic was going to be like, not wanting the driver to have to wait.

She tried to remember what they'd talked about the night before. Stupid shit. Nothing big. Nothing important. Just that she had depositions in LA on Wednesday and Thursday, and that she would be back on Friday. That Chloe was working Saturday. That there was dry cleaning that needed to be picked up.

Until Charlie called, she hadn't even known what flight she was on.

"Chloe. Hey, it's Charlie. Was she on the plane? I mean, did she actually get on?"

"I don't know. I mean, I guess. She left before I got up. I don't even know which—".

"We were booked on the United flight. I was supposed to go with her. But they decided at the last minute that the client wasn't going to want to pay for two people to go. You haven't heard from her?"

"No. I— I've just been here. I was watching. On TV, I mean. The buildings."

She felt herself clinging to these last seconds of not knowing, willing herself not to make the connection between what she'd been watching and what he was saying.

"Well, if she hasn't called or anything, that's got to mean she was on the plane. Shit, Chloe. I'm so sorry."

"Well, yeah. I mean, of course she was. You know Waverly. She's never missed a plane in her life. She's never even late. She'd rather die than—"

Neither of them spoke. Chloe could hear Charlie breathing, sharp quick inhalations.

She wanted to tell him that she had to go, but no words came out. She was about to hang up when Charlie continued.

"So, umm." He cleared his throat. "Sorry. I umm, hang on."

She heard him put the receiver down on his desk, without putting the call on hold. She heard him blow his nose. She waited.

"Sorry. I'm back." He cleared his throat again. "So, okay, Craig is going to— You know Craig, right? Craig Rabson? He's the Managing Partner.

I'm sure you've met him. He's mostly in the New York office, but he's here a lot. Anyway, he's going to call her mom. Like, on the firm's behalf, I guess. He asked Katya to call you, first. To see if maybe she didn't get on the plane. And also to find out if she knows. If Waverly's mom already knows. Like, if you've talked to her yet. Katya didn't want to do it, so she asked me to call you."

"To see if I talked to Waverly's mom? Today you mean? No. I— I didn't even really know until— She and I don't— I doubt they even would have known that she was going to LA. They aren't actually that close. I guess maybe her brother might have known. But, why is Craig going to call her?"

"Look. I'm sure he's going to call you, too. But you know how this place is. Someone is always worrying about protocol or something. HR said she listed her mom as her official contact. Like her next of kin? And I guess because she was traveling on firm business. He's probably going to have to give some kind of statement at some point too."

Some kind of statement? She wanted to tell everyone to slow down.

"I'm hanging up now."

Chloe spent the rest of that day and most of the next three days standing in the kitchen, listening to the television from the living room. There had been moments when she'd been drawn into the room by something she heard a newscaster say. She got as far as standing behind the couch. But she couldn't bring herself to sit down, and she didn't last more than a few minutes before retreating back to the kitchen, standing by the sink, feeling somehow safer among the stone countertops, the appliances and utensils creating a barrier between her and the news being reported in the next room.

The phone rang a lot, but she let the machine pick up. Most of the calls were from friends in New York, calling to let her and Waverly know that they were okay. She didn't pick up, even when her brothers called. Although she desperately wanted them to know, she couldn't say the words out loud. She'd tried, standing in the kitchen, leaning into the open refrigerator, her eyes closed, the cold on her face. *Waverly was on the plane.* No sound came out. She tried to whisper it. *Waverly was on the plane.* Nothing.

The only call she'd picked up since she spoke with Charlie was from Waverly's brother, Dan. He called Tuesday night. Marie had gotten the call from Craig, and they'd been in touch with the airline, who confirmed that she'd been on the plane. He told her he'd come by at 1:00 on Friday. She looked at the clock on the microwave. She had four and a half hours to get it together. She needed to shower, to change out of the clothes she'd been wearing since they went to bed Monday night. But first, she needed to figure out lunch.

She surveyed the contents of the refrigerator and pantry. There was smoked salmon left from the weekend and the sweet peas she'd picked up at the farmers' market. She could make a cream sauce with roasted garlic and cilantro, and maybe some jalapeno, and toss it all together with some pasta. A little fresh lime juice and voila. She took a half a baguette out of the freezer that she would warm in the oven a few minutes before he was due to get there. Fresh would obviously be better, but she knew he wouldn't notice. She remembered having once come home early to find Waverly making herself spaghetti with ketchup for dinner. Ketchup! She hadn't even opened a jar of Ragu. She said that it had been her and Dan's favorite dinner growing up. If Waverly was here now, she thought, she'd be teasing her, how it's always about the food. She'd say that the world could be coming to an end and Chloe would be planning the menu. In fact— She stopped herself from thinking it, turned off the TV and went upstairs to get ready.

"Look," Dan said. "You have to understand, my mother's not acting normal right now. Granted, she's in shock. Well, obviously. We're all in shock, right? The whole fucking world is in shock."

Chloe looked up, and saw that he had leaned forward in his chair, was holding his face in his hands. Please don't let him cry, she thought. There was no way she was going to be able to comfort him if he started crying. She pushed back her chair and picked up their dishes, trying not to make a sound, and carried them into the kitchen. She turned on the coffee maker and returned to the dining room. Dan watched her sit back down.

"Here's the thing. They never really accepted Waverly's relationship with you. I'm sorry. It's not about you. It was never about you. Honestly, it has nothing to do with you. My dad even likes you. But they can't deal with the fact that Waverly is gay. Was gay. Fuck."

"But she came out to them a long time ago, I thought. When she was in high school?"

"She did. And you know, they seemed like they were okay with it. But they weren't really. They were pretending. They treated it like it was a phase. They wouldn't ever mention it, but they indulged it. Like the way you'd have a meat-free lasagna as an extra dish at Thanksgiving because someone who once was a vegetarian was coming. Like, just in case she's 'still not over it'. Do you know what I mean?"

She did, but she was pretty sure those weren't his words, that he was repeating something he'd heard Waverly say. But what was the point? Fine, so they don't accept the relationship. They got what they wanted. There is no relationship.

"Anyway, for whatever reason, she's fixated on keeping you out of it. Keeping your name out of it."

"Out of what? Dan, I have no idea what you are talking about."

"There are already people calling, asking for information. Putting together the victim stories. You know, human interest stuff. About the people who, the people on the planes. And in the buildings.

Victim stories, she thought. Jesus.

"Yeah, okay. So what?"

"She doesn't want anyone to know. About you. That you and Wave were together. So umm. The story is just going to be that she was a loving daughter and sister, and a brilliant and hard-working and dedicated lawyer. And that's it. The firm is going to support that."

"Jesus, Dan. Whatever. Is this seriously what people are worried about? Thousands of people are . . . gone. Missing. Dead. Those buildings are— There is nothing left of them. Can you even imagine? I mean, just think about it for a minute. Think about what was in those buildings. All of the stuff. Where is all the stuff? Floors and floors of offices. Desks, and chairs and conference room tables. And file cabinets. And book shelves. And it's all gone. It all got turned to dust. None of this makes any sense. She's gone. And your mother is worried about getting the firm to go along with a bullshit story that she was single? That she was straight? That is seriously fucked up."

She waited to see if he was going to say anything. He didn't.

"Do you want coffee?"

She went into the kitchen and filled mugs for both of them, even though he hadn't answered. They had talked about making wills, and putting the house in both their names, but they'd never done it. She wondered how long she had, how soon before they told her she had to get out.

She put the cups on a tray, with spoons, napkins, a sugar bowl and a pitcher of milk, which she carried into the dining room and put down on the table.

"I'm sorry, but we only have milk. I needed the Half and Half for the sauce. This is two percent. I hope that's okay."

"Chloe, I'm really sorry. I wanted you to hear it from me. And I wanted to tell you in person. I mean, I wanted to see you. To see if you're okay."

"And?"

"Pardon me?"

"Am I? You're here. You got a good look. So, how do I seem to you? Am I okay? Because I'm not really sure. I think I look okay. But I don't really feel okay."

He stopped stirring his coffee, and put the spoon down on the tray.

"So, what do you think? Based on your recon mission, what are you going to tell your mother? Will I keep quiet, or do you think I might put up a fight? Because she's going to want to be prepared."

"I'm sorry. I shouldn't have said anything. I just—"

"Yeah. You should go now."

September 16, 2001

She woke up Sunday morning, finally back in their bed. Working the night before had somehow made it possible for her to go back to the bedroom, ready to make the phone calls she'd been dreading. She was glad they hadn't canceled the dinner. It felt good to have gotten out of the house, and she was glad to have been busy. The client had seemed pleased.

In-home catering was a funny business, but she liked it. When she'd first started working at Fantasy Foods, she was self-conscious, especially around Waverly's lawyer friends, like she might as well be working at Dunkin' Donuts. But it had worked out, even better than she could have hoped. First, they put her in charge of the prepared foods, giving her freedom over not just the menu, but presentation and pricing, too, and then expanding into catering, last year making her the Executive Catering Chef. She liked going into people's homes, cooking in other people's kitchens.

Last night, it had been four couples, passed hors d'oeuvres and a sit-down dinner, celebrating somebody's birthday. Ruthie was the event captain, serving and clearing, pouring the wine, interacting with the guests, while Chloe stayed in the kitchen. That was how she liked it. It was enough to hear them ooh and ahh over the food, as Ruthie described each dish she was serving. Listening from the kitchen, hearing them talking and laughing, but also sometimes somber—someone they knew from school had been at Cantor Fitzgerald. They could so easily have been friends of Waverly's.

She and Ruthie had the clean-up routine down to a science. They were already completely packed up. Once the coffee and dessert were finished, and the last few dishes were loaded into the dishwasher, they would be ready to go.

"Waverly was on one of the planes."

"Wait, what? Oh my God. Chloe, why didn't you tell me?"

"I couldn't. I couldn't say it out loud. Until just now. I had to do this first. You know? It's okay. I mean, it's not at all okay. But I'm okay. Or not even, really. But right now I am."

"Oh, honey. I am so sorry."

"I know. Me, too. But let's finish so we can get out of here."

She called her mother, her brothers and a few of her and Waverly's friends who she knew would spread the word to the rest of their circle. It was exhausting, even though once she got the words out, "Waverly was on one of the planes," the person on the other end of the phone took over, and she didn't have to say anything more. Everyone she spoke to asked her what she needed, how they could help. She imagined that Waverly's mother would resent the attention she was getting.

The phone rang non-stop the rest of the day, but she let the machine pick up. She retrieved nearly a week's worth of mail from the mailbox, went into the den and sat down at Waverly's desk. They'd always kept their money separate, with Waverly responsible for some bills and Chloe responsible for others. Just opening mail addressed to Waverly felt like an invasion of her privacy. But she felt like she needed to know what was going on, where things stood.

It took about an hour to confirm what she'd already suspected—that Waverly paid her bills on time, balanced her checkbook to the penny and had less than a weeks' worth of paperwork in her "to be filed" basket. Opening the file cabinet, and seeing the folders, with typed labels, arranged alphabetically, she imagined that Waverly must have been her accountant's dream. "Aetna", "BMW Lease", "Brown Alumni", "Carson Danner Cash Balance Plan". She pulled out the folder labeled "Chloe", tucked in between "Chase Bank Statements" and "Crystal Capital K-1", and took it into the kitchen.

She got a box of Rice Chex from the pantry and sat down on the floor, leaning back against the dishwasher. She reached into the box and took out a handful of cereal, eating it one piece at a time, looking at the folder on the floor in front of her. She finished a second handful before she opened the folder.

Waverly wasn't particularly sentimental. So it was shocking to see that she'd saved every note and letter Chloe had written her, every doodle, every card, ticket stubs from three years' worth of concerts and movies, playbills from the shows they would see when they went to New York, a photo of the two of them from Jenna's wedding that she'd never seen before, the boarding pass from their trip last year to Costa Rica. Chloe wiped the tears away with her sleeve. She opened the manila envelope on which Waverly had written MassMutual, thinking it must have been misfiled. It took her a minute to figure out what she was looking at. It was a life insurance policy, with Chloe Toberman named as beneficiary. She read it again, and put it back in the envelope.

She went back to the den, and pulled two heavy cardboard boxes down from the top of the closet. Her mother had had them packed and sent to her when she and Stan were getting ready to move to Florida. She peeled off the tape from the first box and lifted the lid. She dug through the letters and post cards, the old wallets and expired passport, an old Hacky Sack, Annie Lennox' autograph on a cocktail napkin from The 21 Club. She took out the old report cards, class pictures and photo albums, and piled them on the floor. There it was, a brown leather bound book with the words Le Fontane di Roma hand-painted on the front cover. She looked at the pictures, her nine year old self posing in front of fountains, picnicking in the park.

She hadn't realized that she'd been worrying about what she would do, where she would go. She knew she couldn't stay in the house, and without Waverly she had no reason to stay in Newton. As much as she enjoyed working at Fantasy Foods, especially with the catering business starting to pick up, she would only ever be an employee there. She thought of the insurance policy, back in its envelope, back in the folder marked "Chloe". She knew exactly what she was going to do.

The idea was fully formed in her mind, as if she had been planning it for years. She even knew what she would call it. Viaggi per Bambini. Picnics and day trips for children. She'll move to Rome, where she'll do for traveling American families what Jenna had done for her so many years ago. Give the kids a break from the churches and museums. Give the parents a break from their kids. She'll get an apartment and take a few months to get settled, to learn some Italian and get to know the city, come up with some itineraries. Maybe she'll even offer some cooking classes. She would market it in English speaking countries, the US, UK and Australia. She pictured a possible logo.

She looked at the clock and decided to call Jenna, to see what she thought.

Jenna

CHAPTER 18

November 9, 2001

It was one of those rare perfect days, neither summer nor fall, but somehow the best of both. I'd gone out at lunchtime to run some errands, and stopped at the salad place on my way back to the office. Eating lunch at my desk, I realized that I'd just gotten my period. It was that consciousness, that dull cramp accompanied by a mild sense of alarm, an awareness that sent me to the ladies' room. I'd expected it, was prepared for it, but somehow it wasn't until I was back at my desk that it occurred to me—I wasn't pregnant. Again. Still.

I spent the afternoon at my desk, not calling Matt. I knew that I needed to tell him, but I also knew that I didn't want to. I told myself I would call him once I finished the work I needed to do. And then I spent the next four hours staring at a document, not actually reading a word.

Eventually, I gave up. I turned off my computer, and put the papers from my desk into my bag, thinking I'd find some time to read them over the weekend. On my way out, I stopped by Jordan's office.

"Hey. I'm leaving. Don't stay too late. You're young, and it's a Friday."

"Ha! Actually, I think this deal is making me old."

"I know what you mean. Hopefully, they won't want to talk over the weekend, but I'm taking copies of the documents, just in case. I'll be at my in-laws', so call me on my cellphone if you need me."

*   *   *

I finally told Matt once we were in the car, on our way. I think maybe I acted more upset than I actually was, probably because it felt like I was supposed to. It was frustrating, because we were coming from two completely different places. I was done. It was over. The Clomid made me fat and mean and weepy. And it didn't work. We'd tried, we'd failed. We needed to just be happy with all the things we had, and stop fighting for the things we didn't have. He disagreed. He was like a cheerleader. Come on, Jenna, we're just getting started! Mind over matter! It's all in the attitude. He said we just needed to keep going, to try something different, don't quit, don't give up. Yay team.

"Fertility treatment exists for a reason," he said. "We are not the first people to utilize A.R.T."

"What's A.R.T.?"

"Assisted reproductive technology. You know, like in vitro."

He'd obviously been doing his homework.

It wasn't that I didn't want a baby. I desperately wanted a baby. But I wanted it to be a miracle. A miracle of love and passion and biology. Assisted reproductive technology? That was the opposite of a miracle.

"I think we need to accept it. So maybe we aren't meant to have a baby. It's okay. Can't we just let it go?"

"What? How can you even say that? You're going to be a great mom. I'm not kidding, you were born to be a mom. Look at how you are with Mallory. And Chuck and Annie's kids? They are madly in love with you. I mean, just think about the Peanut Girl thing. You're like a kid whisperer. I'm being completely serious—you are definitely meant to have kids."

It must have been him mentioning Peanut Girl that did it. It was like he'd opened a stuck jar. Without knowing it, he'd been squeezing and twisting as hard as he could, running it under cold water, tapping the side of the lid with a knife handle, finally banging it on the edge of the counter. *Phwoom.*

"I had an abortion."

"You what? When?" He turned to me, surprised.

"Jesus! Watch the road. Let's please not die, okay?"

"Wait, you got pregnant? Why didn't you—? When?"

"It was a long time ago. Before I met you. I just mean that's why I can't do this. Why I can't have a baby."

"You mean physically? Why didn't you say something?"

"No. Sorry. I meant— Not like that. Dr. Fleming says I'm fine. She can't find any reason."

"Then, what?"

"Can't you see? I don't deserve it."

"Okay. Now you're being crazy."

"I'm not. I had my chance, okay? There already was a baby. My baby. And I— I chose to— I just think I'm not meant to have another one."

"Will you please stop talking about what you're meant to or not meant to do? Since when do you even think like that?"

"I can't help it. It feels like, I don't know. It feels like fate."

We rode in silence.

"Who was the guy?"

"What? Oh, he umm, it wasn't— He was— You know what? I really don't feel like talking about this. It was a long time ago. I shouldn't have said anything."

"Jesus Christ, Jenna. Would you just this once please fucking talk to me? Why does everything have to be such a goddamn mystery with you?

"It's not. I don't mean to— I'm sorry. It's just that it wasn't that big a deal. I mean, he wasn't."

"I don't believe you."

"You're calling me a liar? Are you serious?"

"Yeah. I am calling you a liar. I really don't understand you. Why are you still keeping secrets from me? I'm your fucking husband."

I opened my mouth, and then closed it. I didn't know what to say.

"Is this even a marriage? I mean, seriously. What the fuck? You've been lying to me for 10 years."

"I haven't been lying. It wasn't relevant. I mean, was there a right time when I was supposed to tell about something that doesn't even matter?

"Not relevant? You have got to be fucking kidding me. We've been try-ing to get pregnant for more than three years. Or at least I thought we were. For all I know, you've been on the goddamn pill this whole time."

"I'm not. I haven't been. I swear."

"If you can't trust me, I don't know what we are even doing."

"I do trust you."

"Then you really need to start acting like it."

Neither of us said anything for what felt like a really long time. I watched him driving, his jaw clenched in anger, a vein showing in the side of his forehead. I never meant for it to be a secret. I just somehow thought that I was doing the right thing, that I was sparing him, that it would hurt him more to know. But maybe not knowing was worse.

I told him. I told him everything. The story of me and John, starting at the beginning, from that first time I babysat for Chloe. He pretty much let me just talk, and I pretty much didn't stop until I got to the end, right up to when Matt and I met on the subway. By the time I finished, we were almost there. We rode in silence the last few miles to his parents' place.

There was an old Celica parked in front of Matt's parents' house as we pulled into the driveway.

"Is that your dad?"

"Where?" Matt asked.

"In that green car. Sitting in the passenger seat?"

Matt got out and started walking to the car, but his dad shooed him away from inside the car, waving him toward the house. Matt's mother met us at the door.

"What's he doing?"

She let us in, ushering us toward the kitchen, asking if we'd eaten. I excused myself to use the bathroom. I stopped halfway up the stairs and listened.

"How's Jenna? She looks tired."

"Mom, who's he in the car with?"

"It's just one of his kids from school. Is she okay?"

"When is he going to stop doing this? It's after 9 o'clock on a Friday night. This is fucking ridiculous already."

"Is she—? I'm sorry. I thought maybe when she went right to the bathroom like that . . . oh, never mind. I guess I'll just wait and let you tell us together."

"Tell you what? Mom, there's nothing to tell. She's not pregnant. Just leave it alone, okay?"

I went the rest of the way upstairs, used the bathroom, washed my face and brushed my teeth. I knew I should go back downstairs, at least for a few minutes, but I really didn't want to. I was spent, empty. I didn't know if Matt hated me for keeping secrets, or for finally telling the truth, if he thought I was a slut, or if he was mad at me for not wanting to do more fertility treatments. At that moment I really didn't care to find out. I got into bed and turned off the light.

I pretended to be asleep when Matt came to bed, and he was still sleeping when I woke up in the morning. I put on a pair of sweatpants, and a bra under my t-shirt that I'd slept in, and went downstairs. I poured myself a cup of coffee and joined Matt's dad at the kitchen table.

"Good morning, counselor. How did you sleep?"

"Good, thanks. I'm sorry I didn't say goodnight. I was just tired I guess. Work's been pretty busy."

"No need to apologize to me. By the time I got in, everyone had already gone upstairs. I should have come in when you guys got here. I tried, but he was pretty . . . I don't know. He's in a tough spot. I didn't want to leave him like that. Maybe Louise is right. She says I have a need to be needed."

"A kid from your school?"

"Yeah. Marcos Cordero. A basketball player. And a pretty good student. He was all set to apply to college, but now he says he wants to join the marines. Since last month anyway. Officer candidates school. His folks support it completely. So there's really not much for me to say about it."

"If his family supports it, what's the problem? Is it just that he has to wait, like until he graduates?

"Marcos has a girlfriend, Lorena. I don't know her. She's over at the Catholic school."

"And, what? She doesn't want him to go?"

"Nothing like that. It seems she found out the hard way that relying on the power of prayer can sometimes let you down."

He must have seen from my face that I didn't understand.

"She's pregnant. Almost four months. And she didn't tell anyone. No one, until she told him yesterday. I guess she'd been hoping for some kind of divine intervention. Personally, I don't get it. It is 2001, not 1951. What the hell was she thinking?"

"Four months. Shit. What's she going to do?"

"She says she'll be kicked out of St. Agnes. That's why Marcos came by. He wanted to see if I can get her into Central. We have a program for pregnant and parenting students."

"Poor thing. What do her parents say?"

"He said they are telling them today. Together. I'm telling you, he's a good kid. He wants to do the right thing. Her family is Italian, very religious. He already talked to his parents, and they said she can stay with them if she can't stay at home."

"He really thinks they'll kick her out?"

"He said that she says they will. Look, on the one hand, it's an absolute disaster. But then, if you think about it, it really could be worse. She has a place to live, right? And she's going to be able to finish high school, get her diploma. That's what I was trying to tell him, that it could be worse. "

"Yeah, but then what? They are kids. You started by telling me about his plans—college, the marines. So what, are they supposed to just scrap all of that?"

Just then, Louise came in through the door from the garage. I hadn't realized she'd already been up and out.

"I have fresh bagels. The everythings just came out of the oven when I got there. And I got nova and cream cheese. Jenna, you like vegetable, right? Not scallion? I got plain and vegetable. And I can make eggs if anyone wants. Is Matthew still sleeping?"

"Yeah. I mean, he was when I came down."

"Would you go get him? I want him to come with me this morning. To the stone place. We need to redo the patio and if I make a decision without him I will never hear the end of it."

Matt was awake and he lifted the blanket to make room for me.

"I'm sorry," we both said at the same time.

He said "I should have respected your privacy" at the same time I said "I shouldn't have kept it from you."

We both said "I love you" at the same time.

I said "Jinx" at the same time he said "Let's stop it before this gets weird."

I curled into him, relieved, knowing that we were going to be okay.

"Your mother says you need to get up so you can help her pick out stone or something."

"You know that they have been talking about redoing the patio for like five years, right?"

"She says the everything bagels are still hot."

"She thought we were coming this weekend to make a big announcement. To tell them that you're pregnant. I couldn't take it. I had to tell her that you aren't. I hope you don't mind."

"It's fine. But you want to hear something weird? That kid, who your dad was talking to? In the car last night?"

"Yeah?"

"His girlfriend is pregnant. Some Catholic high school girl. And she waited too long to have an abortion."

"Yeah?"

"So I guess he wants your dad to help. Just with her school stuff. But it's weird, you know?"

"That he'd want my dad to help? You know what he's like. I've told you that. How everyone always comes to him with—"

"No, I mean it's weird that we can't get pregnant, and here's this random girl, who no one ever even heard of before, pregnant with a baby she doesn't want. I don't know. It sort of feels like fate."

"Wait. What did he say?"

"Nothing. Your dad was just telling me about it. How it sort of screws up all of their plans, but also how they are good kids. They want to do the right thing."

"So are they going to give it up for adoption?"

"I don't— He— You know what? Never mind. Nobody actually said anything about anything. I completely made that up. This has nothing to do with us. I shouldn't have said anything. They'll probably get married and live happily ever after. Really."

"Really?"

"Really."

"Okay."

But I could tell from the way he looked at me that we were both thinking the same thing.

"Let's go," I said. "Those bagels aren't going to eat themselves."

April 19, 2002

The moment the nurse placed her in my arms, all of the doubts I'd had were gone. There was no uncertainty, no fear, no questions about what was or wasn't meant to be. I knew then that my life was forever changed. I held her close, close enough so that I could feel her breath on my neck. I watched her lips part with each tiny exhalation. *Puh. Puh.* I studied her nose, her tiny nostrils, so perfectly round. Her eyes like almonds behind translucent lids. She had some crusty stuff by her ear that I wanted to scratch off with my fingernail, but I didn't trust that I would be able to moderate my strength. She seemed so delicate, fragile, an elaborate sugar sculpture swaddled in a blanket. Like if I moved at all I might crush her. I looked up at Matt, standing beside us, tears in his eyes, and the look on his face was pure joy. I scooted over a little bit, to make room for him, and he sat down and wrapped his arms around us. In that moment, I was both protector and protected. I felt like we were all that there was. I closed my eyes and imagined we might never let go.

I don't know how much time passed. I might have slept. Minutes? An hour? More? We hadn't moved. She was still asleep in my arms, Matt was still beside me, still holding us. I opened my eyes and looked up when I heard someone speaking softly. I was surprised to see the room so small, so crowded. It had felt like it was just the three of us. Marcos, tall, broad-shouldered, stood next to Matt's father, both of them facing the window, their backs to me. I could see their faces reflected in the glass. Matt's father was speaking, too quietly for me to hear. Marcos nodded, rocking up on his toes, cracking his knuckles.

Roberta stood at the foot of the bed. I tried to figure out from the look on her face what was coming. Over the past few months, she'd become a friend, gentle, reassuring, sometimes motherly. But I'd also seen her impatient, brutally honest, asking tough questions, demanding answers.

"So, here we are. It's been a big day." She crossed her arms in front of her chest, took a deep breath in and out. "Okay. I know we've discussed this, but I want to go through it one more time. If that's okay with everyone?"

She was talking to all of us, but looking at Lorena. I'd forgotten she was even there. I looked over at her, lying on her side, her face hidden by the sheets. Matt's dad nodded at Marcos, who turned away from the window and took a step toward the bed. He leaned down and touched her arm.

"It's fine," I heard her say. "Go ahead."

"Okay. As you know, the law requires that you wait 72 hours after the birth before you can give your consent." She turned to Matt and me. "At any time until they give their consent, Lorena and Marcos can decide not to go forward with this." She looked back at Lorena, who still hadn't moved, and then said to Marcos, "That said, we talked about Jenna and Matt taking the baby home with them when she's ready to go. Assuming, Lorena, that that is still okay with you? Technically, they will be acting as foster parents. I spoke with Dr. McCann. She says that should be some time tomorrow. So, Lorena? You don't need to decide now, but you should think about—"

"It's fine."

"Okay. Why don't we just leave it at that for now. I will be back tomorrow. But Lorena, you have my number. You know that you can call me. Any time."

"Can you please just get her out of here?"

I looked at Matt, and I felt myself wrap her a little tighter in my arms.

"Natalie." I hadn't meant to say it out loud.

"What?" Lorena lifted her head and turned to face me.

"Natalie. Her name is Natalie."

"Fine. Whatever. Just— I don't want her in here."

I should have been grateful. This was what we'd been counting on, hoping for, ever since that morning at Matt's parents' house. But I couldn't help it. I was offended by what she said. How could she talk about her baby that way? I opened my mouth to speak, but Matt made a face, shushing me before any words came out.

"Here, let me." Roberta reached down and took her from me. "I'll have them take her back to the nursery. Why don't you two come with me? We can talk to the nurse about the feeding schedule." Matt and I followed her into the hall. Matt's dad stayed with Lorena and Marcos.

They set me up in what they called a nursing room. Basically, it was just a regular room with the beds removed, where they put me in a corner screened off by a curtain, so I could give Natalie a bottle. There was no place for Matt to sit, so he went to see if his dad and Marcos wanted to try to find something to eat. It took a while before Natalie seemed to understand what she was supposed to do. I would squeeze drops of the formula on my finger and then touch her mouth, trying to part her lips like the nurse had shown me. Formula ran down her chin and into the folds of her neck. I finally managed to shove the nipple into her mouth, and eventually she started to suck.

April 22, 2002

Waiting is the worst. Especially, when no news is good news, and bad news would be the worst news. Natalie already felt like my baby, like a part of me, a part of our family. No matter how many conversations we'd had with Roberta to prepare us for the possibility that Lorena and Marcos would change their minds, if we lost Natalie it would be absolutely devastating.

Part of the deal had been that we would we would keep her in New Jersey for those initial 72 hours, so we took her home to Matt's parents' place. The next day, my mom and Ted, and my dad and Deirdre, and Matt's brother Jake and his wife all came over. I was afraid that too much exuberance would somehow jinx it, so the rule was no gifts and no champagne. Each time the phone rang, I thought I might pass out.

I knew that if I could speak with Lorena, one on one, she would agree that the adoption was the best thing. She would remember how much she liked Matt and me, and how we'd all had the same idea from the start about what an open adoption should mean, how we would send them pictures and updates on Christmas and her birthday each year, and how we would tell Natalie about the adoption and about Lorena and Marcos as soon as she was old enough to understand. And how Lorena and Marcos would always make sure we had their current address and phone number so that if Natalie someday wanted to meet them it wouldn't be hard for her to find them.

I also knew that if I didn't talk to her, she was going to change her mind. I thought of her in the bed in the hospital that first morning, when she wouldn't even look at me and Matt, like she hated us. When she didn't want to hold her, didn't want her in the room. I understood that it was because she knew that if she did, if she allowed herself even the slightest opening, there would be no going back. So she looked away, acting tough in a room full of people, and I got that. But alone at night in that room? Knowing that her baby, her beautiful, perfect baby, was right down the hall? Of course she was going to change her mind. I mean, how could she not?

"It's 10:00," Matt said from the rocking chair, where he sat, holding Natalie.

"Sweetie, I know." I had just gotten out of the shower, and was getting dressed. Thinking that what I put on would be what I was wearing when we heard what Lorena and Marcos did or didn't do.

"She was born at 10:17, right? So they can sign the consent at 10:17?"

"Yeah, I guess."

"You guess? Jesus, Jenna, you're a lawyer. 72 hours means that they can sign at 10:17, right?"

"Yes. It means that is the soonest they can sign. But they don't have to sign at 10:17. They can sign at 10:30 if they want to. Or at 11. Or never."

"Roberta's with them?"

"I guess. She said she was going to see them this morning."

"Here, will you take her? I can't sit here anymore."

"Okay. Just let me put on— Okay, fine. Wait, where are you going?"

"Out. Around the block. I don't know."

"What if she calls?"

"I'll be back at 10:17."

I checked my phone to make sure the ringer was on. I looked at my watch—10:04. I fixed Natalie's blanket, so she was wrapped up tight like they'd shown me at the hospital. I looked at my watch again. It was still 10:04. I closed my eyes and promised not to look at my watch again until we knew.

Matt came back and I looked at my watch. 10:15. He sat down on the floor next to me, and leaned his head against my legs. We didn't speak.

Natalie started to cry. I looked at my watch. 10:17. Fuck. Was that a sign?

Matt stood up and then sat down on the bed. I looked at my watch. 10:18.

At 10:19 he went to the window and leaned his head against the glass.

At 10:26 my phone rang. I saw that it was Roberta. I gave him my phone and he walked out of the room with it. He went into the bathroom and closed the door.

I told myself that it was okay that I couldn't hear what he was saying. It didn't matter. The only thing that mattered was the baby, the miracle in my arms. Whatever happened next, I would always have this moment.

I heard the bathroom door open and I closed my eyes. I felt Matt kneel down next to me. He put his hand on mine. I was afraid to see his face, which I knew would tell me everything.

"They signed," he whispered. "She's ours."

Deirdre

CHAPTER 19

July 27, 2003

Deirdre forced a cough, thinking maybe she needed to clear her throat. Her heart was racing. She tried to slow her breathing.

"Are you okay?" Andrew asked, not looking up.

"Yeah. That was so strange, though. It was like I was choking, but I wasn't. Like I wasn't getting any air. I couldn't catch my breath." She made herself cough again. She felt a tingle through her fingertips. It felt like fear.

He picked up the remote and paused the TV.

"Do you want to get some water or something? Because I keep missing what they're saying."

"I'm fine. You can rewind it, you know." She looked at her watch, 10:41, and put her fingers to her wrist, checking her pulse. *Deep breaths,* she told herself. *Slow in. Slow out.*

Six Feet Under was her favorite show, but she couldn't make herself pay attention. She was distracted, anxious. She thought maybe she'd go into the bedroom and call Mickey, see what he was up to. But she felt a headache coming on, and decided she'd call him in the morning.

After the show ended, they got into bed and turned on the news. Andrew was snoring less than 30 seconds after closing his eyes. She was still tossing and turning, adjusting her pillows, thinking that if she could find the right position the throbbing in her head would stop, when Andrew's cell phone rang. She looked at the clock, 12:04. He was doing fewer surgeries these days, and he had plenty of people to cover his patients overnight. Why would the hospital be calling?

"Yeah," he said into the phone, instantly awake. He sat up in bed. "Yes, this is Andrew."

If it was the hospital, they wouldn't be asking if it was him.

"Oh Jesus. When?"

She sat up and turned on the lamp on her bedside table.

"Yeah, of course."

He pressed his left hand across both eyes and squeezed.

"I will. No, I understand. Absolutely. I appreciate that."

She reached over and touched his arm. He shook his head, not looking at her.

"Okay. Tomorrow? Okay. Yes, I will. Thank you. Thanks for calling." He clicked off his phone and put it down in his lap.

"What is it? Are you okay? Who was that?"

"Sweetie, I'm sorry. It's Mickey."

"What about him? Who was that?"

"Come here." He pulled her close to him. "It was someone named Jason. A friend of his. He's gone, Sweetie. Respiratory failure. A little over an hour ago."

"Where was he? What did he say? Tell me what he said."

"Sweetie, I don't know. The guy I spoke to isn't a doctor. All he said is that Mickey went into the hospital on Tuesday. They were with him when he died."

"Who was? Jason and who else?"

"I don't know. He said 'we.' I think he mentioned a woman's name, but I don't—"

"Why didn't you give me the phone? Why did he call you? Mickey doesn't even like you."

"He said that Mickey wanted me to tell you. He wanted to be sure you wouldn't be alone when you heard."

September 6, 2003

Flat on her back, drenched in sweat, she drew in a slow deep breath, and tried to feel the energy, which she tried to envision as a glowing white light, moving through her body, out to her fingers and down to her toes. She'd just completed her twentieth class, Bikram today, and here she was, staying for meditation. Unbelievable. It was just over a month since Mickey died. Twenty classes, as promised. Eyes closed, she took herself back to that first time, four weeks before.

She'd let the door close silently behind her and stopped, just inside the room, her eyes adjusting to the low light. There were four people already inside, two of them busy, fussing, arranging their things around them with the routine efficiency that comes from familiarity. The other two might have been sleeping. Or dead. One lay flat on her back. The other was sitting, or had been at one time, her legs straight in front of her, her body folded in half, her forehead touching her knees. No one acknowledged her arrival.

When she saw the statue in the front of the room, of what looked like a fat seated Goddess with an elephant head, holding a candle in her outstretched hand, she decided that she wouldn't stay. Promise or not, this wasn't for her. She turned and leaned into the door to push, just as it pulled away from her.

She stumbled forward, into the space where the door should have been, nearly knocking over the young woman who was standing in front of her. She was pretty, with wide green eyes and long blond hair, parted down the middle. A generous mouth, she thought, and then wondered where she'd read or heard that description. She had a backpack over one shoulder, and was holding a water bottle in one hand and a cell phone in the other. Deirdre tried to step around her, but was blocked by two more women, talking, distracted, entering the room.

She never actually changed her mind. She just had to get out of the way of the tide of women coming in, more a lack of resistance than a decision to stay. She found herself moving toward the front of the room, drawn toward the woman with the mouth, who had put her bag down in the corner and sat down on the mat next to the statue. There was something about her, so calm, so un-self conscious.

"I'm Andrea," she said, leaning forward over her crossed legs and smiling warmly. "What's your name?"

"Deirdre," she said, unrolling her mat, not sure if it mattered which side was up.

"Deirdre," she said. "Hi. Is this your first time taking my class?"

"Yes. This is actually my first yoga class. Ever."

"That's fantastic! I'm so glad you're here. This is a great class to start with. If you have any questions, you can just sort of wave your hand and I'll come to you. Otherwise," she closed her eyes and took a slow deep breath, in through her nose and out through her mouth. "Just keep your heart and mind open."

The room had filled, some women chatting quietly, some stretching, some just sitting, waiting. The woman to her right was lying down, looking up at the ceiling, with what looked like an oversized brick made of cork tucked under the small of her back. She looked around, and noticed that most people, but not all of them, had one or two of those bricks next to their mats. Just when she'd decided that she would get up to get her own, some music started playing gently, background noise, and Andrea stood in the front of the room facing the class.

"My name is Andrea, and this class is Slow Flow Yoga. Is anyone here today who is new to yoga? First or second time?" She looked at Deirdre and gave her a slight nod. "New to this class?"

Deirdre didn't turn around to see what was happening behind her, but Andrea asked two people their names, which she then repeated back, like she was committing them to memory. Andrea walked around the room while she was talking, and placed a blanket and two cork blocks on the floor next to Deirdre's mat. She explained that this class, any class, is appropriate whether it is your first time or your one thousandth time. She said that even after many years of practice, she herself is still a beginner, would always be a beginner. "Wherever we are, we are at the beginning of a journey, so in that sense all yoga is beginner yoga."

Deirdre rolled her eyes. The music that just a moment ago had been sweetly soothing in the background now seemed irritatingly plucky, like a new age cliché. Which was exactly what she was starting to feel like, a new age cliché. A middle aged cliché. She sneaked a look at her watch. Not even five minutes in. Yes, she'd promised, but now she didn't see how she'd even make it through one class.

Promise me you will find a yoga studio and take twenty classes in thirty days. It's up to you what happens after that. Thirty classes in thirty days would be better, but I know how you are. Trust me, twenty is totally manageable. You might be sore at first. Because you'll probably try too hard. So give yourself a day or two after the first class to recover. But don't quit. Yoga fucking saved me. I know what you are thinking, It's too hippie-ish for me; too many bare feet. Get a pedicure and get over it. And then go.

Once the class got going, she actually didn't hate it. Surprisingly, it wasn't frustrating like she'd imagined it would be, even though she didn't know what she was doing, and she wasn't flexible enough to touch the floor, and she couldn't hold the poses. But there was no need to compete. Instead, she just tried to listen to Andrea, and to imitate what the people around her were doing. It felt like cheating on a test, but it also felt like freedom. And just when she was thinking that she was ready for it to be over, about to check her watch again, Andrea turned down the lights and instructed everyone to lie down on their backs for Savasana.

July 16, 2003

My dearest Dee Dee, Sissy, Twinnie the Pooh. I am sorry that it has to be this way, but I have come to realize that there is simply no way that I can say goodbye to you. It's too hard. I love you too much. I'm beyond ready for this show to be over, even though I am nowhere near ready for it to end. Read that again. Go ahead, I'll wait. It actually does make sense.

I am just going to assume that things have unfolded as I arranged. Someone should have called Andrew. I know you will be offended that you didn't get the call, but I need to make sure you will be okay when you hear.

There are some things you should know. Freddie has the details on all of this. I sold my condo and am living at the Ritz Carlton. My plan is to stay here until the end. I'll check out when I check out. Get it? (Fine, don't laugh. But I thought it was funny.) By the way, I highly recommend hotel living—I should have done it years ago. The gallery deal finally got done. The landlord was a huge pain in the ass. In the end I had to write him a check. I wrote "Go Fuck Yourself" on the memo line, which gave me more pleasure than you can imagine. Anyway, the couple of really good pieces went to MOCA, and everything else is now at Penner Stevens Gallery. Except for my two favorite pieces, which Freddie will tell you about.

Yes, I know. I could have left all of that for you to deal with. And no doubt you would have done a fine job. But it actually felt good for me to clean up after myself, rather than to leave you with my mess. I desperately don't want to leave you, but if I have to, and it appears that I do, then at least I'm not leaving you with a heap of my shit to deal with.

I do, however, have some things that I need you to do for me. I need you to promise me that you will do what I ask. It's not a lot. Five promises. Just say okay. Come on. Yep, before you even know what you are promising. Let's say it together. Out loud. I promise. Very good. Thank you.

Promise me that you will take a step back and let someone else be in charge once in a while. Even if you can do it better yourself. You know what? Especially if you can do it better yourself. Let it go. Let it be someone else's job. Let it not be perfect.

October 4, 2003

Today obviously wasn't the best time to try to let someone else be in charge. Yes, she'd promised, but it was harder than she'd thought it would be. It didn't feel right, standing back there, out of the way, like a child. Was it supposed to feel good? This standing by? This idle uselessness? Normally, she would have positioned herself right up at the edge of the carousel, in what she thought of as the "ideal location", where she would have first access to the bags as they pushed through the black rubber flaps. She would wave off any and all offers of assistance. "No, no. I've got it." She believed that you shouldn't pack more than you could carry. She'd once been carrying a box out to the car and a man walking by offered to help. "It's okay. I'm actually much stronger than I look." He'd stopped, amused, and watched her as she put her foot up on the fender, balancing the box on her thigh and steadying it with one hand, while she unlocked the trunk. The box slipped, its side splitting on impact, books spilling out onto the street. "No, thanks. Really, I'm good," she'd told the man, embarrassed, anxious to get in the car and go. She drove around for weeks after that with the books loose in the trunk.

Watching one black rolling bag after another tumble onto the conveyor belt, she had a sudden memory of the big blue and green plaid suitcase her parents used to have, with one zipper to hold it closed, and a molded plastic handle by which to carry it, neither a pocket nor a wheel to be found. She could picture her father hauling it through the airport, leaning to one side, straining against its dead weight, hyper-extending his elbow, reddening his face. Her mother had tied a white yarn pom pom to the handle, she'd said so that it would stand out in the crowd. She wished she could ask Mickey if he remembered.

She saw her suitcase, recognizable by its luggage tag, and willed him to notice. He wasn't even looking.

"Andrew?" He didn't hear her. "Andrew," she called, louder this time.

He turned. She pointed. He shrugged.

"My bag." She pointed again. "No, that one."

He tried to get to it but there were people in his way.

She read his lips, "Next time," indicating with his finger the oval loop her bag would take.

She wanted nothing more than to push her way in, to grab her bag and to position herself for Andrew's, but she'd promised Mick. They hadn't even made it out of the airport yet. It was too soon to start breaking her promises.

*   *   *

Later that day, at the hotel, she sat on the bed with the TV on, the volume not quite loud enough to hear over the sound of the shower. It felt odd to be in a hotel in Cleveland. This was her first time back since Dad's funeral, and it would probably be the last. As instructed, they hadn't had a funeral for Mick. Just this, tonight. She picked up the invitation. Mickey's Last Chance Dance Party.

Promise me that you will go out and buy yourself the most fantastic dress you have ever owned to wear to my party.

"What party?" you ask. Why, I'd be more than happy to tell you about it. Here's the thing. I don't know about you, but I am plum, full up, done with funerals. Done. When Dennis died last year—did I tell you about him? Dennis Premond, the sculptor? He is actually a pretty big deal. He did these totem poles that people went nuts for. Anyway, it was just a few weeks after Dad. So when Dennis died, I did my best Scarlett O'Hara impression and vowed, God as my witness, I would never go to a funeral again. There have been way too many, and they are just too fucking sad. So I'm throwing what is going to be the gayest disco dance party that Cleveland has ever seen. I have it all planned, down to the motherfucking cocktail napkins. It will be a few months after I'm gone, and Jason will take care of the final arrangements. He'll call you to figure out a date when you and the good doctor can be here. And Freddie has my money, so he'll pay for everything. Stay tuned for details.

But anyway, back to the dress. Go to Barneys. Not Saks. And definitely not Bloomingdales. Go to Barneys. And take someone with you who has a sense of style. I hesitate to say it, because I still think of her as that brat he had you hiding from for all those years, but take Jenna. I know I only met her those two times, but I could see that the girl has taste, and she isn't afraid to spend a few bucks.

She stepped into the dress as Andrew came out of the bathroom, a towel around his waist. He zipped her up and she stepped in front of the mirror. The dress was fantastic. And ridiculous. It cost a fortune, and she was certain she'd never wear it again. And of course, she'd had to get shoes, too. But she felt amazing. And how often does one go to the gayest disco dance party Cleveland has ever seen?

Promise me that you will sprinkle my ashes someplace that you imagine would make me happy. I leave it to you to decide, as you have always exercised better judgment than I. But I do have some ideas.

I've never been to Dollywood. Insane, right? I can't quite believe it myself. As you know, Dolly Parton is my idol, and I can't imagine a better or happier place on earth.

I have always dreamed of walking the Camino de Santiago. (Well, not exactly always. But ever since I first heard about it last year.) Do you know about it? It's a religious pilgrimage where you basically walk across northern Spain. There are longer and shorter routes, but if I were doing it, I'd do the French Way. My friends William and Giacomo did it, and it took them about five weeks I think. They said it was very spiritual, life altering. Life altering, okay? Think about that. I'm not saying you have to do it. I'm just giving you some ideas.

You know, now that I think about it, I imagine that visiting Dollywood could be life altering, too.

December 6, 2003

She'd been standing in the Travel section of Barnes & Noble for more than fifteen minutes, holding two different books about the Camino de Santiago, flipping through the pages of one, then the other, comparing their tables of contents, trying to decide which was better. "Better for what?" she asked herself. "This is ridiculous. I'm not spending a month walking across Spain." She put both books back on the shelf and wandered into Psychology.

She'd been blessed, she supposed, with mental health. Mick had gotten the grace and beauty; she'd gotten the sanity and stability. She was pretty much immune to depression. When things were bad, really bad, she would find herself in a bookstore, looking at self help books. That was as close to rock bottom as she ever got.

She picked up *The Grief Recovery Handbook*, and flipped through it. Umm, no. She put it back on the shelf. *The Power of Positive Thinking.* Yeah, she thought. Tell us something we don't know. Where was the book that tells you what you are supposed to do when your twin dies? When you lose the best parts of yourself? When you are 57 years old and suddenly find yourself completely alone, unattached? Orphan doesn't begin to describe it. She was like a leaf. A leaf in November. Dropped from its tree, brown, brittle, swirling, twirling, blowing in the wind, just a matter of time before it is crushed, drowned, buried.

She wiped her eyes, looking to see if anyone had noticed. Crying in the book store. That's just great. In the self help section, no less. Shit, this is exactly what he didn't want her to do.

Remember how Nana and Bop used to take us to New York every year? We'd have pillows and blankets in the back seat. And we'd stay in that shit hotel in Snow Shoe, Pennsylvania because it was exactly halfway? You used to have to sleep, or try to sleep, or pretend to sleep the whole way, just so you wouldn't get carsick. Remember that one time when we thought we made it and then you puked just as we pulled into the driveway?

I kept the playbills from every show they took us to. I found them when I was packing up Dad's house. I fucking loved those trips. You know why? Because it was a family tradition. It was something that belonged to us because of who we were. Because we were Deirdre and Mickey Schein, and that is what we did in our family. Even when Mom was sick. Even when we were too old to pretend we were having fun.

Promise me that you will be a part of your family. Yes, your family. Andrew and Jenna and what's his name, the husband. They are your family. And Natalie. That precious baby girl is your family. So get off the sidelines and stop hiding in the background. Be her Nana. Or Grandma. Or Dee Dee. Or something. But for Christ's sake, do not be her Grampa's girlfriend who sits quietly in the corner and goes with the flow. Make some waves. Natalie is the luckiest child in the world, and do you know why? Because she's the only one who has you for a grandmother. Promise me that you will give her that gift fully and completely.

Make a tradition. Something that you and she do together. Something that is just for the two of you. It doesn't matter what it is. What matters is that it will be her experience, her memories, that will belong to her simply because of who she is. Because she is Deirdre Schein's granddaughter.

Walking home from the bookstore, she tried to shake off the sadness. She knew that he didn't want her to feel like she was all alone in the world, but she was. It was a fact.

Hey. Cut it out. We talked about this.

"I'm sorry Mick. I can't help it. That's how I feel."

You promised.

"I know. But what am I supposed to do? I'm out here on the street."

I didn't say you have to sing it. Just remember the fucking words. Jesus, you're a pain in the ass.

She turned at the corner onto a residential street. She sat down on the front steps of a brownstone and tried to clear her mind. She focused on her breathing and allowed herself to hear the music playing in her head.

So don't say goodbye
Don't turn away
It doesn't have to end today
Don't say goodbye
Cause I will love you til the end of time
Don't say goodbye

She spilled the uneaten string beans from Andrew's plate into the garbage can. He was like a child, never quite finishing his vegetables.

Feeling better?

"Yeah, Mick. I am."

See? I knew it would work. It makes you feel less alone, right? I'm telling you, that song is magic.

"I don't know that the song is magic. I think it's more like meditation. Stopping me from thinking by filling my head with the song."

Whatever. How was dinner?

"It was good, Mick. But now you have to let me clean up."

You're going to clean up while he lays on the couch and watches TV?

"Leave him alone."

She liked their relationship. It felt like a partnership, equal enough, if not quite equal. She did the shopping and cooking and most of the cleaning. And the planning. And the remembering. And the thinking. Andrew was perfectly happy to stay home, eat in, watch TV, and go up to Connecticut on the weekends where they would do the same things. She wondered, sometimes, if they would have ever gone on a trip, or tried a new restaurant, or had people over if it wasn't for her. She said that he was a creature of habit. He said it was because he was content, that he had everything he wanted right there at home. She didn't really mind most of the time, but it was just another way that she was alone. Think of it, research it, plan it, book it, and tell him where and when to show up.

So, that's it. That's all I ask, five promises:

1. *Let someone else be in charge*
2. *Sprinkle my ashes someplace that you imagine would make me happy*
3. *Buy yourself a party dress*
4. *Twenty yoga classes in thirty days*
5. *Be a part of your family*

You can do it. Do it for me if you can't do it for yourself.

I can't say goodbye to you, so I am not going to. Actually, you know what? I have a sixth promise. You know the Paulina Rubio song Don't Say Goodbye? Of course you don't. Who am I kidding? Anyway, it's been my fucking theme song the past couple of months. It's from her latest album, Border Girl. Go buy it, and listen to the song. Then listen to it again. Listen to it over and over again until you know every word. (Be glad I'm not making you promise to learn the words of the Spanish version.) Promise me that when you feel sad or like you are all alone, you will remember the words to that song and think of me.

You love me, my brilliant and beautiful twin. Know always that I love you, too.

After she finished loading the dishwasher, she went and joined Andrew in the living room. He turned off the TV, sat up on the couch and picked up a piece of paper from the coffee table.

"So listen, I had some ideas. About places I think Mickey would have liked. I wrote them down. I hope you don't mind."

"You did? Really?"

"Yeah. I mean, they are places that I think *we* would like, but I am pretty sure Mickey would have liked them too. I was thinking we could maybe plan to get to some of these places if you want. And we can take Mickey with us. Unless you had another idea."

"No. I've been thinking about it, but I couldn't really figure out what to do. Honestly, it's been making me crazy."

"There's no hurry, though, right? And it doesn't have to be just one place."

"Right. Yeah, of course."

"So I was thinking that Santa Barbara sounds like a place he would have liked, don't you think?"

"Sure. I hear it's beautiful there."

"And Hawaii?"

"Hawaii? Absolutely."

"There is this drive on Maui, the road to Hana? It's not the Camino de Santiago, but I think maybe it could be life altering."

"I bet it could."

"I have some other places, too. Here, come sit down and I'll show you."

Jenna

CHAPTER 20

July 25, 2005

"Hey," Beth said, slipping her arms back into her bathing suit straps, swinging around on her lounge chair and sitting up to face me in one fluid motion. "Will you be around on the 17th? I have to be in the city that day. I was thinking we can have lunch."

"Sure." I put down the magazine I'd been reading, and adjusted the towel that was covering my legs. "You're coming in just for the day? What for?"

"I have to register. For my classes."

Classes? I must have made a face.

"I know, right? Isn't that hysterical? I'm going back to school. I'm totally going to be the old lady who always shows up early for class and sits in the front row."

"Get out, really? For what? How come you didn't say anything?" I picked up the baby monitor from the table between us and turned it off and then back on to make sure it was working. "God, I can't believe she fell asleep. She was so fucking crazy this morning. How come no one told me that three is so much worse than Terrible Two? Anyway, sorry. So, tell me—"

"It's okay. Go check on her. I'll tell you when you come back."

I put my shirt on over my bathing suit and went inside through the sliding glass doors into the breakfast room. The house was somehow both cool and quiet, and warm and inviting. I walked through the kitchen, the dark wood smooth under my feet. Running my hand along the white stone countertop, I felt that familiar pang of jealousy that I always felt with Beth. How is it that she gets to live like this? She's out here for the whole summer, in what has to be the nicest house I've ever actually stayed in. She doesn't even have— Jesus, I've got to stop it. I'm here, aren't I? On vacation? God, can't I ever just be happy with what I have?

I went upstairs and stepped quietly into the room where we were staying. Natalie was sleeping, her hands curled into fists tucked up under her chin. I looked at her rosy cheeks, her arms already tanned golden, and then down at my knees, the tops of my feet, hot and red. Great, I thought. That's very nice. I'm jealous of her too.

It had been a fun weekend, barbecuing, taking the kids to the beach, but I wasn't sorry when Matt and Neil left in the morning to go back to the city. This was the first time in a long time that Beth and I were spending any real time together, just the two of us.

She was in the kitchen when I got back downstairs. She put a bowl of hummus and a plate of carrot sticks on a tray that already held a pitcher of iced tea and two glasses filled with ice cubes.

"My rule is that when Neil's not here I don't drink until after dinner. So I hope you don't mind if we eat at about 3:15."

"Funny. You are kidding, right?"

"Yes, duh. About dinner. But I do mean it about not drinking during the day. Otherwise it would be so easy to just— I have this fear that if I'm not careful by the end of the summer I'll be this bloated wrinkled lizard with orange lipstick on my teeth who talks like Harvey Fierstein. Like my Aunt Syl. Do you remember her? Oh, that reminds me. I have pilates tomorrow at 10. You should come. But we'll have to figure out what to do with Natalie."

"That's okay. I think she and I will just hang out here."

"That's fine. Or you can drop me off and take the car for an hour. Anyway, I made us a 6:00 reservation tonight at Yellow Bear. You know that place? We drove past it yesterday. It will be fine for Natalie. It's all moms and kids during the week. But you should see the looks I get whenever we go anyplace with Devon. You'll see tonight."

I picked up the tray and Beth grabbed a bag of chips from the pantry and we went back to the pool.

"So, wait. I really want to hear about the grad school thing. But first, Devon goes out for dinner with you and the kids?"

"What else would he do? Stay home and eat our leftovers? That would be rude."

"You're right. It totally makes sense. I guess I didn't— It's just that he hasn't really been around, so I figured— I don't know. Forget it."

"Figured what? That I was hiding him? He has weekends off. He's not our slave, you know."

"No, I know. Of course. It just seems weird to me. That Neil leaves and he like, steps in? Or maybe it's not. I'm—"

"We finally found the right guy. He's been working with Wes since October, and it's making a huge difference. Do you see how much better he is? Even just from the last time you saw him, right? It's really helping. So we can't just take the summer off. Plus, this is his job. The only way he was going to be able to keep working for us while we are out here is for him to live here."

"You're right. That totally makes sense. I was—"

"Neil was the one who suggested it. Because otherwise we'd be trapped in the city all summer. He had a live-in housekeeper growing up, so it seems normal to him."

"So, what happens after dinner? Like, after the kids go to sleep? The two of you have drinks and watch TV together?"

"Umm, actually no. First of all, he lives in the guest house, so he pretty much hangs out there. Sometimes he goes out. And yeah, a couple of times we actually have watched TV together. Trust me. It was all very G-rated."

"I didn't mean—"

"Of course you did." Beth poured us each a glass of iced tea. "This may surprise you, but it is actually possible for some people *not* to fuck the babysitter."

That felt like a slap. "I really— I'm sorry. Jesus, Beth, I don't even know what I was—"

"You know what? It's fine. Forget it."

"No. It was stupid. I'm really sorry. You've made this wonderful life for your family. And Devon is amazing with Wes. There is not a single thing to criticize about a single thing you are doing. I honestly don't even know what I was saying. I didn't mean to—"

"I get it, okay? But you've got to stop seeing everything through this lens of you and John and umm . . . you know, the mom. God, why can't I ever remember her name?"

"Do I do that?"

She smiled at me. Then she opened the bag of chips, took one out and ate it.

"Whatever. It's a part of who you are. So, not all the parts are pretty."

I wondered if that was true. Beth tilted the bag of chips toward me. I shook my head no.

"Well, this was good. We've uncovered something new for you and your therapist to talk about. Hey, remind me to get some avocados when we go out later. If they're soft, we can make guacamole tomorrow."

"I don't— I'm not in therapy."

Beth took off her sunglasses and put them down on the table.

"Since when?"

"Since never. I've never been in therapy."

"Never. You've never been in therapy. Like, not ever? Get out of here. Everyone has been in therapy. Even Mallory has been in therapy."

"What? Why? She's eleven years old."

"First of all, because it isn't easy being Wes' sister. And it is going to get harder, not easier. Plus, she had a really tough time in third grade when her teacher went on maternity leave."

I looked hard at her, to see if maybe she was kidding, making fun of me. She wasn't.

"So, like, when Joanne was at her most psycho? And she wouldn't let you see your dad?"

"What about it?"

"You didn't talk to anyone? You just soldiered through?"

"I talked to you. Plus, I was like fourteen. No one ever offered. What was I supposed to do, find myself a shrink from the yellow pages?"

"Okay, fine. But what about later? You seriously never saw someone? Not even when John died?"

"Jesus. You're making me feel like there is something wrong with me. Like I was too stupid to even know that I need that I needed therapy."

"Not stupid. Just maybe a little too . . . stoic? You do this thing that when something is hard or awful or hurts you, you act like it's this punishment you deserve. And then, instead of fixing it, or changing it, or finding a way to make it stop, you just sort of wrap yourself in it, so it becomes a part of you. Do you know what I mean?"

I wasn't sure I did.

"Look, all I'm saying is that therapy is great. It's like, I don't know. It's like a deep tissue massage for your psyche, getting rid of the toxins, or maybe like one of those intense facials where they extract all kinds of crap that's been clogging your pores for, like, ever. Plus, you get to sit there and talk about yourself the whole time, and he has to listen and pay attention, and he doesn't get to talk about himself at all."

"I guess that's what I use my journal for."

"Oh, bullshit."

"What?"

"We all know what your journal is for."

I didn't know what she was talking about.

"Your journal is just a way for you to be a writer until you finally cut the shit and actually be a writer. And by the way, exactly what are you waiting for? You might want to explore that, too."

"First of all, I have a job. Remember? And who says I even want to be a writer?"

"Oh my God, seriously? You hate your job. You've always hated your job, from the very first day. Just because you're good at something doesn't mean you have to do it forever. You're a writer. Who do you think you're kidding?"

"You mean because I once wrote down a bedtime story that I made up?"

"Yeah, that. That's what writers do. They make up stories and write them down. You're a storyteller, and you always have been. It's who you are."

"I love that you think of me that way. But I honestly don't know why you do."

"Wow. Okay, here's why. If I was going to tell you that I went to the store, I would tell you that I went to the store. If you were going tot tell me that you went to the store, you'd tell me a story about going to the store. And when you were done I'd know what it was like outside, and what you were wearing, and what you bought and why you needed it. Because you are a storyteller. It's a good thing. Why are you fighting it?"

We sat for a few minutes, not saying anything. I reached over and took a handful of chips out of the bag. Was I fighting it? Did I want to be a writer? I had to think about that. Which actually meant I was going to have to write it down to figure it out.

"Enough about you, let's talk about me now. So, guess what I'm going to school for."

"You want me to guess? Okay, wait. Let me think for a second."

"It should actually be pretty obvious."

"Something in fashion? No. Wait, I know. Interior design. Am I right?"

"That's funny. That was Neil's suggestion when I first said I wanted to go back to school for something. He said he thought it would be nice if I was buying furniture with someone else's money for a change. And I thought about it for a while. But, nope. Come on, guess again."

"It should be obvious?"

"Yeah. From our conversation just now."

"Writing?"

"No, stupid. You're the writer. I'm going to get my masters in counseling. At NYU. Counseling for Mental Health and Wellness, to be precise."

"Really? That's so cool! And you'll be so great at it. Seriously. It's perfect."

"You think?"

"Absolutely. And now we know why I never needed to be in therapy. I have you."

"I always figured I'd become a something someday, you know? Just because I don't need to work doesn't mean I can't or shouldn't. Plus, this will give me some independence, you know? So I can make some extra money after Neil leaves me."

"What are you talking about? You guys seemed so good."

"We are. We're fine, relax. But honestly? I feel like it's inevitable. I can't imagine that we'll stay married forever. I mean, do you? You and Matt? Actually, you guys probably will. He doesn't strike me as the type who would leave you."

In a weird way, that felt like a criticism.

"I guess I never really thought about it."

"See, that's the thing. I think about it all the time. Especially now that we've got Wes sort of figured out. Plus, he's always got these little work girlfriends. You know, his assistant, or some new analyst. I stopped paying attention."

"He's cheating on you?"

"Mmm, I actually don't think so. Not yet, anyway. For now, I think they are just little flirtations. Work crushes. Or maybe he is. I sort of feel like I'd know, though. As long as he's just screwing them, and doesn't fall in love? I don't think I'd even really care. Would you?"

Would I? I was thinking about that when I heard Natalie over the monitor.

"Ha! Saved by the bell." Beth stood up, putting our empty glasses on the tray. "Or should I say, 'it looks like our time is up'? Can you get the door for me? Devon and Wes will be back from the library soon. They usually go right into the pool when they get home. And I have to leave at 4 to get Mallory from tennis, but you don't have to come. I'll be 20 minutes. We'll pick up where we left off after dinner. With drinks."

July 31, 2005

It was a good week. The weather was great. Mallory was sweet and patient with Natalie, who followed her everywhere she went. And having Devon there made it possible to include Wes without him taking all of the attention away from everyone else. I checked in with my office a few times, and it seemed clear that they actually could survive without me. We sat by the pool, walked in town, shopped, cooked, and watched a couple movies.

I spent a lot of time writing in my journal. I had to try to make sense of the stuff Beth had said, to process it. She was probably right, that I see things through a lens of me and John and Mara. But is that so bad? It isn't judgmental. Maybe it's just realistic. She was funny about the therapy stuff. It sounds great. And I believe it can really help people. It wasn't like I ever decided that it wasn't for me. I honestly never thought about it one way or the other. Which probably proves that I really need it.

I spent the most time thinking about writing. It was weird. I don't think of myself as a writer, and I never really had a plan to someday become a writer. But I do know that I am always telling and retelling a story. Watching and listening, and then recreating my own version of it. Mostly in my head. Sometime in my journal. Sometimes out loud. But what was weird was that Beth somehow knew that about me. That she perceived it. I started wondering if it was possible that she knew something I didn't know. Maybe she was right. Maybe I should give it a try.

Matt and Neil came out on Friday, and we had a late dinner after we put the kids to bed. On Saturday, they played golf and Beth and I took Natalie, Wes and Mallory to the beach. It rained overnight and Sunday was cool and cloudy, so we left right after lunch, thinking we'd avoid the traffic. We were wrong.

After we got home, Matt picked up Hermione from the boarding place and I gave Natalie dinner and a bath. Matt read her some stories and put her to bed while I was at the supermarket. After I got back, I did laundry and watched TV while Matt did some work. We got into bed at 11.

I picked up my book but didn't even open it. Maybe there was a way I could cut back at work. They'd been talking lately about alternative work schedules. There was a guy in the DC office who had recently gone down to three days a week. But I couldn't see how that would work for my clients and the kind of work I did for them. When a deal was hot, it was seven days a week. No way could I tell them "sorry, I don't work on Mondays or Fridays." But maybe there was a way I could work on just certain deals.

With time off in between. I wondered if the firm would go for something like that. Maybe, if they thought it was a choice between that or me leaving.

I turned to Matt and saw that his eyes were closed. I looked at the clock, 11:10.

"Are you sleeping?"

No response.

"Matt?"

Nothing. God, he is unbelievable. How do you fall sound asleep in ten minutes?

"Sweetie. Are you still awake? Matt? Matt! Are you sleeping?"

"You mean now? Or before you woke me up just now?"

"Sorry. I was just thinking about something. You know how it's a really big deal at law firms how many women lawyers they have? And women partners especially? I mean, those statistics get reported in the American Lawyer every year. And it's one of the things law students use to compare one firm to another. Although I seriously don't get why law students care about that. But anyway, they're always talking at work about how they want to retain women, you know? Matt? Are you listening? Matt?"

"Can we talk about this tomorrow? I have to get some sleep. I'm meeting with Simon at 8."

"With Simon? What's it about?"

"Jen, please. I'm sleeping."

"Is it that thing in Atlanta? Do you think he's going to ask you to lead the team?"

"Jen—"

"Okay, sorry. Good night. Go back to sleep."

Maybe that's how I can do it. If he leads the pitch and they get the business, it'll be like a promotion. And it's a big job. And he'll probably have to travel. So maybe that's a reason for me to quit. Plus, I can't expect my mom and Deirdre to keep watching Natalie forever.

August 1, 2005

The next night, we ordered in dinner after we put Natalie to bed, and Matt opened the bottle of champagne he'd picked up on his way home.

"So tell me what Simon said. He liked the design, obviously. But what else? Does he think you'll get it? Do you know how many firms are pitching?"

"He loves the preliminary design. He said he thinks it perfectly realizes their concept. That's what he said, 'perfectly realizes.' I told you about the whole live/work/play thing, right? It's pretty cool, actually. If you're young, anyway. I don't think I'd want to live there. But who knows? The whole world is changing."

"Who else is on the team? Manny, right? He works on all your stuff. And what about the German guy, Reinhold?"

"Reinhard. He won't work on this. It'll be me and Manny, and this guy Jonathan Millhouse, who I haven't really worked with before. And Brianne. I think I've mentioned her. She was the one who worked with me on the White Plains project."

"I don't know. Maybe. She's new?"

"Not really. Well, yeah, I guess. She started last year, right after she graduated. So it's been about a year."

"Cool. When is the presentation due?"

"Not until the end of September. We're fine, timewise. But I'm a little worried about having Brianne on this."

"How come?"

"Simon wanted me to fire her. I mean, he told me to fire her. And I convinced him to give her another chance. So now she's pretty much my problem."

"Why did he want to fire her? Does she suck?"

"She doesn't suck. But she's a little . . . scattered. She comes in late. A lot. And she just— I don't know. She's a little bit of a mess. Like, sometimes she looks like maybe she slept in her clothes or something."

"Fascinating. So why'd you want to keep her?"

"Her work is okay. And, I don't know, it just seems like if she's struggling, losing her job isn't going to help. I think maybe she just needs to grow up a little."

"Sweetie, you're so nice. And she's really lucky. But you have to make sure she knows what's going on. If this is her last chance, she should know that, right? Plus, she needs to know that you saved her ass."

Matt poured us both some more champagne and we clinked our glasses together.

"To the Crossroads at Thornton Park."

"To the Crossroads."

Something changed after that. For the first time in my life, I wasn't reading a book. When I finished the one I had been reading, I didn't start another. Instead, I started writing a story. Two stories, actually. But just in my head. It was like I was watching something on TV that I would pause when I needed to do something, but then I could hit play and resume where I'd left off. On the subway, in bed at night before I fell asleep, walking around at lunchtime, I let the characters come to life. I could picture them, hear what they were saying. I could see what they looked like, what they were wearing.

After a couple weeks of that, I started writing. It turned out it was harder than I'd thought it would be. Slower, anyway. The ideas I had in my head didn't quite spill onto the page the way I'd imagined they would. I wrote a couple pages of one story and then got stuck, so I started another. A few pages in, I went back to the first one. I went back and forth between the two, reading and revising the first few pages, changing a word, moving a sentence. But never getting any further. Maybe Beth was wrong. Maybe I couldn't do this.

But really, what did even it matter if I could or I couldn't? I realized that I had no idea what I would do with a story if I ever actually finished it. For the first time in a long time, I wished that John was still alive. He would have known exactly what to do, and he'd have had the perfect person for me to talk to. Roger probably still knew people in the business, but

I hadn't spoken to him since he retired. Plus, they were stories. It wasn't like I was going to have a whole book to show anyone. And no one was going to be interested in a couple of short stories.

I went to the big Barnes & Noble at lunchtime the next day and looked at every short story anthology and collection they had. Eventually, I figured out that a lot of stories were reprints, and that they'd first been published someplace else. I recognized the names of some of the magazines where they'd first appeared, but it was only with the help of an enthusiastic salesperson that I was able to figure out what the rest of them were. I bought every literary journal they had. Just before I got in line to pay, I went back upstairs and found a couple of how-to books on fiction writing that looked like they might be helpful.

Over the next few days I read every word of everything I'd bought. I realized that a short story was going to have to be more than just the idea, the characters and the snippets of conversation I played out in my head. It was frustrating, because I couldn't see the whole thing in my mind. It was like trying to do a complicated math problem in my head, where the numbers would disappear, and be gone when I needed them.

The best advice I read was the most obvious. If you want to write, write. Sit down, start writing, and keep at it until you are done. So that's what I did.

It was weird. Once I pushed myself to just keep going past those first couple pages, past the part that already existed, that was fully formed in my mind, the story sort of took over. I didn't really know where it was going until it went there. It was still slow, one word at a time. And I still kept going back to the beginning, editing as I went along, changing a word, changing it back. But I did what they said to do in the book. I kept going until I was done.

I remembered seeing that one of the journals ran a short story contest every year. I dug through the pile of magazines, flipping pages until I found it. The Bloomington Review Short Story contest. Five thousand words, unpublished work, submission deadline four days away.

I hadn't paid any attention to word count, and it turned out I was a little over, but that was pretty easy to fix. I read and reread the story over and over, to the point where I practically had it memorized. I finally got to the point where there wasn't a single word that I wanted to change. It might not be perfect, but it was done.

I didn't say anything about it until after I'd submitted it. I'd let Matt think I was doing work, or writing in my journal. So he must have been surprised when I told him about the contest and asked him if he wanted to read my story. But he just said okay, turned off the TV and started reading. I went into the bedroom and waited.

"It's good, Jen. It's really good."

"Really? You think so?"

"I really do."

"Good, like, for the first story written by someone who isn't a writer? Or good good?"

"Good, like, really good. Like, well-written and engaging."

"But do you think it's fiction? I mean, it's basically a true story."

"Of course it's fiction. I mean, yeah, it's obviously the story of Marcos and Lorena, but you tell it from her perspective. And you only met her those three times. Also, everything else that's in it, besides the pregnant teenager story, their families, and histories and all the religious stuff? That dream she has? That's all you."

"So you don't think they would mind?"

"I don't think they'll know. First of all, it's not like it's that unique a story. I guess they might recognize their circumstances, but so what? Besides, I doubt they'll ever stumble across it."

"No. I know. But I don't—"

"I like how the reader never actually sees or hears the adopting couple. How all we know about them is what Maria thinks and says about them. What are their names again?"

"Kate and Gary."

"I thought it was cool how when you're reading it, you don't really know what is motivating them. What did Maria call them—'privileged shitheads'?"

"Yeah. Something like that."

"Well, I like that you can't necessarily trust her opinion, so you don't really know if they are good and selfless, or if they are using this adoption to try to prove that they aren't horrible people."

"Wow. You got all that?"

"Yeah, but actually I think I want to read it again. Oh, you know what else is really good? It's suspenseful. I really felt like I didn't know what they were going to decide to do. I mean, I guess I did, because . . . Natalie. But I really believed that they didn't know what they were going to do until they did it. Jen, I'm not kidding. It is really good."

"Thanks."

"So when will we hear?"

"Hear what?"

"About the contest. When do you find out if you won?"

"Oh, not for a really long time. Months. Like, sometime in the spring, I think. I figure we'll have forgotten all about it by then."

"But you'll keep doing this, right?"

"You think I should?"

"I do. I mean, did you like it? Did you like doing it?"

"Yeah, I think so. I mean, yes. Definitely. It was challenging. But sort of gratifying, too."

"Have you shown it to anyone else?"

"Not yet. But I think I'll send it to Beth. And I guess maybe my mom. Oh, and probably your mom, too."

"You should. You should see what other people say about it."

"It feels sort of silly. Like to wake up one morning when I'm 42 years old and declare myself to be a writer? It's sort of arrogant, don't you think? Plus, shouldn't I have written more than one story before I go out and start calling myself a writer? I don't even know if I have another story in me."

"I don't think you're declaring anything. You're letting your friend and your mother and your mother-in-law read something you wrote. And I am certain you have another story in you."

"You really think so?"

"It seems like this is something you have been wanting to do for a long time. So yeah, you should do it. And I can help more with Nat. To help you free up some time. Promise me, okay? That you'll keep doing this?"

So that's what I'll do. I'll write some more stuff. And if Sinners and Saints wins the contest, I will quit my job.

"Okay. Yes, I promise that I'll keep doing this."

Chloe

CHAPTER 21

July 14, 2007

He put his napkin on the table and leaned back in his chair. "No shit, Chlo. I think that that was the best meal I have ever had."

She looked hard at his face. Relaxed, satisfied, happy. That's it. That look. That's why she cooks.

"You really think so? I'm glad you liked it. But the best ever? I think maybe you might be a little biased."

"Because you're my sister? Definitely not."

"Okay. But come on. It's just food."

"But that's what I mean. It was— I don't know. It was like more than food."

"Wow, really? Thank you." More than food. Yes, she thought. Exactly. "But if you could improve one thing, what would it be?"

"Chloe—"

"I mean it. It's important."

"There's not a single thing. I'm not kidding. It was perfect."

"Oh, quit it," she said. "Nothing's perfect."

"I'm not—"

"Rick. I need you to give me feedback, okay? Real feedback. I want you to be brutally honest."

"Really? You really want me to tell you?"

"Yeah. I really do. Whatever it is."

"And you're sure you'll be okay with it? Because I wouldn't want to—"

"Rick, what? Was it the crab cakes? Shit. I knew I—"

"Well, okay. If you're really sure . . . ."

"I'm sure. What?"

"I think maybe I could have used a little more ice in my water."

"You know what? You're an ass." She picked up the empty wine bottle. "We killed this. Should I open another one?"

"I'll take a beer if you have."

"Okay. Yeah, me too. Here, take these," she said, handing him two bottles. "Go put on some music, and let me put this stuff in the dishwasher. I'll be in in a sec."

After she finished in the kitchen, she joined him in the living room where he was flipping through the records that filled the shelves along one wall.

"I can't believe you still have all of these. It's like a time warp to the 1960s."

"I know. I should probably just sell them or something, but I can't bring myself to do it. My mom wanted to throw them out, and I was like 'no fucking way.' Now it's like a piece of him that I can't let go of."

He pulled a record off the shelf without letting her see what it was. As he put it on the turntable, his back to her, he said "Name that tune."

She listened to the strumming of the guitar for three seconds, maybe five, and she joined Van Morrison when the vocals kicked in, singing "If I ventured in the slipstream . . ." "Easy. Astral Weeks."

"Damn, you're good." He sat down at the other end of the couch.

"Well, I kind of cheated, actually. I could tell that you were in the M's or N's."

"Remember how he used to always say that, in his humble opinion, this was one of rock music's most important albums? I must have repeated that a hundred times in high school and college. Including the 'in my humble opinion' part. It's amazing I didn't get my ass kicked more."

She pictured him in high school, remembering how she looked up to him, and realized that yeah, he probably did get his ass kicked some. "So, hey, can we talk for a minute about this thing I'm doing next Saturday? I just need to sort of think it through out loud with someone. It's going to be twelve people, so I'm thinking I will just have one long table. But I laid it out on the floor the other day and I figured out that if I move the couch and coffee table out of the way, I can actually fit 24 people for a sit down dinner. You know, in the future. I mean, I would have to rent tables and chairs. But four round tables would totally fit in here. Anyway, Saturday it will just be twelve—"

"I need you to tell me again what it's all about. I am not sure I'm getting it."

"Why this is so hard for you? It's catering. It's pretty much the same thing I've been doing since I got back. Except that it's my business instead of me working for someone else. And it's interactive. And I do it here."

"Yeah, so when you say it is interactive—"

"We all cook together. It's like a cooking class. Actually, forget that. I hate how that sounds. It's a cooking experience, where the guests participate. So, like, for Saturday? This woman Erica is the host. She and I already set the menu, and wine and flowers. I do all the shopping and some of the prep. Just the stuff that would take too long if we first did it when everyone gets here."

"Okay, so she invites twelve people to dinner at your house. And when they get here you're going to make them do all the work?"

"I'm not going to make them. Or yeah, actually, I guess I am going to make them. Shut up, it's going to be fun. We'll open some wine, and I'll have music playing. There will be these different work stations set up, and I'll go around from station to station and tell them what to do." More than Food, she thought. "I found this place that will customize aprons. So everyone will get an apron to take home, and I'm going to print copies of the recipes on these cards. What?"

"I don't know. It seems—"

"It seems what? It's a thing to do. I mean, it's not like you decide at 7, 'hey I'm hungry, should we order a pizza, or should we go to Chloe's and cook something?' It's an event, okay? Like a party. That you plan in advance. Because it's a fun thing. Jesus."

"Okay. I'm sorry. It does sound fun. I mean, if you know how to cook. But I—"

"Oh my God. You don't have to know how to cook. I'm going to tell them chop this, mix that, boil this. Whatever. It's not magic."

"Okay. If you say so."

"And then when we're done cooking, they come in here and sit at a beautifully set table and I serve them this lovely meal that they cooked. Then I clean up and they pay me a shitload of money. It's really the exact same thing I've been doing, except now I get to do it here, using my own pots and knives. And instead of having to pay people to help me, the guests are my helpers, and they pay me. Admit it, it's actually kind of brilliant, right?"

"So how are potential customers going to know about you? Like, what would you google to find this?"

More than Food, she thought again, but she didn't say it out loud. "I'm still working on that. So far, it's just word of mouth."

"Because wasn't that the problem in Italy? Not being able to get the word out?"

"Actually, the problem in Italy was that I was so sad I could barely breathe."

"I'm sorry. I should have come to visit. It was bad, huh?"

"Yeah. It was pretty bad."

"Well, I'm glad you're back. And better."

"Me too."

"So how did this Erica chick find you?"

"She's a friend of a friend of Jenna's. Something like that. Oh yeah, I think she works with Jenna's—"

"Wait, Jenna? As in Dad's Jenna? No way."

"'Dad's Jenna'? What are you talking about? She's *my* Jenna."

"What? Oh, umm. Nothing. I just— Jenna the babysitter, right? That's what I meant."

"Yeah, Jenna the babysitter." Dad's Jenna? She thought. Why would he have said that? She felt a shiver, like an itch, just under her skin.

"So anyway, I guess this woman Erica wanted to do something for her husband's fortieth birthday, something different. And I'd been talking to Jenna about this, you know, this idea of interactive catering. So somehow

Jenna told her friend and the friend told Erica. And I figure those twelve people all know other people, right? So if it works, hopefully they tell all their friends."

She took a long swallow of beer as the oven timer went off in the next room. "Hang on" she said. "There's dessert."

"I was hoping you'd say that."

She took the baking dish out of the oven, and put it on a tray, with a cake server, two plates, napkins and forks. She was turning off the oven when Rick walked in.

"Ta-da! Blueberry clafoutis. We just have to let it cool for a minute."

"Wow. That is gorgeous. No kidding. It looks like something you'd see in a shop window in Paris."

More than Food. "Do you want coffee? I can make decaf."

"Nah. But I'll take another beer. You want one?"

She nodded, and turned toward the refrigerator.

"That's okay," he said. "I'll get them."

"Thanks. I'm sorry Deb couldn't come tonight. Is everything okay with her? With you guys?"

"It's okay. Or it will be. We're fine. But marriage is hard, you know?"

"I guess. I actually thought you guys made it look pretty easy. No?"

"It's just tough right now. Did I tell you that her sister is sick? That's been hard for her. And— You know what? It's fine. We're fine. She just felt like staying home tonight. What's up with Mara? She's still married to that guy, right? What's he like?"

"Oh, Stan? He's okay. I mean, he's fine. He's a nice guy. He's nice to her. And thank God for him. She's his problem now. But I still barely know the guy, you know? I mean, why should I though, right? Yeah, he's my stepfather, but it's not like you guys are with Roger."

"Well, that's different. We were kids. He lived with us. He pretty much raised us. I mean, Dad was Dad, and Roger never wanted to compete with that. But it was— It's just that he was there."

"Yeah. I guess."

"I mean, look at me and Sam with Mara. She's our stepmother, right? And we don't have any relationship with her at all anymore. Seriously. Not since Dad died."

"Trust me. You should consider yourself lucky. I was always so jealous of you and Sammy. That you got to be— You know, that you lived with your mom and Roger. You guys were like a family on TV or something. I used to have this fantasy that my mom and Dad would get divorced, and I would go live at your house, with you and Sammy and Roger and Viv, and we'd see Dad on weekends. Which obviously doesn't make any sense. But that's what I wanted."

"You were jealous of us? Because Sam and I just wanted to be around Dad all the time. And you always came first with him."

"You think I came first with him? I always thought his work came first."

"Yeah, I guess. But when he was around, you were everything. Which, looking at it now, totally makes sense. You were just a little girl, and we were supposed to be these young men. Plus, we had our mom and Roger. But I was always trying to come up with these problems, you know? Like I would make up some issue that I'd need Dad's help with, something with a coach, or a kid at school, just to have something to talk to him about. A connection. Do you know what I mean?"

"Not really. I mean, yeah, I guess I do. But I really can't imagine it. I was always just trying to get out from under my mom's microscope."

"I know she drove you nuts, but you could tell she always meant well."

"I don't know how Dad could stand it. Don't you think he must have been miserable with her?"

"I never really thought about that. We weren't really around like you were."

"She was impossible. She's still impossible."

"She loves you. You were her whole world, even before Dad died. No one will ever love me the way she loves you."

"The way she loves me? It's aggressive. And suffocating. To this day, she would breathe and swallow for me if she could. That's why I stayed in Rome so long. Because she's like a magnet. One of those super strong electro magnets. And if I had been weak, if I had allowed myself to get too close, she would have pulled me in and I never would have left. She and I would be roommates right now, sitting by the pool in Sunny Isles basking in our widowhood."

"I guess I—"

"You want to hear something crazy? I'm not allergic to peanuts. How messed up is that? For real. I have a jar of peanut butter in the kitchen. Wait here. I'll show you."

"Don't show me. I believe you. Maybe you outgrew it?"

"I don't know. Can you do that?"

"Yeah," he said. "I think so."

"Well, maybe. But she totally could have made it up. It definitely fits with how she always treated me, doesn't it? Like I was so, I don't know. Fragile. Like I was this rare tropical orchid. And she was my orchid keeper."

"Orchid keeper?" He smiled. "Easy there, champ."

She got up and looked through the stack of cds. "U2 okay?"

"Which one, Joshua Tree? Yeah," he said. "That's good."

"You know something? I feel like I was happiest, like maybe in my whole life, during the time before anyone knew I was gay. Like after I'd figured it out, but before I told anyone. You hear all the time about how kids struggle with it, and how scary or lonely it is. But for me? God, I loved having that secret."

"That's funny because the thing that made me the most jealous of you was when you came out to him. I really hated you for that. For having that big important thing to share with him, to like, you know, work out together."

"You've got to be kidding. It was nothing. Seriously. He was like yeah, whatever."

"Really? Because when he told us, me and Sam— I guess he was afraid we would act like doofus big brothers and give you a hard time about it or something. So he said he was telling us so we wouldn't be surprised, and we would, you know, act right I guess when you told us. Anyway, he made it seem like you and he had had this really beautiful sharing moment. Like where you sort of transcended the whole father daughter thing, and connected as adults on this new intensely personal and emotional level. Which I couldn't even really imagine with him." He picked up his empty bottle. "Hey, I'm going to grab one more beer and then I have to go."

"No way. I mean yes to another beer. I want one, too. But you're not going home. It's— Oh my God, it's almost one in the morning. And if you're twice as drunk as— If I'm half— Shit, okay. If you are half as drunk as I am, you're too drunk to go home. Stay over. I'll make you breakfast. I make these eggs, with tomato jam? They're really—"

"I can't. Deb is going to—"

"So call her. Tell her she should come for breakfast, too."

"There's no way she'll believe that I'm here. Think about it."

"So let me call her. Or you call and then give me the phone. Plus, don't you have caller ID? It's the best."

July 21, 2007

Erica and her husband had arrived first. It wasn't a surprise—he'd known that they were having dinner with a group of their friends—but he'd assumed they were going to a restaurant. Everyone arrived pretty close to on time. Once they had drinks she'd explained what they would be doing. Some of them had seemed nervous, like she was handing them a scalpel and asking them to perform heart surgery or something. Erica had told her who should be grouped with whom. She'd said that splitting up the couples would be more fun.

She didn't recognize Beth until she introduced herself, and reminded her that they'd met at Jenna's wedding. It was Beth who had told Erica about More than Food, so she supposed she should have thanked her for that.

The apartment looked great, and the menu was perfect. Crab cakes to begin, seared duck breast with cherries and port sauce, spinach salad with warm bacon dressing, and blackberry clafoutis for dessert. It was actually all pretty easy, and presented beautifully. Surprisingly, things were more hectic after everyone went and sat down and she was left to plate and serve the appetizer, and finish the duck, all at the same time. For a group larger than twelve, she would definitely need a helper.

After serving the crabcakes, she'd stood just inside the kitchen doorway and listened for a minute. She wished she could see their faces, but she didn't want them to see her, to know she was watching. They raved about the food, partly she knew, because they had prepared it. It had all turned out pretty well. Someone had overdone it with the salt in the salad dressing, but she didn't think they would notice.

She cleaned up while the duck rested, wondering if the music was loud enough to cover the noise. She would have to test that before the next time, how loud was loud enough but not too loud.

Clearing the starter plates, she listened to their war stories about chopping the shallots and forming the patties only minutes earlier. It was funny how she'd had their full attention in the kitchen, when she was telling them what to do, and showing them how to do it. Now that they were her guests, and she was their server, she'd become invisible to them.

Wanting to get an idea of what Beth thought, and how she might describe the evening to Jenna, Chloe had been watching her all evening. After she served the main course, she walked around the table refilling wine glasses. They were talking freely now, about what a cute idea this was. That it would be fun for a bridal shower. And how it would be good for corporate team building. She was at the sideboard, opening another bottle, when she saw Beth lean across the man to her left. She lowered her voice, and spoke to the woman next to him.

"You remember my friend Jenna? Who's married to the architect? They're the ones who did a private adoption. I told you about that. Anyway, Jenna used to babysit for her." Beth had nodded toward the kitchen. "Plus, she was screwing the dad, her father. For like ten years, starting when she was still in high school. Right up until he dropped dead."

Chloe put down the bottle and the corkscrew. She stood still for what felt like minutes, waiting for the roaring in her ears to stop. As she stepped into the kitchen, she heard a man's voice say, "At least it sounds like he died happy". She leaned against the refrigerator and closed her eyes. Her knees felt week and she had to force herself to remain standing. Not now, she told herself. Don't think about it. Don't mess this up. She set up the coffee maker and got out the dessert set up so she would be ready to serve once she'd cleared the dinner plates. She checked the oven. Two more minutes. She turned off the timer so they wouldn't hear it go off.

She peeked into the next room. They were still eating, talking, laughing. Someone had gotten the bottle she'd opened, and it was now on the table. Don't think about it. Not now. It's working. They are having fun. They are going to tell their friends about it. She thought of what Ricky had said. "Dad's Jenna?" No. Stop it. Not now. She turned off the oven and took out the clafoutis. Golden brown and bubbly. Perfect.

Twenty more minutes, she thought, thirty tops, and they'll be gone. In five minutes she'll clear their plates, ask who wants coffee, and serve dessert. And then, when they are done, she'll stand by the door with a smile. She'll hand them each their apron, that she'd rolled up and tied with a ribbon that morning, the recipe cards tucked inside. She will shake their hands and thank them for coming. Erica and Jason will be the last to leave. She will count the bottles of wine that were opened, and add them to the invoice. Erica will pay her the balance that she owes and then they will leave, too. And then she can think about it.

It was finally over. They'd lingered longer than she would have liked, opening one more bottle of wine with dessert. They sang happy birthday and a few of them had presents for Jason, even though Erica had apparently said no gifts. There were huge laughs over the bottle of Viagra someone gave him. Assholes, she thought, standing in the kitchen.

She cleared the dessert plates from the table and unloaded and reloaded the dishwasher. Not yet, she told herself. Just finish first. She took the leaf out of the table and moved the folding chairs into the closet in the guestroom. She cut a piece of clafoutis, poured herself a glass of wine and put them both down on the coffee table. She stood in front of the wall of records. What did she want to listen to? Something that wouldn't make her think of him. Something that would remind her of Waverly.

She put on an Eva Cassidy cd, and sat down and closed her eyes, just listening. She picked up her glass. What was she supposed to think, to feel? She'd had the information for a couple of hours already, and now that she was free to think about it, to feel something, she felt completely detached. Like when you hear something terrible about someone you don't know.

She considered possible reactions that might be appropriate. Sadness? Anger? Betrayal? Dramatic, certainly, but not really applicable. She felt like something had been taken from her, but she couldn't say what it was. He'd been gone for sixteen years. And she'd figured out a long time ago that you don't get anywhere being angry at a ghost. Jenna hadn't done anything to her. She hadn't even broken up her parents' marriage. And besides, maybe she made him happy. Maybe that was how he was able to stay with her mother. Maybe it even made sense.

She wondered if Ricky actually knew something, or if he'd just misspoken. Maybe he'd sensed it, from the way Dad had talked about her. She could call him, but she didn't think she wanted to say it out loud. Or to hear anything more about it than she'd already heard.

She thought instead about what they'd said over dinner. What a cute idea More Than Food was. Bridal showers. Corporate team building. She wasn't so sure about corporate team building, but maybe. Why not?

Jenna

CHAPTER 22

August 8, 2010

I was in my office on Friday, trying to get through these documents so I can do some work on my thing that is not yet, but might someday be, a novel. I was apparently so absorbed in what I was doing that I didn't even notice that Cute Smart Ben was standing there until he cleared his throat.

"Hey," I said. "What's up?" He asked if I had a minute, and I said sure. I always say sure. It's my thing. I make time for the associates, no matter what. I remember what it was like to be a young lawyer with a question, when there was no one who would take the time to answer it. It really sucked. So, yeah. I always have a minute.

He closed the door before he sat down. He was obviously not there to ask me how to calculate the closing adjustments, or if a purchase and sale agreement needs to be notarized. If I'd had to guess, I would have bet that he wanted some help prioritizing his work. I knew that he was working on two deals for two different partners, both of whom tended to think that their work was the only work that mattered. I'd have tried to help navigate that minefield, but I also would have told him that it is a good problem to have—when you are good at what you do, everyone wants you on their deal.

It turned out that he wanted some career advice. He'd been offered a job, not as a lawyer but on the business side, and he didn't know if he should take it. I told him that it was a pretty safe bet that Porter & Gray wouldn't be his only job ever, and it was almost as likely that his next job wouldn't be his last job. I talked about how, at this point in his career, he should be looking to expand his opportunities, to open doors, not close them. The question, I said, that he should ask himself was whether this opportunity would take him any closer to his dream, whatever that might be.

He asked me what I would do if I were him. I hadn't anticipated the question, so I answered without thinking about it first. I told him that if I'd been offered that job when I was a second year associate I would not have taken it—I would have figured that I had invested too much time and money becoming a lawyer to walk away without having gotten some return on that investment. I also said that I was pretty sure that I would have regretted the decision for the rest of my life.

He thanked me, and told me that he was going to think about it, and that he would let me know what he decided to do. And then I spent the rest of the day in my office with the door closed, asking myself why it was okay for Cute Smart Ben to pursue his dreams while I continue to sit here not pursuing mine.

After we put Natalie to bed that night I asked Matt what he would think if I told him that I think that I'm ready to do it. To quit, resign, retire. He was totally cool and supportive. He swore that he had absolutely no reservations about it. He actually looked at me like I'm crazy when I asked him if he would resent me, if he would hate me each morning when he left for work and I stayed home. I said it felt like I was breaching some essential contract in our deal, violating this unwritten but binding agreement we had. I mean, I know how I would feel if he decided one day that he was going to quit his job and I'd just have to keep working. He told me that I was acting nutty, that he has no interest in quitting his job, that he loves what he does. And besides, he said, it's not like I'll be staying home watching soap operas, right? I will be writing, which is still work, even if I am not getting paid for it right now. It still counts, he said, even if I don't hate it.

We then spent the entire weekend talking about it. I explained to him for the millionth time how my compensation works, and I said I'd stay until they pay out the deferred portion at the end of they year. He said I shouldn't wait, that there will always be reasons that it is not the right time, and that I have a novel to finish. He told me to stop worrying about money, that I was just looking for reasons not to do something that we both know I am ready to do. We agreed that we would get rid of the nanny, and cut the cleaning lady to every other week. He said yes, I can keep going to my regular haircut place even though it is stupid expensive (he actually has no idea how expensive it is), and yes, we can still go on vacations. And that we will still be able to send Natalie to college (in ten years).

So that's it. I am going to do it. I am going to tell them. Tomorrow. Gulp.

September 9, 2010

It was my third day of not working. A bunch of people had August vacations scheduled so I ended up staying on through the end of the month. Then, we were up at my Dad's for the weekend, and we got back pretty late Monday night because of the holiday traffic. The plan was for me and Nat to have some special together time this week before school starts. Then, on Monday, we'll take her to school together, Matt will go to work, and I'll come home and get down to business.

We had lunch with Deirdre on Tuesday, and my mom came shopping with us for new school shoes. Yesterday we went to see Ponyo, which was this trippy Japanese animated movie that Natalie absolutely loved. We were supposed to meet Matt for lunch today and then he called at the last minute to say he couldn't make it. I ended up taking her to the paint-your-own-pottery place on Columbus, and then we stopped at Fairway to pick up some stuff for dinner.

I knew something weird was going on when Matt was there when we got home. Before I could ask him why, Natalie saw the goldfish in the little tank on the dining room table and absolutely flipped. Ponyo! Her very own magical goldfish! She might actually be the happiest child on earth right now.

We had dinner and played with Ponyo (which means petting the side of the bowl and whispering baby talk to it), and we read books and played some more with Ponyo, and the whole time I was trying to figure out why Matt came home in the middle of the day. Whenever I tried to ask him, he brushed me off, gestured toward Natalie, said "not now."

We finally got her to bed, and I followed him into the kitchen. "What's going on?"

"What? Oh, nothing. It's going to be fine."

"What's going to be fine? Matt, you're being weird."

"It's really not— I just— Someone said something. Someone at work. Simon told me I should stay home while they complete the investigation. I'm sure it is going to be fine."

"Someone said something? What about?"

"I don't know. They wouldn't tell me."

"Matt, Jesus. Would you leave the dishes and talk to me?"

"There's this girl, Cassie. And she apparently said I did something. Simon wouldn't—"

"Did what? Are you serious? Matt, what did she say?"

"I'm trying to tell you, but you have let me finish. Simon wouldn't tell me what she said. He said the lawyer told him not to discuss it with me."

"They already talked to a lawyer? Matt, what did you do?"

"Are you kidding? I didn't do anything."

"Are they firing you? How could you let this happen? You have a family."

"I didn't— I swear to God, Jenna. I never touched her. I never spoke to her inappropriately. I never even made a joke."

"You need to tell me exactly what happened."

"I keep telling you. Nothing happened. I swear to God."

"We're going to have to hire a lawyer. Someone good. Shit. I don't even know who—"

"Jenna, please. Just stop for a minute. You have to believe me."

He had a look in his eyes that I had never seen before. Stunned. Frightened. Scrambling. Like in those cartoons, where the ground falls away and he stays suspended in mid-air for a second before he falls too. Maybe that is what guilty looks like.

"No I don't. I don't have to believe you."

He opened his mouth to say something, but nothing came out.

"You know what? I need you to leave. Seriously, just go. I can't even look at you right now."

"Jenna, please don't. We need to—"

"Fine. You stay and I'll go." I went into our bedroom to get my shoes, and I slammed the door as hard as I could. I sat down on the floor, leaning against the door so he wouldn't come in. I couldn't bear to see that look on his face. How did he think I was going to react?

How could he do this to me? After all that talk about how this is going to be my time. About how he supports me. How he loves his job and how well everything is going for him at work. And how we can afford to live on just his salary.

Someone has accused him. Of something. And is threatening to sue. Sue him? Sue the firm? I have no idea. Just that Simon told him not to come back until they complete their investigation.

It doesn't take a genius to figure it out. Either they had an "inappropriate relationship" or he somehow created a "hostile workplace". Right? What else could it be? But it doesn't even matter. What matters is that I just quit my job, and now there is a really good chance that he's getting sued. And fired. So what am I supposed to do now? Go ask for my job back? Hey guys, thanks for the party. Remember how I just resigned my partnership? And I told everyone—literally everyone in my contacts— how I was leaving the practice of law to pursue other interests? Yeah, well, it turns out I was just kidding. I'm back.

He won't even tell me what she says he did. Oh, and like I'm really supposed to believe that he doesn't know? Wouldn't he have asked? Whatever it is, I think we have to assume it's probably true. I can totally see how it would be. I know what girls are like, and I know what they can do. Especially to someone like him, who has a soft spot for girls who are a little damaged, a little bit broken. It's that superman hero thing he has.

I don't know who Cassie is. But let me guess, she has daddy issues. He probably left when she was little. Or he drank too much. Or maybe he knocked her mother around. She was always smart, strong, independent. Tough on the outside, but fragile, breakable beneath the surface. She left home the first chance she got, put herself through school, never looked back. She didn't need anybody's help. And then boom, he walks in. All handsome and well dressed. Charming and successful, and totally safe. A grown-up, somebody's dad. The dad she'd always been looking for. I know how it works. I was there. I was her.

How can this be happening to me? He promised that it would be okay, and I believed him. I trusted him. I gave up my career. I walked away from this hugely prestigious, lucrative, secure career because he promised me that it would be okay. And it's not.

If Beth were here she would tell me that I am being narcissistic. And I'd point out that anyone who ever took Psych 101 can use the word narcissistic in a sentence, but that doesn't mean it's true. "Fine," she'd say, "you're being selfish." Are you serious? "Yeah," she'd say, "you're being totally selfish. This isn't all about you." Well wasn't it supposed to be about me? She'd tell me that I am jumping the gun, getting ahead of myself. Then she'd say, in that totally matter of fact way she has, that if he actually did something wrong, if his actions put his livelihood, our family's livelihood, at risk, she will personally kill him for me. But I should consider the possibility that maybe I'm not the only one getting screwed here. Maybe Matt is being treated unfairly. Think how terrible it would feel to have your business partner automatically assume that it is true. And then think about if your wife did, too. Plus, she'd probably say that he doesn't have it in him to behave inappropriately anyway.

She's right. Or, if she was here, and if she really said those things, she would be right. I'm being an asshole. If it were me, if someone accused me of something that I said I didn't do, there is no question in my mind that Matt would take my side. Automatically and without question. And it would take an awful lot of evidence to convince him otherwise.

"I'm sorry that I slammed the door. Did it wake her up?"

"She didn't come out. I just checked and she's sleeping now."

"I overreacted, and I'm sorry. Can you just tell me what happened?"

"I already told you. Nothing happened. Jesus, how many times—?"

"I mean today. What happened with Simon. What did he say?"

"He didn't say anything. Just that I should stay home for a few days."

"I need you to start at the beginning."

"Fine. I was about to leave to come meet you and Nat. Simon's secretary called and told me to go to the conference room. I asked if it could wait because I was on my way out, and she said no. So I go in and he's there with MaryPat. And—"

"MaryPat is the one with the big ass?"

"Yeah, the office manager. You know her."

"Right. But what does she do? Like, what is her role?"

"She orders the pencils. I don't know. She's in charge of the admin staff. She's the one people call when they're calling in sick."

"HR stuff. Okay. Keep going."

"I go in and they're both sitting on one side so I sit down across from them and it's like an interrogation. She starts reading these questions off a legal pad and I tell her to leave and Simon says he needs her to stay. So then he asks me about Cassie. And I say that I think she's going to be okay. That's she's getting better. And MaryPat says—"

"Getting better from what? What do you mean?"

"People were complaining about her. This was a couple of weeks ago. Simon and I went out for lunch and he asked me to talk to—"

"Wait, is this that same girl? The one who sleeps in her clothes?"

"Who?"

"I don't know. Someone you once told me about. A long time ago."

"I don't think so. Cassie's only been there for a few months."

"So not the same girl. Keep going."

"Right. So after lunch I asked her to come to my office. I closed the door, and I told her that there had been some complaints, some problems with missed deadlines. I said that it didn't seem to be an issue with the quality of her work. It was more a matter of managing expectations. I said that I would make myself available to work with her, to help her manage her workload. I did what Simon asked me to do. I did what I always do."

"How did she react?"

"I don't know. Like a kid whose boss just told her that people have been complaining about her. Like she was going to cry. I told her that she shouldn't be upset. I said she could sit there if she needed to take a few minutes to get it together. To calm down. I don't know what I said. I left her sitting in my office with the door closed."

"That was it? You didn't hug her? Or squeeze her hand?"

"Of course not. I'm not an idiot."

September 12, 2010

I just got home from drinks with Beth. I finally told her about what's been going on these past couple days. I'm not angry. I believe that he didn't do anything inappropriate, but I am sort of resigned to a bad outcome. Matt swears he can't think of a single thing that he said or did that she might have misinterpreted. I keep telling him that I believe him and I trust him, but that whatever did or didn't happen doesn't actually matter. It's going to be his word against hers, and the lawyers will always push to settle, just to make it go away. So I fully expect that this means that I am going to have to back to work. Even after this somehow gets resolved, I can imagine him saying that he can't go back there, that he can't work with people who questioned his integrity. Oh well.

For some reason, whenever I try to play it out, to imagine how it is all going to unfold, every scenario ends with us getting divorced, with me alone, a single mother, struggling financially. I even imagine that Matt and Cassie somehow end up together, living happily ever after. And every time, I end up alone.

Beth said that I need to stop expecting Matt to let me down, to leave me. That he is not my dad, and he's not John. And plus, she reminded me, we got over all of that a long time ago, right? I guess. But does anyone ever really get over anything?

September 14, 2010

Matt just got off the phone with Simon. And just like that, less than a week after it began, it's over.

As part of their investigation, they got in touch with Cassie's prior employer. Apparently, they didn't check her references when they hired her. Idiots. Anyway, it turns out she'd done this before. At her last job she claimed that her boss had come on to her, and that he threatened to fire her if she didn't go along with it. The guy was apparently enough of a creep that they wrote her a big check without ever taking too close a look. Maybe it was true. Or maybe not. Who knows? Either way, maybe it seemed like a really good way to make a living, going from town to town, from job to job. Anyway, I haven't gotten all the details yet, but when Simon asked her about the last job, she admitted that whatever she'd said about Matt wasn't true, that she'd made it up. She retracted her statement and resigned.

I feel pretty terrible about how I reacted when Matt first told me what was happening. Luckily, he will never know how angry I was, or how quick I was to assume he'd done something terrible. It was completely wrong and unfair of me. All I could think about was how it was going to affect me.

So now I am going to take him out for lunch to celebrate. Actually, since I no longer have an income, I guess he's taking me. Whatever. Later we will go together to pick up Natalie from school. It's nice out, so we'll probably go to the sprinkler park before dinner. And then tomorrow will be the first day of the rest of my life.

Deirdre

CHAPTER 23

April 10, 2012

Oh, for fuck's sake, said Mickey's voice in her head. *You are 66 years old, and you're sitting here chewing on your fingernails?*

Deirdre pulled her hand away from her mouth. "Shut up. I was not."

How is it possible that you are still intimidated by that bratty teenager?

"She's not a teenager, Mick. She's almost 50 years old."

My point exactly.

"And I'm not intimidated by her. I just get nervous sometimes about being alone with her."

She looked up and saw Jenna walking toward her, head down, looking at her phone.

Whoa. It looks like Daddy's little girl might have put on a few pounds. Dee, am I right?

She wondered if she would ever stop hearing his voice in her head. Actually, she realized, she hoped not. Deep breath in, deep breath out. She stood up from the bench, and waved to get Jenna's attention. "Is this too early? I'm sorry. I probably should have said 10."

"No, this is fine. It's good," Jenna said, putting her phone in her pocket and pulling the sleeves of her sweatshirt down over her hands. "I just hope it warms up a little."

"It'll be better once we start moving."

"Good, then let's start moving."

They walked east, heading out of the park.

"So, I usually go along the river to 125th. Maybe across to Randall's Island if I feel like it. But if that's too far, we can—"

"How far is it?" Jenna asked.

"From here? Probably about four miles. Maybe a little more. So figure there and back will take about three and a half hours. But like I said, we don't have to do the whole thing. If you need to be back—"

"It's fine. Are we allowed to stop for coffee?"

"Of course. There are no rules. It's just walking."

"You do this twice a week?"

"I try to. When we're in town. I usually do it when your dad goes to the office."

"Why does he still go in? I mean, he doesn't see patients anymore. What does he even do there?"

Deirdre felt herself bristle, defensive. "He still consults a little. But mostly I think he goes to the office for the same reason I do this. For something to do." Something separate, she thought. "He and I spend an awful lot of time together these days, you know? Sometimes it's good to just— Well, you must know what I mean."

"Oh God, for sure."

"I think it's good, you know, that we don't spend all of our time together. I guess I just like to have a little space. To think."

Tell the truth. You take these walks so you can talk to me.

"Well, whatever you're doing, it seems to be working for you. I mean, you look fantastic."

"Oh, thanks. I've really been trying—"

"I seriously have to start doing something. Either that, or I'm going to have to buy all new clothes. I'm getting so fat."

Ha! Didn't I tell you?

"Don't be silly. You look good. You always do." She did look good. Softer, in a good way.

They walked in silence.

Somebody better say something or this is going to be one long walk.

"Your dad told me that there's something happening with your book?"

"Not exactly. I mean yeah. Maybe. Did I tell you about the thing I'm going to next week? The conference?"

"Your dad mentioned that you were going to Providence, but he was a little light on the facts. Is it next week? We'll be around if you need us to take Natalie."

"No. I mean, thanks. But Matt's going to go to his mother's with her. Anyway, it's this annual writers' conference called Words and Pages. And part of what they do is this thing called the Emporium, where they hook you up with an agent who will read 20 pages of your manuscript before you get there. And then you meet with them one on one when you're there. It's all about getting feedback. I mean, they go way out of their way on their website to say how it's not about getting you signed with an agent, that you shouldn't expect that. It's really just for exposure. You know, from an actual person in the industry."

"That's such a good idea. I wouldn't have thought that there would be something so—"

"They hooked me up with this woman, Deanne Hoffman. As in Warden Hoffman Literary Agents. Not that I've ever heard of them before, but still."

"So you'll meet with her when you're there?"

"Yeah, but here's the amazing thing. She emailed me and asked me to send her the full manuscript. Which I don't even think she's supposed to do. She said to send it right away so she'll have time to read the whole thing before we meet next week. Which has to mean she really liked it, right? She said she did. She said that she was intrigued by what she'd seen so far and looked forward to seeing more. Which is really amazing, don't you think?"

"Wow, yes. Or no, actually. Not so amazing. I think your writing is really good. I loved your story. The one that was in that magazine? I forget—"

"Yeah, thanks. Two Years Ago Tomorrow. I know I shouldn't get my hopes up, but I can't help it. Can you imagine if she says she wants to represent me? Or if— Okay, I need to stop. Because just meeting with her will be good for me, you know? Hearing what someone thinks who actually does this for a living. And doesn't feel like they have to tell me that they loved it."

"Can I read it? Your book? Only if you don't mind. You know, I don't think I even know what it's called."

"The title is The Truth About Parallel Lines. But actually, that could change."

"Well, I would really love to read it. I don't even have to tell you what I think if you'd rather I don't."

"Are you kidding? First of all, I'd love for you to read it. But you have to promise to tell me what you think. And be honest. But kind. The only people who have read it are Matt, my mom and my friend Beth, and they sort of have to love it. So yeah, if you really mean it, I'll email a copy when I get home."

Very nicely done. You definitely earned yourself some points. But who's keeping score, right?

"Well, Mick. It does sort of put me in her inner circle, doesn't it?"

"So, what does it mean?"

"What?"

"What is the truth about parallel lines?"

"Oh. That sometimes they actually do intersect."

"Interesting."

"Hey," said Jenna. "Want to hear something weird?"

"Always."

"Okay, do you remember my friend Chloe?"

"Sure. She's the one who lost her partner, right? On 9/11?"

"Yeah. But it's funny. I mean, it's not funny at all. But it's funny to hear you describe her that way. It's like the last thing I think of about her. She was the kid I used to babysit for. And the lesbian at my wedding. And the one who does that cooking class catering thing. I mean, I obviously get that losing your partner on 9/11 is a hugely defining thing. But it's just not— Anyway, yeah. That's her."

"Didn't she move abroad someplace?"

"Italy, but she's back. She's been in New York for a long time. Years. I don't know, like six? Maybe seven? It's weird because we stayed in touch all those years, right? I mean, the whole time she lived in Boston, and then wherever their house was, her and Waverly. Someplace with an "N" I think. Needham, maybe? No. Newton? I don't know. Anyway, who cares? So, the whole time I've known her we'd always write letters and talk on the phone. It was sporadic, but regular. Or at least consistent. Does that make sense? I mean, it wasn't every week, or even every month. But usually at least every couple of months. And always when something big happened. And we'd always get together when she came to New York. So then, she finally moves back, and we're living in the same place at the same time for the first time since she went to college, right? And we just sort of, I don't know, it's like all of a sudden we fell out of touch with each other."

"Well, that happens sometimes. I used to know this woman Frannie, and we—"

"But that's not the weird thing. I mean, it was weird, because it seemed so sudden and for no reason. Like, all of a sudden she wouldn't respond to my emails. And I left her a couple phone messages, too. I guess I didn't actually try that hard, because at first I was kind of irritated. Like, what did I do? And then I just, I don't know, got caught up in my own stuff."

"Well, of course. Life gets in the way. And these past few years you've certainly had a lot on your—"

"I knew she was still in New York. But she's not on Facebook. Which is actually kind of weird, don't you think? I mean, she should at least have a Facebook page for her business."

"Really? What would that even do? I mean, I obviously see how Facebook is good for catching up with old friends. But for a business? I honestly don't understand. There's this cute knitting store near our apartment. A fancy yarn store. It's a little too precious, maybe. But it's cute. And they have a sign in the window that says Like us on Facebook. I asked your dad, why would I do that? And he had no idea. Do you know? What would my liking them on Facebook get me? I've been trying to figure it out."

"You knit?"

"Do I knit? No. It was just an example. I was trying to make a— Never mind."

"When you like something, it shows up on your feed. You know what that means, right?"

"Yeah, sure. Of course. I was just—"

Come on. You have no idea what that means.

"Mick, will you please shut up? I'll figure it out later. How hard can it be?"

"I'm sorry," Deirdre said. "Go ahead. I didn't mean to change the subject."

"That's okay. I'm probably making too big a deal about it. But anyway, I finally heard from her. Like, totally out of the blue she posted a message on my blog. We're having dinner tonight."

She has a blog?

"You have a blog?"

"Yeah. But it's barely anything. I literally have like twelve followers."

"Oh. Okay. So she posted a message. That's good, right? What's the weird part?"

"Well, the message itself was weird. She seemed kind of distant. I don't know, careful. Like she'd spent a long time writing it, or thinking about it before she wrote it."

"That makes some sense, doesn't it? If it's been years since you'd been in touch?"

"I guess so. But it feels the way it would feel if we'd had a fight or something, and then we had these years to cool off. And now we're ready to move past it."

"So that's good. If she's ready to move past whatever it was."

"But there never was any fight. I mean, nothing ever happened. I even went back and read my journal from that time. From around when I last talked to her."

"And?"

"And, nothing. Hey, can we walk over to First Avenue? I really need to pee. Maybe we can find a place with a bathroom."

"Sure. There must be a Starbucks. If you want, we can—"

"I don't think I've been a very good friend to her," Jenna said.

"Why would you say that? I thought you've— How do you mean?"

"I don't know. It's sort of hard to explain. I've known her forever. And I feel like I know everything about her. She's always known that she can tell me anything."

"That's exactly what a good friend is. Isn't it?"

"Yeah, but it's totally one-sided. It always has been."

"That sounds like maybe she hasn't been such a good friend to you."

"But I think it's my fault. I mean, I know it is. It's something I'm doing, or actually not doing. I haven't ever really shared with her the way she shares with me. It's like I'm withholding some essential part of myself. Do you know what I mean? Like, when I talk to her I'll ask her a million questions about her life, about what's going on. And I'm always just like, 'Oh, I'm fine. Busy. Matt's good.' And then I'll tell her some cute Natalie story and turn the conversation back to her. I can't really explain what I mean."

"I think you're being hard on yourself. It sounds to me like you've been a very good friend to her."

They went into Starbucks, and took turns waiting, on one line for the bathroom, and the other line to order. After they got their coffee, they went back outside and continued walking.

"Sometimes it's like I forget that John was her father."

Deirdre looked at her, confused. "I'm not sure I know what you mean."

"You remember John, the guy I was seeing? He was Chloe's father."

"Yes. Of course. I know that. But what did you mean about forgetting? It always seemed to me like your relationship with him was very much a part of your relationship with her. Am I wrong?"

"I guess. But I've been thinking about it lately. And it's like the person I was who was with John wasn't the person I was who was her friend. I don't know. That doesn't make sense."

"I'm not sure I follow. Certainly, who you were with John was different from who you were with Chloe. But isn't that true of every relationship? To some degree anyway?"

"I think this is different though. Because she knew me with her, but she also knew me with him. Do you know what I mean? It wasn't separate. She was around, you know? Not all the time, obviously, but I didn't just have a relationship with each of them. There was also my relationship with both of them. I don't know. Maybe it's just that there is this big piece, this big secret, that she doesn't know about."

"It can be tricky when you have a secret. When you can't be entirely candid with someone. That can definitely affect a relationship."

"Wait, is this weird?"

"What?" Deirdre asked.

"For you and me to be having this conversation? I mean, because of you and my dad and everything."

"I don't think so. Besides, this is completely different."

Jenna stopped walking and turned to face her. "Different how? Because it was a long time ago? So was this."

"Yes, but—"

"Do you think it's different because John died and you and my dad are living happily ever after? Because I don't think that has anything to do with it. It's really just a question of what was happening when. Which, by the way, no one ever told me."

"You never asked."

No, no, no. Deirdre, you did not just say that.

"Okay, fine. So, when did you and my dad—? When did you start—? Did my dad cheat on my mom with you?"

Good one, Deirdre. Now what?"

"Jenna, listen. I really don't see how that's even relevant. And besides, as you just pointed out, it was a long time ago. And your dad and I are happy. And your mom and Ted are happy. So I really don't think there is any reason to get into any of that at this point."

"Yeah, but you see? That's not really a satisfactory answer."

"I'm sure it isn't. But think about it for a minute. Is there any answer that would really be satisfactory?"

Chloe

CHAPTER 24

September 10, 2012

Chloe got there a few minutes early. She wanted to be there first, to be in control. She'd chosen the restaurant, her friend Leonard's new place. She'd arranged for him to bring an assortment of food, sort of a casual tasting, and keep their wine glasses filled. That way there would be no menus to distract them, no choices to linger over. She'd asked to be seated away from the bar, where there wouldn't be a lot of traffic. She had been practicing for days what she was going to say. She was ready.

Jenna was a few minutes late, and rushed in, flustered, her phone ringing. She dug around in her bag for it, knocking over a full water glass that spilled mostly onto the floor. Her phone stopped ringing just as she retrieved it from her bag.

"Oh my God. I seriously hate that thing," tossing it back into her bag. "Hi. How are you?" She put her bag down, and leaned over to kiss Chloe on the cheek. "I'm so sorry I'm late. I had a ridiculous day. First, I went on this like 10 mile walk with Deirdre. She calls it urban hiking. I swear, it was like being in boot camp or something. And then Natalie was impossible. She announced tonight that she wants to be a vegetarian. Seriously? She's ten years old. Anyway, sorry. I'm a complete mess." She leaned over to pick up the ice cubes from the floor as a waiter arrived with a towel. "Sorry about that," she said, handing him the glass of ice cubes she'd picked up.

"Do you realize that you've said you're sorry three times in the fifteen seconds since you got here?"

"You're right. Okay. You know what? I'm not sorry. So there. Is this mine?" She picked up her wineglass. "To old friends." They touched glasses. "This place is nice. Is it new?"

"Yeah. It just opened a couple of weeks ago."

"I'm never down here. I can't even remember the last time I was in this neighborhood."

"The chef is a friend of mine. I asked them to just go ahead and bring us a bunch of food and wine if that's okay."

"Sure, absolutely. That sounds great."

Chloe sipped her wine, and reminded herself that there was no reason to rush. It had waited this long, it could wait a little longer. She noticed that Jenna still seemed anxious, talking too fast.

"I was so happy to hear from you. I mean, it came as such a surprise. A good surprise. I really can't believe how long it's been. You need to tell me everything that's going on with you. How is the catering business?"

"It's really good actually. Busy."

"And it's working? Your idea, I mean. The interactive—? Is it going like you thought it would? Because I think the last time we talked about it you were just getting started. You were still sort of in the planning stage."

"Yeah, it is. Here, try one of these figs. Do you like goat cheese? So, yeah, it took a while to really get off the ground. But yeah, it's good."

"I knew it! I knew the minute you told me about it. I mean, it's such a good idea. It's sort of like a book club or something. Not a book club. But like, a get together with an activity. But why am I telling you? I mean, you obviously know better than I do."

"You're right, though. That's pretty much how I describe it. A participatory approach to fine dining. Or interactive entertainment. Here, take my card."

"More Than Food? That's perfect."

"Thanks. Tell your friends. Word of mouth has been the best source of my business. That and the law firms."

"Law firms? What do you do with law firms?"

"The same thing, with the law students that they hire for the summer. You know, the interns. It's actually become a really popular thing. I already have seven firms booked for this summer."

"The summer associates you mean, right?"

"Right. Summer associates."

"Oh my God, that's so perfect. How did you think of it?"

"I remembered how Waverly used to have to do stuff sometimes with the summer associates. You must have, too, right? Bowling parties and baseball games?"

"Yep. Some of the events were so lame. But your thing—" She picked up the card Chloe had given her. "More Than Food. It sounds like it would be really great for that. God, I wish I'd thought of it. You know, so I could have suggested it to you."

"Have one of these." Chloe put a mac and cheese bite on Jenna's plate, and one on her own. "And you're really not a lawyer anymore? Not at all?"

"Really not at all. Pretty weird, huh? I stopped almost two years ago."

"Because I tried emailing you and it got bounced back. So then I googled you. That's how I found your blog. Jenna Writes."

"Yeah. My blog. It's pretty much just stuff that I write in my journal that I occasionally feel like I don't mind sharing. It's actually pretty random. This food is seriously good."

"Why do you do it?"

"What, the blog? I'm just trying to put myself out there. To get used to the idea of having an audience."

"And you wrote a short story, right? That's pretty cool."

"I've written tons of them. Well, seven. But only one has been published. Mostly I've been writing a novel. I mean, I wrote it. Already. It's finished. But now—"

"Are you serious? You wrote a novel?"

"Yeah, but honestly? It took me forever, and now that it's done I don't even— You know what? I enjoy it, and it gives me something to do while Natalie is at school. It's really okay if that's all it ever is."

"What's it about?"

"My novel? Oh, it's, you know, sort of character driven. About relationships. Family dynamics. Sort of about becoming who you are meant—"

"Jenna, what's it about? Like, what's the description going to be that'll make me want to click on the button that says add to my cart?"

"Oh, right. Okay. It's about these two kids, sisters actually. The parents were just kids, in high school, when she gets pregnant with the first one, and they put her up for adoption. A few years later, they're married and they have a second kid, who they raise. It's basically the story of these two families raising these two sisters who are living these parallel lives even though they are very different, culturally and economically. Eventually, unexpected circumstances bring the sisters together. It's called The Truth About Parallel Lines. But I might—"

"I would read that."

"You would? I'm not sure it will ever see the light of day. Outside of my computer, you know? But anyway, I really want to hear more about what's going on with you. Aside from the business. Like, how have you been? What do you do when you're not working? How's your mom?"

"Everything's really good. I still live in the same place, on 20th Street. I was doing Cross-Fit for a while but it started to feel really culty so I quit."

"That's the thing where you flip tractor tires?"

"Yep. All kinds of stuff. It's really fun, in a totally ass-whipping way. But you have to be all in, you know? You can't do it just a little."

"Yeah, I don't think it's for me. I really have to start doing something, though. Just walking with Deirdre today almost killed me."

"You said ten miles? That's a lot."

"I don't know if it was really that far. I may have been exaggerating."

"Well, here. Have another one of these. You earned it."

"Right? I was starving, and everything is so good. And Mara? How's she?"

"She's good. Still a little crazy, but way better since she and Stan got married. Like, there haven't been any calls from the Four Seasons lately."

"Yeah, remember that? That was pretty weird."

"That was so nice of you. I wonder sometimes what would have happened if you hadn't been around that night. She probably would have ended up in a mental hospital."

"It really wasn't—"

"Anyway, they're in Boca, and she's Stan's problem now. Thank God for him."

"Believe me, I get it."

The waiter put down new wine glasses and poured them each a glass of red wine.

"Thank you," Jenna said, picking up her glass. "This is nice. What else? Are you seeing anyone?"

"I am. For a while now, almost two years. Her name is Lauren. She's actually pretty amazing."

"Chloe, that's so great. I'm really happy to hear that. What does she do?"

"She's umm . . . she's the Recruiting Manager at Mattis Henderson. She runs their summer associate program. We actually met when they came to my place for an event."

"Ha! That's perfect. Love at first bite?"

"Something like that. She likes to say that I made her cook me dinner on our first date."

"How long did you say it's been?"

"It'll be two years in June."

"So it's pretty serious?"

"Yeah, I guess. I mean, it is. It's so different though, from how it was with Waverly. This feels more, I don't know, equal. Like we're partners, but I don't mean that in an unromantic way. With Wave it always felt like we were living her life. Even though I was a part of it, it was her life that I was a part of. Does that make sense? Like, we lived in her house. Our friends were her friends. If it had been me who died, her life would have continued without me. I know that sounds bad, and I don't mean it in a bad way. I'm not saying that she didn't love me, or that she wouldn't have been sad, devastated, whatever. That's not what I mean. But when she died, there was nothing left. There was no life for me to continue without her. It was like I had to completely start over. Anyway, this is different. With Lauren, I mean."

"I think I understand what you mean. I do. It's like— God, this is so weird."

"What is?"

"Okay. So there's this thing that I've been trying to write for a long time, but I'm sort of . . . It's like I'm paralyzed or something. It was the second thing I tried writing, and I'm still wrestling with it."

"What was the first?"

"The first thing I wrote? It was a short story for this contest I heard about. I didn't win. I mean, of course I didn't. But I secretly sort of thought that I would. Anyway, I was really proud of it. Eventually, it ended up becoming the first part of Parallel Lines."

"Okay. So go ahead. What's this other thing, the second thing?"

"Right. So all of this was years ago, years before I stopped working even. I was writing whenever I could, whenever I had free time. Mostly just to see if I liked it, and if I thought it was really something I could do. So first I wrote Sinners and Saints, that was the story for the contest. And I wrote it in like ten days. So I was like, oh okay, this is so easy. And then I started working on this next thing, but for some reason it was really, really hard. I could never get anywhere with it. I just keep writing and rewriting the first eight or ten pages. Over and over again. And then I'd give up, and write something else. But I kept going back to it. Even now. It's like I can't do anything with it, but I can't give up on it either. So I keep going back to it, and getting nowhere. Anyway, it's kind of about what you're talking about. Never the Same Love Twice. It's probably wrong to have a title first. But it's been in my head for years. Do you know that line? From The Great Gatsby?"

"No. I read the book in school, but I barely remember it. What's the line?"

" 'There are all kinds of love in this world, but never the same love twice.' And it's like I know that there is a story there, but for some reason I can't get to it."

"What's it about? I mean, what do you have in mind?"

"It's about a girl. You know, a woman. Sort of a coming of age story, I guess, but then it keeps going. She has this relationship. This sort of defining, life-changing relationship. But then umm . . . It ends. And it's about her healing, and growing, and finding love again. And it's different, because she's different. I don't know. There's so much there in my head, but then when I try to put words to it, even just telling you about it now, it disappears. I can't see it. It's like something is in the way.

"I think I know what it is," said Chloe.

"You do?"

"Yeah. And I think you do, too."

"You do?"

"Don't you?"

"Do I? Honestly Chloe, I don't even know if I know what we are talking about right now."

"I'm telling you that I know. About you and my dad."

"What about us?"

"Jenna, I know. Okay? I know about you and my dad."

"You do?"

"Yeah. I do. I mean, isn't that what we're talking about? Isn't that what the story is about?"

"How did you find out? Who told you?"

"It doesn't matter. They didn't mean for me to find out. It was an accident. Just an unlucky accident."

"I'm sorry. I was going to tell you."

"Right."

"I'm serious. I've been thinking about it lately. I swear to God. Just today I was thinking that I would tell you. Tonight even."

"Why? I mean, why tell me now? Why tonight?"

"Because— I guess I thought— Chloe, you were the most important thing in the world to him. You know that, right? All he ever wanted was to be your hero, your protector. You have to understand, he was never going to leave you. If he ever had to choose between you and me, between you and anyone, he was going to choose you. Every time. And he made sure I knew that. In a weird way, that made him my hero."

Chloe nodded, biting her upper lip.

"He was a good guy. The best guy. He was always honest with me, and careful, and respectful. You need to know that. I learned so much from him, about life and love and also, weirdly, about marriage and parenting.

Whatever he and I had, and there was a lot about it that was wrong and bad and fucked up, it was exactly what I needed."

"Keep going," Chloe said.

"So anyway, when he died, I knew that the most important thing for me to do, the best way that I could honor him, was to make sure that you were okay. I've always sort of felt like you being okay was more important than me being okay."

"So why were you going to tell me?" Chloe asked.

"Honestly? I always assumed that I would never tell you. It was over, right? No one got hurt. Life went on. He's been gone for so long, Mara has a whole new life, I'm this wife and mom. It's practically ancient history. Why would I ever turn over that rock, you know? But at some point, it started to feel like keeping it a secret was more about protecting me than protecting you. And that was never how it was supposed to be."

"I think I sort of knew for a while. Subconsciously. And then when I found out, you know, found out for real, I honestly didn't know how I was supposed to feel about it. I really couldn't figure it out."

"Chloe, I am so, so sorry. I was so young, so dumb. I never meant to—"

"Jenna, I'm not mad at you. I was never mad at you. I thought at first that I should be. I hated the way I found out, and I've always really hated secrets being kept from me. But you loved him, right? And he loved you?"

Jenna nodded, wiping her eyes with her napkin.

"Don't ever be sorry for that," Chloe said. "You shouldn't apologize for loving someone."

"I still miss him sometimes."

"I still miss him all the time."

"He'd be really proud of you. You know that, right?"

"I think he'd be pretty proud of you, too."

"I hope so."

"What's that quote again? From The Great Gatsby?"

"'There are all kinds of love in this world, but never the same love twice.'"

"Never the same love twice. Yeah, I think you've definitely got a story there."

Jenna Writes

The occasional musings of Jenna Kessler, writer, mother, wife, daughter, friend

May 23, 2015

A Book Tour, a Wedding and a Picnic in Ridgewood . . .

I got home late last night from Philadelphia, the final stop on my tour for my second book, The Worst House on the Block. Whew! It was a fantastic (and exhausting) two weeks, and I am absolutely overwhelmed by the response the book is getting. Thank you to all who turned out, and to those of you who tune in here. I couldn't do it without you. Actually, I suppose I could, but it wouldn't be nearly as much fun.

One of the things I missed the most when I stopped working as an attorney was the social aspect of the workplace. I had some great friends at work. And yes, there are a few I still see, or speak to, or bump into occasionally on Facebook. But by and large, my work friends were just that—work friends. Those friendships got me through, providing a welcome respite to the tasks that filled my day, whether it was chatting about a show we both watch, bragging or complaining about our children, complimenting each other's shoes. I miss that. As much as I craved the freedom, the quiet, the solitude, the time to just *write*, it's a tradeoff.

It can be a lonely business. You spend months occupying a world that exists only in your own head, spending time with people you've conjured, having both sides of every conversation. And it is hard to turn that off at the end of the workday. When a book is going well, when the characters have come to life, when I can hear their voices, and trust them to take me toward what happens next, then even when I am away from my desk, back out in the world, there is a part of me that remains in the book, that is not entirely present. It is a joy to sometimes occupy two worlds, to be able to step from one into the other and back again.

A book tour is different. By the time the book comes out, there is a certain distance from it. That world is a memory, a place I once lived and remember fondly. And the travel, the schedule, the new names and faces, require that you be in the moment. As much as I enjoyed it, the tour was sometimes lonely. There is a lot of time in between readings and signings. Many hours alone in airports and taxis and hotel rooms. Lots of solitary restaurant meals. And by the way, why do waitresses always make that same sad face when they hand you your menu and take away the extra place setting?

So, what's my point? (Yes, Jenna. What *is* your point?) One of my closest friends is a chef. She told me that to her, the idea of writing a book and then waiting months, years even, for publication would be like cooking and serving a meal and walking away, not sticking around to see if anyone ever ate it. So, my point? Feedback. It's all about the feedback. Hearing what people think. Actually, it's not even that. Sure, I love a positive review. Who wouldn't? To me, it feels like getting an A on a test. But just to hear from people who read what I wrote, to know that what I put out there into the world has been received, that is what feeds my soul.

Speaking of feeding the soul, it was my great honor to be asked by that same friend, the chef, to perform her wedding ceremony. On a cool and cloudy Saturday afternoon in April, under the auspices of the American Marriage Ministries, I officiated the marriage of Chloe Toberman and Lauren Meyer in Fort Tryon Park in the presence of a group of their dear friends and families. My daughter Natalie led the procession as their maid of honor, followed by Chloe, who was accompanied by her brothers, and Lauren, arm in arm with her father. It was intimate and deeply moving, heartwarming and overflowing with love. The brides were radiant, the food was exceptional and the party lasted late into the night.

As many of you know, my husband Matt and I adopted our daughter Natalie at birth. It was an open adoption and we have remained loosely in touch with Natalie's birth parents. (Although they were not married at the time of her birth, they have since married and are raising a daughter and a son.) Over the years, we have exchanged pictures and holiday and birthday cards. We have always been quite open with Natalie about her adoption.

Last month, right around her thirteenth birthday, Natalie said that she thought she might be ready to meet her birth parents. This didn't catch me completely off-guard, although I hadn't expected it quite yet. She surprises me daily as adolescence begins to assert itself. (Who are you and what have you done with my little girl?) Matt and I had a long talk with her, before I even contacted her birth mother, to try to manage her expectations. I was comfortable with the idea of her meeting them, but I wanted to be sure that we were not setting her up for disappointment. She readily agreed that Matt and I should be there as well.

After a number of emails back and forth, and some frazzled nerves that morning, we met them for a picnic at Graydon Park in Ridgewood, New Jersey, not far from where they live. It was a little awkward, with the adults trying way too hard and all of the kids acting shy. I can't say if it was just curiosity on Natalie's part, or if there was something that she was looking for. But I do know that everyone seemed happy to be going home at the end of the day with the people they'd come with. That night Natalie let us tuck her in to bed and told us she was glad we'd adopted her. I'll take that over a slammed door any day. She leaves for camp in a month. I can't wait to see who she'll be when she comes home in August.

Thanks for reading. I hope to see you back here in a few weeks.

xo

Jenna

the end

Acknowledgments

Sitting down to write these acknowledgments, I find myself at a loss for words. How do you acknowledge everyone you have ever known, without whom you simply wouldn't be here?

Thank you to my fourth grade teacher, Mrs. Judkins, for showing me that I was smart.

Thank you to my fifth grade teacher, Mr. Harsanyi, for showing me that being smart was a good thing.

Thank you to my seventh grade homeroom teacher, whose name I can't remember, for showing me that being smart wasn't always enough, and that sometimes you had to fight for what was yours.

Thank you to my twelfth grade English teacher, Mr. Marks, who planted a seed when he gave me an A on my first short story.

Thank you to my father, Lawrence Block, who 30 years later watered the seed that became the shoot that became the flower that became the garden that became this novel.

Thank you to my mother, Loretta MacKay, for showing me that I really can be anyone and do anything.

Thank you to my stepfather, Alan MacKay, who would be prouder of me than I am of myself.

Thank you to Amy Reichel, my first sister, my first friend, my first reader. What a tremendous gift you have given me, by reading over my shoulder and cheering me on at every word.

Thank you to Julia Dahl for a brilliant edit, and for shining the light in the dark corners to show me what I couldn't see.

Thank you to Jonathan H. for a brilliant edit, when I didn't even know that that's what it was, and for reminding me that getting to the end isn't the same as being done.

Thank you to my girl gang of early readers—Alison, Resa, Maria,

Sara, Marisa, Lynne, Erin, Twist, Leah and Heather. Your encouragement is everything.

Thank you to Ann Patchett, Elena Ferrante, Kent Haruf, Joyce Carol Oates, Roxane Gay, Marisha Pessl, Anthony Doerr, Elizabeth Strout, Kristin Hannah, Jami Attenberg, Bill Clegg, Colum McCann, Delia Ephron and everyone else whose books have inspired me (once I stopped being jealous that I didn't write them myself).

I love you all.

Jill D. Block was born in Buffalo, NY, raised in Titusville, NJ, and spent her formative years in New York City. She attended Stuyvesant High School, Clark University and Brooklyn Law School.

A voracious reader, Jill is a partner at a global law firm, practicing real estate law. In between billable hours, she writes the kind of fiction she likes to read.

In 2015, Jill published her first short story, "Like it Never Happened", in *Ellery Queen's Mystery Magazine*. Since then, her stories have appeared in *Title Magazine* (Australia) and the anthologies *Dark City Lights, In Sunlight or in Shadow* and *Alive in Shape and Color*. *The Truth About Parallel Lines* is her first novel.

Jill lives in New York City.

You can contact her at jill@jillblockbooks.com

www.jillblockbooks.com
Follow on Facebook: facebook.com/JillBlockBooks

CPSIA information can be obtained
at www.ICGtesting.com
Printed in the USA
LVHW01s1946110618
580319LV00012B/1646/P